The Eagle
and the
Songbird

A novel

by Sara Schneider

Copyright © 2020 by Sara Schneider
All rights reserved. This book or any portion thereof
may not be reproduced or used in any manner whatsoever
without the express written permission of the publisher
except for the use of brief quotations in a book review.

ISBN: 978-1-09833-957-9 (softcover)
ISBN: 978-1-09833-958-6 (eBook)

To Jim, with love and gratitude

Ruht wohl

1

What Gifts Can I Give You, For Such a Song?

MECHELEN, *March 1518*

A woman's voice summons him from dreams.

"Majesty... Emperor Maximilian?"

He opens his eyes, absorbing the small fire-lit library, the explosion of papers on his desk, the portraits on the walls, and his secretary at the writing stand.

"I was not asleep, nor even dozing," Maximilian focuses on the woman and the lute she's holding. "Catherine, thank you for coming."

He offers his hand; she takes it. Her skin brings comfort like turning the pillow over during a feverish night.

His eyes rest on her face, pale skin over sculpted bone. His favorite Flemish painters, Van der Weyden and Memling, could not have done better. He sees she is still wearing her hair like an unmarried girl. "Why aren't you married, Kathl? You must be nearly..." He pauses, thinking.

"I'm twenty-three, Majesty." Catherine gazes at his face, unlike other young ladies who stare at the floor when he speaks to them. Her eyes are the color of polished stones in the bed of a stream, and the light in them makes him wonder what she sees.

"'Time is flying, never to return.' You should marry soon."

The cold of the stone floor seeps through the soles of his shoes. One of his daughter's dogs lies under his desk. He presses his feet against its flank.

"Duchess Margaret tried to arrange a marriage for me about two years ago. I liked him; he loved music. But his family found a bride for him whose heritage is...unambiguous," Catherine says.

"I don't understand why my daughter Margaret doesn't simply adopt you. You would grace the house of Austria, and that problem of yours would be solved."

Watching her face reminds him of those changeable days of weather in the north—sun, storm, then placid skies within minutes. The clouds gather when he mentions being adopted by his daughter.

"I am quite the matchmaker, you know," he says. "Sometimes I think that's all they'll remember me for, linking my house to Spain and Hungary. There's someone you like, I assume?"

"There is someone, Majesty," she says.

"I need not ask whether he's a nobleman. Flemish?"

She hesitates. "German."

"Surprising choice. He must be known to me. You have met him here?"

"Yes Majesty, several times. But I suspect he doesn't see me as a wife."

"You will point him out to Margaret when you see him next, and we will see whether it is advantageous or not. If he is not married, he should be."

"You're not married, Majesty,"

"I have been married twice. Never again. Not for money, nor beauty, nor love." He gestures to a chair. "Please sit and play for us while Treitz and I finish our correspondence, then I wish to hear you sing. That will be my reward. You see, I have not forgotten the last time." The slow spread of warmth across her cheeks is rewarding too, but now she lowers her eyes.

Catherine sits and curves her upper body over her lute as she tunes it. His eyes follow one of her braids as it slips from behind her shoulder, and rests against the bare skin of her neck. She begins to improvise on an old German tune when he interrupts her, mostly to divert his thoughts from a happy, agitating picture: a labyrinth of limbs and bedclothes.

"I hear enough German music. Hearing beloved music from the past is like meeting old friends, not that you would know, at your age. Play me anything you like by one of your compatriots: de la Rue, Binchois, Dufay... surprise me."

"With pleasure, sir."

He watches her. She does not become flustered, at least not outwardly. She stares into space while making her choice, then begins again.

The emperor listens for a moment before returning to his tasks. He rubs his forehead to clear his mind. Clarity evades him. He is nearly sixty, and it seems the fog will last as long as he does. He looks down at the letters and other documents littering his writing table. His memory has become as weak as his bladder, so lists dominate his life now: names, ideas, plans; extensions of his overflowing mind.

Cages of larks and thrushes hang from a beam near the window; the music from Catherine's lute enhances their soft chirping. Tapestries of hunting scenes on the walls make Maximilian long to be outdoors again; they remind him of the many hunts he enjoyed with Mary. He doesn't understand his own mind; how can he still think of them with pleasure? He takes up his pen and resumes his letter:

'We, Maximilian, by God's Grace Elected Emperor of Germany, Archduke of Austria, Duke of Burgundy and Brabant do require and charge you, Electors, Princes, and representatives of Imperial Free Cities, to appear at the Diet at Augsburg, which we desire to convoke on the First Day of June, 1518.'

He insists on writing vital communications himself while his hand is still firm. His father, Emperor Frederick, was unfit to rule in his son's opinion, but Maximilian did learn one thing from him: he who holds the pen wears the crown.

"The estates ignored my first invitation, Treitz, so I must summon them again. My charm works on women, dogs, and children, not on electors, popes, or the king of France."

"Offer to pay their way, Majesty. That should bring them running." The vowels of Treitz's Tyrolean accent are as broad and deep as the valleys there. Most scholars smoothed their dialects into a Latinized accent as soon as they could, but Treitz still wore his like a standard. Unlike the valleys, the accent is not beautiful, but it reminds Maximilian of home.

"Your wit would make you more useful to us as a jester than a secretary. How can we do that, when we cannot pay for ourselves? Our first visit in Augsburg will be to Jakob Fugger, and we shall not be passing the time of day."

The emperor writes a line, then stops again. He straightens his back and looks at his secretary. "Although you do bring an idea to mind. I *will* offer to pay the expenses of certain key electors. That will indeed bring the rest running, since they would not wish to give their adversaries an advantage during the voting. The money will turn up, it always does!"

"It always seems to, Majesty," Treitz says, handing Maximilian a package. "Here are the sketches from Kölderer—the revised drawings for the Tyrolean coinage, reflecting Your Majesty's image."

Maximilian glances at the sketches and flings them down on the desk. He snatches the top sketch again, scrawls a large black X over the design, then crumples the page and hurls it at Treitz.

"Return this monstrosity to Innsbruck!" His leg hurts too much to get up and pace the room, so he shouts where he sits. "Tell him we are very displeased. We do not like it, for it looks nothing like us! Our nose is too high, our face is too long, and our chest is too thick." The storm passes, and he regulates his voice again. "Tell him to prepare new designs with the changes we have outlined. Then he is to travel to meet us in Augsburg, where we will examine the improvements."

His voice drowns out the sound of the lute, but Catherine plays on, unperturbed. She watches her fingers on the strings, or stares in the direction of the windows, watching the wind-blown shadows dance on the wall. Maximilian leans back in his chair, listening. He wonders where she cultivated her powers of concentration— it's not something court women are trained to do, like needlework. He recognizes a look he has seen on the faces of painters, woodcut carvers, composers, and other workers of miracles: an absorption in work that comes from hearing the whisper of the muse, and shutting out all else.

"What is that you're playing now?" he asks. "I don't recognize it; it's lovely."

"You sent Duchess Margaret some music a few months ago, and this song by Heinrich Finck was included. I think he may be German." Her eyes spark, but her hands keep up their work, recognizing no authority but themselves.

How good it feels to laugh. "Treitz, it seems we have another character on our hands. What do you propose we do with her?" He nods at his secretary. "I am feeling better. Go and tell my daughter that I will meet with her this afternoon as originally planned. Wait for me there. I'll come shortly. Oh, and take my little friends back to my room. Then we may hear and enjoy the voice of our human songbird without distractions."

Treitz moves to the windows, covering the birdcages before carrying them away.

Maximilian takes his pen up again and aims it at Catherine. "You make my point for me. Yes, Finck is German, but he has entirely absorbed the styles of your country. Your arrow has missed the mark."

"I'll try harder next time, Majesty. So, to grant your wish, here is something from Madame's songbook that might suit. The composer is not German, nor is he Flemish, though he may as well be." Her teasing smile vanishes like the sun in winter.

5

The prelude is so quiet that Maximilian leans forward at his desk. Then he hears her voice—as transparent and agile as any of the boy sopranos in his Hofkapelle, but with depth, and an edge verging on ecstasy. He closes his eyes. Nothing is real for him except her voice and the sigh of melody; a blade finding no resistance.

All the sorrows in the world
Come to me wherever I am.
Take my heart in its sadness,
And cleave it, so that suddenly
my lady can see my pain.

He listens for the pictures in the music, which illuminate the words more clearly than any poet could: the way the voice flings itself in a long descent, then resolutely climbs back up, like a mind bearing down on its own tortuous thoughts. But there is comfort, too; is it her voice or the bright harmonies? Or the relief of the visible heart, finally unburdening itself?

"What do you know of regrets and pain, to make you sing like that?" He says when the song ends.

Their eyes converge in the stillness—what could she see in his face to make such a change in hers? The placid waters of the stream are turbulent now, and her face seems lit from within.

"The notes tell me all I need to know, sir. I know, it's not the same..."

It's more of an answer than he was expecting.

"No, it's not the same, but it is a magnificent artifice." He looks down at his letter and sees that he needs to begin again—his tears have warped the paper, smeared the ink, and scattered the meaning. He takes a linen cloth from his sleeve and dabs his eyes.

"May I show you something, Catherine? Bring this candle with you." Maximilian grips the arms of his chair and lurches to his feet, taking her arm to make his limp less noticeable.

"I rarely show this to anyone. Draw aside the curtain, if you will."

He pushes the door open, and motions for Catherine to enter. He takes the candle from her and uses it to light others in the narrow inner room. A long, low object yields itself to the light: a coffin. Its construction is simple and rough, and the wood is unfinished.

"I call this my *Schatzruhe*, my treasured rest. Or is it where my treasure rests?" Maximilian says. He winks, and feels the return of something akin to lightness. "German is so expressive, allowing both precision and vagueness, sometimes at the same time. You speak it excellently, Catherine, and I have no doubt you can appreciate this ambiguity. As Charlemagne said, 'To have another language is to possess a second soul.'"

Maximilian walks around the coffin so that it stands between them. "Are you afraid to look inside?" he asks.

"No, Majesty."

Together they remove the lid and place it on the floor. Standing side by side, they look down at the contents: books, folios, scrolls, and carved wooden boxes. The emperor lifts a bulky object wrapped in silk, which he cradles like a long-awaited heir. He watches Catherine reach for something, then draw her hand back. "Please examine anything you wish."

Her fingers grasp a small box of pink and white Italian marble. Maximilian watches as she examines the carved exterior, before removing the lid. It is empty.

"It's beautiful, Majesty. What's it for?"

"I will keep that secret a little longer." He smiles and unwraps the bundle he's holding, handing her the cloth. "Lay this out here before us, will you?" She does as he asks, and he places an unbound volume on top of the silk.

"*The White King: A Tale of the Deeds of Emperor Maximilian.*" Catherine reads the title aloud. She turns over the leaves, admiring the woodcuts and the beauty of the script. One illustration captivates her: a room full of musicians and instruments.

"I have labored over my remembrance for most of my life. What you see here makes up just a small part of it." The emperor gestures at the book, and the contents of his casket. "It is not yet finished, but I hope that Treitz and I may make an end of the White King, before I meet mine," He nods at Catherine. "I have seen the signs myself, and my astrologers have confirmed it." He rearranges the pages in a neat stack, then wraps the volume in its silken covering. "One vital piece is still lacking, but we will see to that in Augsburg."

Catherine replaces the marble box. "Are you afraid?" she asks.

He smooths the silk with his long fingers. At least his hands don't look old. "Any soldier will tell you, the worst part of battle is the night before."

She is silent again, weighing her words. "Is there anything I can do, Majesty?"

"There is. I hope you will consent to join my Hofkapelle, and travel back to Germany with me." He reaches for her hand. "I am like King Saul, set upon by demons. You are my little David—you drive them away with your harp. Will you come?"

Before Catherine can reply, motion in the doorway draws her eyes from him. The apparition is as familiar to Maximilian as his own face, but a stranger to Catherine. Maximilian sees her astonishment at the sight: a barrel with short legs, a woolly mass of a face and a promontory where others have a chin. The person has her lute, which she left in the outer room. He drops to one knee in front of her, fingers bringing forth cacophony from the strings, while he croons a song about cocks crowing in the month of May. His voice takes all the music out of it. He has deep lungs, but when he finally draws breath, Maximilian intervenes.

"Kunz, those whom the muses have not blessed must find other ways of serving them. Yours would be to sit quietly and let Catherine sing. Let me introduce this person to you, Catherine. This is Kunz von der Rosen, my advisor, bodyguard—"

"—and fool," Kunz says.

"If you see me," the emperor says, "Kunz is not far. But beware of him—he is capable of saving your life in the morning, then hiding a rotting fish somewhere in your chamber by nightfall."

"But Majesty, I never play pranks on ladies. They never see the fun of it—they just gaze upon you with mournful eyes, and make you long for death," Kunz says.

"Kunz, this is Catherine de Croÿ. Take care of her, for she is our pearl of great price—"

"Beware, Miss, else you'll end up in pawn with the rest of the emperor's jewels!" Kunz interrupts again.

"Give her the lute, you ape. Instruments are items of value, and must be treated with care, like those who play them."

2

Look with Favor upon a Bold Beginning

Catherine stops trying to count the hours spent in the saddle, watching the back of the rider in front of her. Maximilian had not wanted her to ride, saying it was not seemly for a woman to be seen riding in the company of men, but he had not forbidden it. She keeps it up out of stubbornness, though her *achterwerk* feels worn open with saddle sores. She gives up counting the number of overnight resting places, an odd assortment for an imperial contingent. She sleeps in the houses of rich merchants in small market towns, where the owners seem overjoyed to offer free hospitality to the royal locusts, as well as sagging country inns, where it is definitely unwise to examine the straw mattress too closely.

She learns quickly, and now knows most of the two hundred knights, advisors, secretaries, friends, artists, musicians, and servants who make up the emperor's retinue. A small group of ladies tags along, which, he jokes, is necessary to prevent his itinerant company of noblemen from devolving into barbarians. Finally, someone whispered the truth to Catherine: it's the entourage of his favorite courtesan. The emperor insists upon discretion—the courtesan does not appear in public with him or put herself forward, and she does not exercise power at court. The ladies travel in coaches.

Catherine's fellow musicians turn away when they see her coming, but she feels their eyes at other times, cleaving to her with a mixture of curiosity, resentment, and the male emotion that follows her everywhere.

Hoffman, the assistant chapel master, does not stare. He is about forty, soft around the middle, with a walk that reminds Catherine of a hen struggling to lay an egg. When he gives her directions during rehearsals, he seems to regards her as he would a well-trained dog or a dancing bear—she is performing a good trick, but not making real music.

In an attempt to improve relations, Catherine shares the music she brought with her from Mechelen with Hoffmann. With a patron like Maximilian, a constant flow of new music is vital.

"Here," Hoffmann says, slapping a pile of manuscript pages down in front of her, as though paying off a debt. "These are songs by our imperial court composer, Ludwig Senfl, in return for the music you brought. You'll meet him when we join the rest of the Kapelle in Augsburg. He's very gifted in song, both singing and writing them." He indicates the manuscripts with his chin. "Read them. You'll see."

She reads and plays them all, exhausting several candles and giving herself a headache. The pages contain German songs. Some are well-known folk tunes given original settings by Senfl; others are newly composed melodies and texts. The simple complexity of his style makes her hold her breath. The relationship between music and word is as natural as walking and breathing, but she recognizes the formidable talent it takes to create this apparent simplicity.

Some of his music surprises her, and she laughs aloud alone in her room. One song layers multiple melodies and texts atop one another. What might have been a disastrous soup of disparate elements is a harmonious whole under his hand, sounding sweet, salty, and delicious.

She likes his handwriting, and the way he signed his name 'Ludwig Senfl, Schweizer'. So, he is proud to be Swiss, and wants to set himself apart from his German and Austrian peers. The unusual curves and strong leaps of his melodies fascinate her, as does his sense of humor.

As the emperor's cavalcade nears Augsburg, the Hofmeister pulls Catherine aside.

"Madam, er... customs are different here in Bavaria... ladies discouraged from riding... most improper... we've made room for you with the ladies in their coach."

Every pit and stone in the rutted path jolts and jars her bones. She sits like Daniel among the lions, ignoring the whispers with heat throbbing in her face. She doesn't mind not belonging, but being deliberately shut out is no easier at twenty-three than it had been as a child.

The duchess had been kind, and had always had time for her, but most of her childhood was spent among children who knew she was beneath them, and never let her think otherwise. The noble house of Croÿ is one of the oldest in Flanders, but the name is useless to her. It was her mother's name. There's no shame in being the natural child of a nobleman, but there's no lack of it if your father doesn't accept you as his own.

In the days of Philip the Good, Duke of Burgundy, being called a bastard wasn't necessarily an insult. A couple of his favorite illegitimate sons even used it as an honorific, such as Anthony, Bastard of Burgundy. As Catherine grew older, she gleaned some comfort from that thought, but never breathed a word. All she needed was for her tormentors to find out his other nickname and start calling her *le grand bâtard*.

Maximilian's courtesan, a dark-haired lady from Salzburg named Barbara, attacks her with eyes like poisonous darts, but also relishes inducting the young provincial into the mysteries of *circus maximilianus*. The courtly veneer must be kept shining.

"Apparently you are going to stay with us at the Fugger palace, in the *Damenhof*. Nowhere else for you to go, I suppose, and the emperor wants his favored servants with him everywhere. You are in for a treat—the Fugger palace makes your court at Mechelen look like a stall!" Catherine's face wears a polite mask, while her mind paints satisfying pictures of the lady from Salzburg's slow and painful death. She wonders how Maximilian can bear that voice—affectedly high, thin and white like strained milk.

The coach trundles through the streets of Augsburg, near the end of the procession, and Barbara gives her an account of the action. Catherine can't see anything, but only hears the shouts of the people standing along the route. Before they entered the gates, a servant closed the curtains on the ladies' coach. Discretion.

"Outside the gate, the emperor is welcomed by the mayor and the council. Four prominent citizens carry a litter. It's considered quite an honor. But he always refuses to get in, to show his humanity. Common people love him for his kindness. On one visit, before his leg was so bad, he walked all the way to his residence near Holy Cross."

"The streets are clean and decorated—no dung between here and the Weinmarkt to offend the imperial nose. Can you imagine?" Barbara's laugh shatters Catherine's last nerve. "Every horse in Augsburg is in attendance! The riders don't wear armor, naturally, since he is welcomed as a guest."

Examining the lady from Salzburg, Catherine sees traces of a familiar face in her features. She must be the mother of her childhood persecutor-in-chief, a boy a few years younger than herself named Dietrich. Catherine knew he was the emperor's natural son, since the battles for supremacy with Charles began as soon as the two of them could ball their hands into fists. She unconsciously rubs a small scar on her right index finger. She had irritated Dietrich once, and he had bitten her finger, twisting her hand as he did so. The result was torn flesh. She had been unable to play the lute or the viol for nearly two months while it healed.

THAT evening she plays and sings with a small group in Jakob Fugger's smaller, more intimate dining hall, for about one hundred guests. The emperor displays her to the music-loving businessman. Catherine sees his motivation clearly: 'Look, here's something I have that you do not.' Jakob Fugger praises her performance, smiling without showing his teeth.

It is long past midnight when she makes her way to her room, guided by a servant who clearly thinks things have traveled too far down the wrong road if itinerant musicians are staying in the *Damenhof*. Another servant speeds toward them, and whispers something Catherine cannot hear. They turn around.

"The emperor wants you," the servant says. Catherine's bones ache, and she clenches her jaw in an attempt to stop yawning.

An armed doorkeeper waves her in. She opens the inner door, and is dazzled by the light, and the rich furnishings of the room. Every surface is decorated with tapestries, frescoes, and paintings; even the ceiling is adorned. Blood pulses in her face. She is standing in the emperor's bedchamber.

The first person she sees is not the emperor, but another man, slightly older than herself. She stares at him, her tired mind wondering why a stonemason in shabby clerical clothing is visiting the emperor in the middle of the night. His bulk makes the room seem smaller. She sees his profile illuminated by the hearth behind him, then he turns toward her. He looks at her; the brown of his eyes is so dark it melds with the blackness of his pupils. There are shadows beneath his eyes, and the whites are not as white as they might be. He nods to her, and one corner of his mouth tugs upward. She bows her head slightly, then her eyes flick back to his face. No, not a stonemason after all.

The emperor appears from an inner room, supported by Kunz, who helps him walk to a chair near the fire.

"I have warned his majesty about the evils of drinking to excess," Kunz says to Catherine, "especially while drafting the agenda of the Diet! If he is not careful, the Turkish sultan will be elected emperor, and we'll make war on the king of Spain!" After depositing the emperor safely in his chair, the jester drags a hassock across the room and plants himself at Catherine's feet. She looks down, and sees him plucking at the hem of her skirt, gazing up at her with hopeful eyes while muttering about her cruel disdain for him. She jerks her hem from him, upsetting his balance. He topples off the hassock.

The emperor is fully sober. He extends his hand to the man in the cleric's robes.

"Herr Senfl, you were missed on the journey."

Catherine gapes, then recovers herself, but not before she hears Kunz's voice from the floor.

"Catching flies?"

Maximilian says, "Senfl, this is the newest member of the Hofkapelle, Catherine de Croÿ."

Senfl nods slightly with a tight smile.

"It is our wish that you prepare duets for our private entertainment as soon as possible. I suspect your voices will blend like something heaven itself had in mind."

"I'd be delighted, Majesty," Catherine says. "I've been very eager to meet you, Herr Senfl, after reading your songs."

"No thought for what I am suffering," Kunz sighs.

Senfl barely glances in her direction.

"Your Ladyship is too kind." His accent lilts and sways, but his words sound like an insult.

"I have an idea that concerns Catherine, but you also, Senfl," the emperor says. "With so much at stake during the Diet, we feel a strong statement is needed at the opening Mass, when we will be adorned with the consecrated papal sword, and declared the chief defender of the faith. If the Hofkapelle could sound even more celestial than usual, all would know that the Almighty has chosen us for this task."

Something cold tickles Catherine's stomach, then creeps up to the base of her skull.

"Catherine, be at ease. It will be arranged with all possible discretion. You will not come to harm, and we will not lose face." The emperor rings a small bell, which stands on the table next to him, and after a few moments a servant enters the room carrying a bundle.

"Give that to the lady," the emperor directs the servant, and then dismisses him.

"Majesty," Catherine hears the bleat in her voice, "they will know, sir. They'll guess!"

"Nonsense. The mind will not accept what it knows to be impossible. I will rest now. Don't forget about my duets."

"Don't worry, Miss!" Catherine looks down and sees Kunz's cheerful grin. "You'll look like the kind of pretty choirboy priests love to grope in dark vestries!"

Senfl bows and leaves the room, and Catherine prepares to follow him.

"Catherine, stay a moment," the emperor says. "Do you have your lute with you?"

"Yes, sir."

"Would you fetch it, and play for me while I fall asleep?"

Catherine collects her lute and gives the bundle of clothes to the servant, whose mood has not improved in the meantime. She dismisses him, hoping she can find her way alone.

When she returns, Kunz has propped the emperor up in bed, and drawn up a chair for her.

"Don't stop playing until the snoring starts. Instrument makers should study his nose for its resonant qualities." Kunz says as he leaves the room.

Catherine begins to play a melody, one of the popular ones that every composer has set. Tonight, she chooses Josquin's. Though she's not singing, the words unravel in her mind like a scroll:

Desperate fortune,
Unjust and accursed,
Who have blackened the name
Of such a noble lady.

"All will be well, don't worry so much. Surely you've always longed for a chance like this." Apparently the emperor has been hearing the words in his mind, too.

Catherine nods, but her stomach still feels full of snakes.

"I will give you something in return for your service to me. It is rather out of the ordinary, after all," Maximilian says.

Rather out of the ordinary, Catherine thinks. A woman singing in a cathedral full of sacred and secular princes. She's not sure what would happen to her if she were found out. She pictures excommunication, prison, and torture.

"Do you always negotiate with your subjects?" Her hands continue to make music.

"The Diet is nothing more than one long negotiation. The sovereign petitions his subjects, as if he were a commoner, and not the kingdom itself. Tell me what you want."

She decides to show him instead, in the way of good storytellers. She finishes playing the song, sets her lute on the floor, and stands.

His face is warm between her hands. How soft his lips are—what a contrast with the roughness of his shadow of a beard. She can't bear for it to seem merely affectionate, so she parts her lips, daring him to go further. By her own volition, or his action, she finds herself lying beside him. Her body thrums with the resonance of a plucked chord—exhilarating, but nearly unbearable without resolution. Like music.

He takes his lips from her. She hears only their combined breathing, sounding ragged and sticky. She wants to bury her face in his neck and breathe him in.

"Why did you do that?" His voice is heavy and dark like red wine and clove.

How can she explain? There wasn't a clear beginning, not like turning the page in a book of hours, and seeing an illuminated initial. It simply always had been. *In saecula saeculorum, amen.*

"Because I wanted to, Majesty."

He laughs. "I think we can dispense with that formality, for the moment. Call me something sweet that you like."

The name belongs in her thoughts; she can barely say it aloud. "Because I've always wanted to, Maxi, ever since I was little."

He smoothes her hair with his hand. His face is so close, looking like it always had in her dreams.

"How you surprise me. I had such a passion myself when I was a young boy. I loved one of the ladies of my mother's chamber. When they sent her away to be married, I did something very foolish." She loves the conspiratorial tone in his voice.

"What did you do?"

"I stole gunpowder from my father's armory and stockpiled it in the cellar. By the time they found it, it could have blown up half the castle. My father locked me up for three days with nothing but bread and water."

"And you deserved it! Was your lady very beautiful?"

"She was, and I can still see her face. But I am old and ill, what could possibly attract you? You are not the kind to angle for the title of empress; besides, I've told you I will never marry again. Not even for a face like yours."

His hand runs the length of her cheek, stopping at the bare expanse between her neck and shoulder. Catherine wills an invasion, but the emperor retreats.

"I don't want to be empress. I want you. Is that so hard to believe?"

"No, not now that I have felt that kiss," His hand moves back to her face, brushing her lips with his thumb. "But these feelings you have for me are unnatural."

It's a good sign that he has not moved away, Catherine thinks, nor evicted her from his bed. She wishes she could memorize his scent. It reminds her of the forest, a whiff of something tangy and resinous carried on the wind.

"Why are they unnatural? We're not related, are we?"

"No, we are not. I wondered whether I might find myself in Lot's predicament one day, but that is not the case with you." What she hears in his voice could be pride or self-mockery, she's not sure.

"Why then?"

Maximilian separates himself from her in stages, as if he's still deciding. He finally moves away. "Your guardian, my daughter Margaret," Catherine cringes at the emphasis, "would find a way to place me under the imperial ban if I touched you, and rightly so."

She hears the lie, clear like silence.

Catherine wipes her eyes before sitting up and looking at him. The smile she attempts feels watery and not very convincing.

"Will I be banished from court for taking liberties with the imperial person?"

"Our person was far from offended, as I think you know. Now go to your own bed. Ring that bell, will you? I may as well get a few hours of work done. You are useless as a sedative."

So are you, she wants to say. She could barely think from exhaustion when she walked into the room. She can't think now either, but weariness had fled.

Catherine collects her instrument and walks to the door. The air around her seems heavy and unstable, like it does before a thunderstorm.

"Sleep well, Kathl."

She looks back. What she sees in his face works on her as sunshine does after rain.

"Good night, Majesty."

3

From the Emperor's Book of Days

Augsburg is like a lover I can't wait to return to. She's not as beautiful as Innsbruck, but cities are like women: the right combination of other charms makes up for a lot. A very special lover is needed to hold the attention year after year, as I know—one of my mistresses has been with me for twenty years. She has changed with age, as I have—but sometimes I crave her, and nothing else will do.

I feel at home in Augsburg, as far as is possible anywhere, with my frequent travels. I visit so often that some wit decided to nickname me the mayor. The city council always ensures that the streets are full of cheering people to receive me. My subjects love me, even when they hate me.

Augsburg is home to several of my creditors. The amount I owe Jakob Fugger would keep most men wakeful at night, but fortunately I am not a worrier. I would have had my fill long ago if I allowed such things to affect me.

Fugger delights in displaying his artificial Venetian palace on the *Weinmarkt*. He is also never seen without his golden Venetian headgear, perched above that insipid face with its strangely elongated upper lip. He seems always to keep this thought in his mind when he receives me: *I am wealthier and more powerful than you, Habsburg. If you've accomplished anything, it is thanks to my capital.* He is correct, of course, but he also cannot forget that my father gave him his coat of arms (you cannot go anywhere in this city without getting an eyeful of Fugger lilies), and I gave him his nobility. But in name only—true nobility is a gift from God and is in the blood and bone, and in that light, Jakob Fugger is beyond all help. I know it, and his wife knows it. Sibylla Fugger stems from one of Augsburg's oldest patrician families, and all of Jakob's money and influence can't smooth over the rough texture of wool trading in his family background. She did not tell me this—it is there to be read in her face when she looks at him.

Sibylla and I had a comfortable understanding for many years. She was never an exciting mistress, but bedding Fugger's wife helped even out the ledgers for me somewhat. And women are all alike. Princess, patrician, or pretty burgher's daughter—they will give you the sun and the moon if you use your tongue.

When deciding on the venue for my last imperial Diet, Augsburg was the natural choice. The council does not stint on hospitality or ceremony, and what is the Diet besides one long pageant, punctuated by feasts, tournaments, dances and celebratory masses? While we are resting from these exertions, the estates and I like to gather in council chambers and harangue one another with our various points of view on taxes, law and order, and political reform. I say this in jest. The Diet is serious business, and the entertainments are simply diversions to keep the temperamental participants in a good mood, where possible.

One of my great challenges during any Diet is reminding the estates who the sovereign is, and who the subjects are. In Germany, the electors, princes, and freeholders do exactly as they please, with little regard for the wishes of their sovereign. Truly, I am a king of kings. Yet I manage to have my way with them occasionally. It must be done subtly. If I sit upon my dais issuing commands, they ignore me and drone on about who made me emperor in the first place. You see how they miss the point in their narrow view of things. Yes, they elected me, but in doing so they merely served as God's instruments, carrying out his divine plan.

But I am a hunter, used to stalking skittish prey. My first tactic is to ensure I have the largest entourage upon entering the city: seven hundred knights in armor in addition to my usual retinue. My imperial crest flutters everywhere—from every halberd, every standard. Every foot soldier wears it. My double-headed eagle roams the streets, seeking to devour Fugger lilies, at least in my imagination.

I lay aside my hunting garments and appear in splendid array at all times: brocade with gold thread, studded with gemstones and pearls. I send my chamberlain to reclaim jewels left in pawn in moments of need: glorious treasures of my Austrian and Burgundian inheritance. I appear at festive services in the cathedral in my mitered crown, with scepter, orb, and cloak of ermine.

My musical tastes set the standard in the empire, and all the princes and electors align their court chapels according to what they have heard the Hofkapelle perform at the Diet. I stock my Hofkapelle like I do my fishing ponds, to remain two steps ahead of current musical taste, both in composition and performance.

When my musicians perform at the opening service in Augsburg cathedral, the assemblies will hear something remarkable. I have been enjoying this unique sound during my private devotions, and it seems a pity to hide such a flame under a bushel basket. It will remain suitably hidden, of course—to do otherwise would be to lose face. But it will be heard. What the Diet doesn't know will make me the prince with the best choir in Europe, even better than the Medici pope, who loves his music more than most. His Holiness will hear of it from his bland little legate Cajetan, and he will not be pleased to have been surpassed by me.

4

A Woman Leads the Way

Catherine peers out of a small door at the rear of the Fugger palace into the morning sunshine. Anyone watching her would see a young court musician, hardly more than a boy, dressed in a black cloak with wide slashed sleeves and a felt hat with a broad brim worn at angle. A few red-gold curls peep out from under the hat.

Before edging out the door, she looks left and right. Once out on the street she trots, keeping her eyes on the ground. Her movements feel awkward, as though she's only just figured out how her limbs work.

The *Weinmarkt* is full of people: servants and messengers rushing here and there carrying baskets and bundles, ragged beggars with outstretched hands, lawyers and scholars, important people high up in litters or on horseback, surrounded by mounted soldiers with halberds and flapping coats of arms. *Landsknechten*, imperial soldiers for hire, parade around in their overbright costumes, puffed and beribboned, with slashed bicolor sleeves and feathery hats. The emperor exempted them from the sumptuary laws himself, to make up for the other privations of their violent lives.

Catherine passes one of the beggars, who seems to be an old imperial soldier himself, judging by the remnants of the emperor's crest still visible on his tattered cloak. The beggar turns his face to follow the slight figure hurrying by, and calls out some incoherent request. His face is a mask of pustules the size of small pebbles, with a hole where his nose had been. Catherine flicks a penny into the beggar's hat and walks on, disturbing a cloud of flies with her movements. Her first glimpse of the new plague: the great pox, or the French sickness, named for its habit of spreading wherever French soldiers have been.

The emperor's residence near Holy Cross is across town from the Fugger palace. During her walk, Catherine wonders why the emperor is not staying in his own house. The answer comes when she sees it. If she had not seen the Fugger palace, this house might have seemed grand. She's already learned how crucial appearances are at the Diet.

She stands in front of the house, out of breath. Her face feels a bit green after her encounter with the beggar. Suddenly, she dashes into a small alleyway and vomits. She slumps against the wall, breathing hard, and wipes her mouth with the back of her hand. She stops at a pump, swishes some water around in her mouth, then spits. Then she turns and enters the courtyard, stopping a servant who points to a door. Catherine adjusts the angle of her hat, straightens her back, and walks into the house, looking almost calm.

Once inside, she roams the halls, looking for the music library. She passes an open door, stops, reverses, and glances in. A burly man scans the shelves. He is muttering, pulling out volumes, not finding what he wants, and shoving them back again. Catherine sidles into the room without making a sound. Then she clears her throat.

"Yes," the man sounds as though his last measure of patience is needed to control his voice.

"Herr Senfl," Catherine's voice sounds strange in her own ears.

The man whips around. He stares, opens his mouth, then shuts it again.

"Well?" Catherine's hands signal a question.

Senfl laughs. "I wouldn't have believed it. Kunz was right—take care around priests. In fact, I'd guard my bunghole with my life if I were you."

From you too? Catherine lacks the courage to ask.

She removes the hat, releasing a flood of red-gold hair. She reads the question in Senfl's eyes while he stares at her. Before she dressed, her servant helped her wrap long strips of cloth around her upper body, to conceal her shape under the tunic. The wrappings impede her breathing, which is no way to make music with the voice. She reaches under the tunic, makes an adjustment, exhales, and begins to feel somewhat like herself again.

Senfl walks around the long central table, and shuts the door. His graceful movements are at odds with his size.

"Welcome back to earth, Ganymede. Are you here to sing to me of Olympus, and how you escaped the eagle's talons?" Senfl asks. His bow is a caricature of courtly manners. "To what do I owe this honor?"

Catherine hands him a bundle of rolled-up music, wondering why his voice always sounds like a weapon of war when he speaks to her.

"Duets, by his majesty's command. These are from Duchess Margaret's library. You may know some of them already, but there are some new ones, by de la Rue and Cornysh."

Ludwig absorbs this information in silence while paging through the music. The song by Cornysh holds his interest. "This is quite good. Pity that English is not one of my many languages."

"How many do you speak?"

"Two and a half. Swiss-German, Latin, and enough Italian to find a whore and not starve, in that order."

"I know enough English to teach you this song," Catherine says.

"Don't trouble yourself. Some of our singers spent time at the English court—I'll ask one of them." Senfl turns his back on her and the music, returning to his perusal of the bookshelves.

Catherine folds herself into a chair. Breeches are so much more comfortable than skirts. She watches Senfl as he continues his search, remembering her reaction to his music. Her mind can't unite this peevish antagonist with the composer of such clever and humorous songs.

She takes a deep breath. "Why don't you like me?"

Senfl doesn't turn around. "I don't know you; I neither like nor dislike you."

"But you have something against me."

"My teacher Isaac and the chapel master built this Hofkapelle into something to be reckoned with. Germany was once a musical wasteland—now we can stand up to the choirs of Burgundy and the papal chapel." Senfl grabs a large volume, sticks his long arm through the gap, and rummages around behind the row of books and folios. "Isaac died last year, and Kapellmeister Slatkonia is off playing bishop in Vienna, so I do both jobs, plus singing—I don't have time to prop up dabblers."

Catherine clamps her lips together to prevent something rude from escaping. When she can speak calmly, she says, "I was privy musician to Duchess Margaret of Austria—the person who maintains the musical traditions of Burgundy you admire so much. She knows music, and doesn't tolerate anything short of excellence. I learned from some of Flanders' best, like de la Rue. If that's what you call dabbling, then I don't understand the meaning of the word."

"Very impressive," Senfl says. His tone indicates he's a long way from impressed. "Kaiser Max doesn't usually try to pass his *Schlafweiber* off as musicians. He's getting imaginative in his dotage."

Catherine doesn't know the term, but figures it out from the components—a woman one sleeps with. It's too late to try to keep her voice steady—the words have already breached the ramparts.

"I would have expected Isaac's favorite pupil to have a few more fish in the pond than you seem to. Strange, we Flemings usually have a better sense of people." Senfl has finally turned to face her, and she sees that he doesn't like anyone sneering at his teacher. "I'm no more a concubine than you are—I'm a musician in the emperor's employ. Do you really think he would place a 'dabbler' front and center at this Mass?"

"When it comes to the emperor, I don't think. I make the sign of the cross and say 'thy will be done'."

"That makes you a fool, doesn't it?" Catherine says.

The sound of church bells reverberates through the open windows, forming a rainbow of sound one layer at a time. The smaller bells are the heralds, and the tone color deepens as the larger bells join in.

"Forgive me, for a moment I forgot my Christian charity. You're just a Swiss boor, and people like me make allowances for people like you." Catherine stands up and puts her hat on, vigorously stuffing her hair back underneath.

"Ah, here it is," Senfl finds a small flask hidden in the shelves. He uncorks it, takes a long sip, then offers it to Catherine. She shakes her head, guessing the source of redness in his eyes. "Are you sure? It's *Weinbrand*, nature's own restorative. It will settle your nerves…"

"I'm not nervous!"

"Suit yourself." Senfl stows the flask in his leather pouch.

"See you in church, if you don't fall into the river first," Catherine says from the doorway.

"The river's nowhere near here. Are you sure you know where—?"

Catherine obliterates the end of his sentence by slamming the door. She soothes her injured pride by wishing a variety of ills on Senfl in Flemish. She finds her way outside again, and realizes she doesn't know exactly where the cathedral is. But she'd rather have a blind leper take her by the hand and show her the way than ask Senfl for directions. No lepers volunteer their services, so she follows the sound of the tolling bells.

The first eruption of sound from the trumpets and sackbuts makes Catherine jump, although she was expecting it. One of the choirboys has his eye on her and smirks.

The sweet spice of incense melds with the musk of the bodies surrounding her. Before she stood among them, she had observed the singers at Mass packed around the large, ornate music stand, the older men with weaker eyes crowding the little boys in front so that their chins nearly rest on the ledge. She thought it looked collegial, this great brotherhood of singers, hands resting on shoulders, sides brushing sides. But nothing is like it seems from the outside. The bass behind her crowds her unnecessarily, and she feels a part of him, sullen and leaden, jutting into her hip. She waits until the brass instruments surge to a loud finish before driving her elbow into his ribs.

Augsburg cathedral is decorated for the opening service of the Diet like a bride adorned for her husband, as the emperor had said. Catherine stares at her surroundings: the high vaulting, the radiated color of the stained glass, altarpieces shimmering with gold leaf, flowers, satin hangings, and linen altar cloths, whiter than cream. The perpetual twilight softens the sense of sight, hinting at the presence of unseen things.

She peers across the nave and can just discern the brass players, cheeks puffing into half-spheres, faces turning the color of a cardinal's robe. Catherine makes the comparison easily, since there are three cardinals in sight: the two papal legates, Cajetan and Lang, and a newly consecrated member of their exalted ranks: the former archbishop of Mainz, Albrecht of Brandenburg. The negotiations have begun, and so have the payouts.

The electors and other representatives of the estates process into the cathedral to the sound of brass instruments. When they rest, Paul Hofhaimer plays the organ near the choir. He stands as straight as a larch at his instrument while his calcant pumps the bellows. He improvises on *Te deum laudamus*; his lithe movements make him seem like a much younger man. He plays a reed organ with pipes shaped like bulbs; the sound is both sweet and strident. His long, narrow face and strikingly pointed nose give him the look of a learned fox. Even though he is concentrating on his task, not looking in her direction, Catherine senses the acuteness of his eyes. She has heard his students discussing the power of his stare; how his gaze wilts them when displeased, or how his eyes shine approval when he is satisfied.

While Hofhaimer plays, the procession continues. Catherine knows very few of the participants. All interactions at the Diet are dictated by the strictest protocol, and the procession is emblematic of it, as though they had taken the words of the gospel of Matthew literally, while missing their meaning. The last were indeed first, and the first would be last: the emperor would be the final person to process down the long aisle to his place near the altar.

Catherine sees the elector of Saxony, who she barely recognizes from his visit to Mechelen in 1508, since Frederick the Wise is now overweight and gouty. "Not so wise as he makes himself out to be, if he imagines he'll be elected King of the Romans!" Maximilian's advisor Renner had said. "He pretends he can't be bought, and says the whole electoral process is corrupt, whines about 'free elections'. He'll open his purse once he sees how the wind is blowing: a storm from Spain, right in his fat face."

Catherine recognizes a few of the high-ranking families already standing in the sanctuary: Welsers, Langenmantels, Meutings. She has sung in their dining rooms and reception halls. How little it would take for one of them to look her way, look a little too closely, stare a bit too long, and remember where they had seen that face before. A cold current makes its way down her back.

"Patricians notice musicians as much as they do servants," Hoffmann said before they took their places in the nave, attempting to put her fears to rest. He gave her another reassurance. Maximilian had personally discussed her performance with the Hofkapelle with them all, and had charmed them into silence. "You don't know how much we count upon your loyalty to us at this, our last imperial Diet." Then he gave them each a few guilders. Everything else is for sale at the Diet, why not this? Catherine thinks of the irony of paying musicians and singers for their silence.

At the chapel master's signal, the singers turn their eyes to the huge volume of music. They sing a Magnificat composed by Senfl. He stands beside Catherine, looming like a city gate at dusk. As long as you're on the correct side, all is well. She follows the music with her eyes, listening to the voices around her, especially Senfl's. His pitch is solid and precise, and she navigates to it like a sailor to the pole star. She checks herself, reining in the full power and richness of her voice, letting it blend with the voices of the boys. Her moment has not yet come.

When the emperor comes into view she takes a furtive look, though the music should command her full attention. He is draped in the pale brightness of his ermine cloak, and his scepter and jeweled crown gleam like sources of light themselves. He walks with a measured pace, a bit stiffly, but he is not limping. Even in everyday dress, his inward dignity makes him look regal; his gift is to seem at home anywhere, doing anything. But today, walking alone down the aisle of Augsburg cathedral, he looks elevated, as if he has surpassed the level of his creation, and taken his place a little higher than the angels. When Catherine looks back at the music, the notes dissolve before her eyes.

The singers begin to sing a Mass in alternation with the organ. Each part takes the plainchant as its basis: Hofhaimer plumbs every note, interval, and fragment of melody for material on which to improvise. Isaac's Mass gives the melody a superb six-voice edifice in which to live, ornamenting the chant delicately, showing it off in imitation between two voices, or spreading it out over all of them, his music transposes, modifies, and glorifies.

Near the end of the Mass, Cardinal Cajetan stands before Emperor Maximilian. Kunz von der Rosen has helped the emperor to kneel. A priest holding the blessed sword and hat stands beside the cardinal. Cajetan's reedy voice drifts through the sanctuary like dust.

"In the presence of all assembled here, in the name of His Holiness, Pope Leo X, vicar of Jesus Christ, successor of the Prince of the Apostles, servant of the servants of God, I bestow upon you, Maximilian, emperor-elect of the Holy Roman Empire, King of Germany, Archduke of Austria, this blessed sword and hat, and the title of chief defender of the faith. Receive the pope's blessing, and His Holiness' sincere desire that by the grace of God you win the holy war against the Turks, retake Constantinople and Jerusalem, and live to see the expansion of Christianity and the Holy Roman Empire, to the ends of the earth."

The cardinal makes the sign of the cross, and the emperor receives the pope's gifts.

"Please relay to His Holiness my humble gratitude for the honor done to me today. Although I am no longer in the full vigor of youth, I intend to lead the armies of the faith in our holy war. I will not spare myself, my limbs, or my life's blood for the survival of Mother Church or the true faith. It will be done to the glory of God." The emperor uses his voice to great effect—it is not loud, but the stones of the cathedral walls ring with it, and it seems to come from everywhere at once. Catherine's limbs wash warm from within, the quiver in her gut breaks outward and up to her heart.

The last echo of his voice fades. One thousand living breathing bodies inhabit the moment in silence.

The chapel master raises his hands. There is no time, energy, or cause for thought. Catherine puts herself aside, and becomes a vehicle for something else. The tenors and altos form the bedrock, and her voice catapults out of their solid ranks, cascading from the vaults and columns. The power of her voice eclipses the choirboys; she breaks through their veil of sound as the sun sears though mist:

Join the queen of birds to yourself, the king of beasts, that once the Chimaeras are driven away your flock may be restored to you as your own. Then kindle the united wrath of your noble heart against the Turk, wolves and monsters of Canopus. No beast nor hostile bird shall withstand the flock, when they see the eagle as leader, and the true lion. These holy prayers the praise-singers of Caesar re-echo.

She raises the message as the celebrant raised the Host, hoping and trusting for transfiguration: earthly to divine.

5

The Power of Wine and Song

After Mass, the members of the Hofkapelle crowd into a tavern tucked away in the steep alleyways behind the Rathaus. In the normal course of events, Catherine would have held her breath even passing such a place. The ceiling is low, grudgingly held aloft by enormous, cracked beams. The tables are greasy, the cups dented and filmy from years of indifferent cleaning. The musicians shout for wine and brandy.

She's never experienced such a lingering euphoria after singing. Good spirits, yes, but this is different. If her feet are in contact with the earth, she isn't aware of it. Her mind rebels at the thought of going back to another long afternoon of solitude in the *Damenhof*, so she follows the group of men to the tavern.

The trouble is, the musicians didn't actually invite her to come along, so she finds herself alone, standing near a window. Lorenzo, a Florentine sackbut player, gives her a pat on the back on his way by, while shouting some unintelligible words of praise, but she understands the admiration in his tanned face.

She sees Senfl approaching her, and her back stiffens like an agitated cat. Would he initiate a public sparring match for the amusement of the Hofkapelle? She doesn't know him well enough to guess.

"Hello... Ganymede." He hands her a cup of wine. "By way of apology."

She hesitates, then clinks her cup against his. "Accepted."

"As the leader of this august company, it falls to me to confer an alias upon you." He sprinkles a few drops of wine on her head. "I christen you Johann Flamme. 'Flame', like your hair. Hannes for short. Hannes, I drink your health," he smacks his cup against Catherine's with so much animation it nearly flies out of her hand.

"And what do I call you?" Catherine asks after savoring her first sip of wine.

"You may call me Herr Hofkomponist." He drinks, then looks back at her and grins. "I jest. Call me Ludwig." He takes a deep breath, which he releases in a long, low whistle. "You left us all with our faces in the mud. I can't say I've ever heard anything like that. You have more balls than anyone here."

Catherine's face radiates like sunburn. "I've never heard my voice in a space like that."

"Now you know why we all think so highly of ourselves."

"Does the rest of the Hofkapelle feel as you do? I mean, can they be trusted?"

"Not to spread it around? I think so. Things aren't great, but it's better than singing in the square on market day holding out your hat. Even if they do throw you in prison, Kaiser Max will probably bail you out. He got one of his favorite sculptors out of prison in Nuremberg. Saved him from having his hands cut off."

Her palms begin to sweat. "What about the choirboys?"

"They didn't even notice you. Choirboys care about two things: mealtimes and the hour each day when they are finally released from servitude, and can go amuse themselves. In their eyes, one adult is much like another, and all of them are boring. I know this because I was one once."

Catherine tries to imagine a miniature Ludwig, and fails.

Ludwig drains his cup, and refills it from a pitcher on the table next to him. "Drink up, you're falling behind. Not that this stuff is worth putting in your mouth—only if you want to get drunk. It's swill compared to Italian wines."

"Were you really in Italy?" She takes a big sip. It doesn't taste that bad to her.

"Yes, with Isaac. Beautiful country. Beautiful women."

"I bet they loved you. Called you Ludovico, right?" She's gratified to see him looking a bit embarrassed for once.

"It is about the time for it, isn't it? You first." Ludwig says, bobbing up and down on his toes.

Catherine can't imagine what he means.

"Life stories. Go on. I've got money riding on this."

"Meaning…?"

"You know the bass who got so friendly during Mass? He thinks you're Kaiser Max's bastard child. I say not. Now that I know you're not his *Schlafweib*, my money's on that you're the bastard of his son Philip."

"Well, you are both wrong. Does that mean payoff for me? I could certainly use it." Catherine studies the interior of her cup.

"Don't get irked. It's all in fun. Go on."

Catherine shakes her head.

"All right, I will then. Do you want the long version, or the short version?"

Silence.

"'A silent woman is more precious than carbuncles.' That's somewhere in Proverbs, right? Here's the short version. Once, on a mountainside in Switzerland, a fifth child was born to a poor farmer. Four more come after him, and maybe more. When he's about five, the boy starts singing in the village church. A few years later, he's heard by a visiting nobleman who gives the father some trifle, and promises a bigger payoff later."

"Sounds like the start of a fairy tale," Catherine says.

"Yes, the kind they tell small children to frighten them into good behavior. The nobleman takes the child to Vienna. He can barely understand when anyone speaks to him, even though they're supposedly speaking the same language. Luckily, the child was big for his age, and could hold his own. But not against the assistant chapel master, the so-called 'Master of the Boys', who was a brute. Loved to beat us all for no reason, but me especially. Remind me to tell you about the first time I ever laid eyes on the emperor."

"'Time is flying, never to return.' Why not tell me now?" Catherine says.

Two seats on a bench have cleared, and Ludwig invites her to sit down. He keeps his distance from her by crowding the man next to him. The man glares at him but doesn't dare say anything, since Ludwig could certainly snap his wrist with no noticeable effort.

"I was about seven, I think," Ludwig says, getting comfortable on the bench. "God only knows what my offense was, but the assistant chapel master pulled me out into the courtyard by my ear and started thrashing me, and I was howling my head off.

"The emperor was walking across the courtyard with a group of men, but I didn't know it was him, since he didn't look very imperial, and I was getting the devil beaten out of me. All of a sudden the beating stopped, and I was led by the hand somewhere, still yelling. Someone took me to the kitchen. Everyone stopped what they were doing, bowed and said 'Majesty'. That's when I realized who it was. I stopped crying so fast you'd think I'd been gagged.

"He lifted me up, and sat me on the table, and he sat too, straddling the bench. We were nearly eye-to-eye that way. Someone handed me a bowl of something. Well, I was upset, but I was also hungry. We were always hungry. Whatever was in that bowl was the best food I had ever tasted—something sweet with fruit in it. I wish I knew what it was, since it's still the best thing I've ever eaten, at least in my memory.

"'You're one of the new Swiss boys, aren't you?' the emperor asked. I nodded, and he asked me my name.

"He asked me why I was being beaten. Because I was crying, I said. 'Of course you were crying, he was beating you! These people who think thrashing children is the way to get them to learn, or to obey... What were you crying about before?' I was a bit embarrassed to tell him, honestly. But he teased it out of me. I miss the mountains, I said. I miss my mother. I hate Vienna.

"He almost whispered to me: 'I'll tell you a secret which you must never reveal: I also hate Vienna, and I miss my mother too. She died when I was about your age. It gets easier. But the good news is, you'll see some mountains very soon. We're going to Innsbruck, which is my favorite city. I hope you decide to come with us, because you'll like it there too, and I'd be sorry if you went back to Switzerland, since I like your voice very much.'

"The emperor told me all this while the kitchen staff bustled all around us. I looked down at my bowl and realized I'd eaten nearly all of whatever was in it, and was guilty of very bad manners. There were a few bites left, and I asked the emperor if he'd like some.

"You know what happens when he gets that big smile on that hawk face of his. You don't know quite what hit you. He said 'No thank you, that is all for you. I'm going fishing. You'll remember what I said?' I said I would. And he got up, and everyone in the kitchen stopped what they were doing again and bowed as he left, and I finished my heavenly dish. I loved him for that."

Ludwig takes Catherine's hand, and peers into her cup. He pours some more wine for her, then himself. "Your turn, Hannes."

Catherine takes a long drink. "You were partially right. I am someone's bastard, but no one knows who. I grew up in Flanders at the court of the emperor's daughter. My mother was one of her ladies-in-waiting. She died when I was born. You know, the usual story. Seduced by some nobleman."

"Yours sounds like the same kind of fairy tale," Ludwig says. "They always say, 'she got into trouble'. Trouble got into her, is more like it."

"The emperor swears it wasn't him, and I believe it."

"So do I. Now that I look closely, there's no sign of the House of Austria in your face, lucky you. Besides, he seems to take care of his little accidents."

"The duchess insisted on propriety, and I think he respected that while at her court, so as not to subvert her authority. She's governor of the Low Countries, you know. She raised me out of loyalty to her former lady-in-waiting, who she loved like a sister."

"And when did you take up music?"

"Duchess Margaret tells it this way: one day, when I was four years old, I disappeared from the nursery, and was the cause of quite an uproar when they couldn't find me. Where do you think I was?"

"Listening to the *chapelle* sing?" Catherine tries not to laugh at his clumsy pronunciation.

"They found me in the music room, doing my best to play the viol. I was even holding the bow correctly! Thanks to that, the duchess decided that music would be my vocation. She grew up at the French court, where she had an excellent education, so she believed in teaching girls just like boys. So I learned music, but also Latin and the liberal arts."

"And German, obviously."

"So on the emperor's last visit, he asked me to come back with him. You know how he loves novelty. Apparently, he encountered a woman musician long ago, before he was even crowned Roman king. He loves to show me off—"

"Like a prize heifer?"

Catherine looks away from him, silent.

"Sorry. You obviously care about him." Ludwig pauses and dips his head a little so that he can look out of the window. "So do I. Just don't trust him so absolutely. For your own sake."

"Why? What do you know?" Catherine says, following his gaze, as though the answer could be located out in the streets of Augsburg.

"Like I said, I've lived in this chamber of wonders for most of my life, and I know what goes on. Musicians are used as spies all over, did you know that? Isaac spied for Kaiser Max in Italy for years. People talk to musicians. More importantly, they talk near them. Even if you are the emperor's pet, if he can use you in some way that will give him an advantage, he will deliver you up, trussed and garnished."

Catherine shakes her head. "I've known him all my life, Ludwig. He's fond of me."

"People are trinkets to him, nothing more. Like his cherished gemstones. He takes them out once in a while, coos over them, pretends he can't live without them, but when he needs something, off they go to be pawned or sold outright. He fills the need of the moment."

"And why should I trust you? In the space of one morning you go from adversary to ally. I can't keep up."

"Because of my guileless face," Ludwig pours them each some more wine. "Drink up. I can still feel my feet."

The wine begins to affect his tongue, strengthening his Swiss-German accent. It is drawling and wave-like—almost lyrical compared to the marching cadence of other German accents.

"Listen to this: you may not know about the emperor's interesting habit of using anything at hand as security when he can't pay his bills. Anything or anyone, I should say." Ludwig pauses to let his words take effect, always performing even when not on stage.

"Once, in Cologne, he pawned the entire Hofkapelle, including me. We were left at an inn until his chief steward arrived and paid for our release. We were lucky in some respects; our imprisonment lasted only four weeks. But only because Kaiser Max needed us somewhere else then! It was awful—the innkeeper wouldn't let us leave for any reason, not even to get a breath of air. Imagine twenty men trapped in a small inn for a month."

Catherine tries to bite her tongue, but it is too much to hold in.

"Go ahead and laugh—I can see the humor in it myself now too." Ludwig's voice is dry.

"But why didn't you leave under your own power? Surely twenty men could have pulled off some sort of escape and found their way back home again."

"Because, dear child, it takes money to travel, and none of us have any. I haven't been paid in years. The emperor gives us trifles at Christmastime, but no actual salary. We're all supposed to receive new clothing twice per year as part of our terms of service." Ludwig holds up his frayed sleeve. "I'll leave the state of my linens to your imagination."

"Cheer up, Ludovico. As Horace said, 'Let us delight in banishing fear and anxiety for Caesar's affairs, with sweet wine.'"

"I'll drink to that. But since all we have is this Rhenish vinegar, it will have to do."

*

High up in the mountains
There is a tall house
Every morning, three pretty girls come out.
The first one is my sister...

Ludwig Senfl, Schweizer
AUGSBURG, *1518*

6

From the Emperor's Book of Days

Whatever quarrels the estates and I have had, I cannot fault them for consistency. The only real surprise was how quickly it happened.

The spirit of unity and concord kindled at Mass lasted one day. When the negotiations opened, Cajetan read a speech in the pope's name. It was intended to rouse the spirits of the hearers in favor of the crusade, and keep the fervor at a high pitch. Spirits were roused, without a doubt—against their emperor and the pope, instead of the Ottomans. The estates unanimously refused to shoulder the financial burden of such an enterprise. Let the pope pay, they said, since he is richer than Maecenas. They refuse a crusade tax, and reject the idea of indulgences.

Ever since that angry monk named Luther shot his flaming arrow into the door of Wittenberg Chapel last year, a new discontent with the church has been smoldering. Leo and Cajetan will see to it, of that I have no doubt—they will water him down, before his blaze spreads. Naturally, I read his theses, and found much to commend in them. I am the last one to reject the idea of church reform; I've called for it often enough myself. But it must go no further than that. The empire needs a united Germany, and that is only possible when all worship at the same altar.

My plans for a crusade have been thwarted over and over again by the stiff necks of my subjects, and their inability to see the severity of the

THE EAGLE AND THE SONGBIRD

danger, or its proximity to our doorstep. They clutch their purses like miserly housewives, making noises about the expense, refusing to send men and materials, refusing taxes, refusing me my Common Penny. Who will they cry to when the Turks besiege their cities, burn their castles, and carry off their daughters?

The realization of the Turkish threat has been a part of me all my life—it was in the material the Almighty used when he knitted me together in my mother's womb. I was born just six years after the fall of Constantinople. To say it cast a shadow over Europe is to call a hurricane a small gust of wind. My mother even wanted to name me Constantine, but, as in so many matters, she was overruled by my father.

We will make war on the Turks, and they will be vanquished, but we will not destroy them—that is not the object. The object is the expansion of Christendom, and the reclamation of Constantinople. They will be made to convert. Once they have embraced the true faith, they can be as noble and upright as any Christian knight. One of the boys who grew up beside me at my father's court in Wiener Neustadt was a converted Turkish prince named Otman Kalixt. He was a true friend and comrade, with an honorable heart.

When the estates become fractious, they use any means available to make a point, even printed matter. It's all the same: hastily printed with primitive woodcuts and hateful slogans, such as, 'the pope is worse than the Turks!' The broadsheets flutter like a veil on a plain woman, and with the same effect: once you get behind it you quickly realize there's nothing to see.

Naturally, I stand ready with countermeasures. I prefer to use artistic means, rather than the printed word. You reach a broader audience that way, including the unlettered. They do not sway the business of the Diet, of course, but public opinion counts for something. It never hurts to have the people singing your praises. Some may doubt the effectiveness of art in influencing politics. They may wonder how much power a carved block of wood can have, rolled with ink and pressed on paper. They will see it all. I will show them myself.

Everything I desire to accomplish at the Diet is laid out in a woodcut. All things center on three large figures in the foreground: the animals, and a man on the left.

The estates must be confronted with the strong alliance between Rome and the empire. The prominence of the Medici coat of arms is also meant to flatter Leo, since his sanction and blessing are needed to crown my successor.

Hand in glove with the message of this print is Isaac's motet, sung at Mass. There can be no doubt who the eagle is—I am kneeling near the altar. The lion is a play on the pope's name. The other animal is intended to be a wolf in a posture of submission, as in the text: '*Then kindle the united wrath of your noble heart against the Turk, wolves and monsters of Canopus.*' (I have seen both a lion and a wolf. Weiditz, the artist, has clearly seen neither. But we will overlook this, as both time and money are short.)

The obvious nobility and prominent chin of the man in the foreground on the left will tell my audience all it needs to know. I instructed Weiditz to make him appear a bit older than he does in life—his appearance is still youthful, though he is a man and a king. He holds all of my eggs in his basket. To my great sorrow, my faith in him is just as fragile.

The 'praise-singers of Caesar' are there—my Hofkapelle: Hofhaimer at his organ, Senfl towering over the choir... you must be clever to discern my Songbird, but she is there too.

AFTER Mass, I was seated next to Cajetan at dinner at the bishop's palace. He brought his own phalanx of singers along with him from Rome, and heard how completely overshadowed they were by my choir. He said, "Majesty, His Holiness will want to know how you achieved the remarkable sound we heard today. Your choir boys from Vienna have been famous for years—are you employing eunuchs now?" I told the dear cardinal it must be kept quite secret. Otherwise, everyone's choir would sound like that, and where would be the novelty?

In moments of quiet reflection, of which there are precious few at the Diet, I think of her startling revelation to me, and her mouth, sweet and surprising, as unexpected as the taste of a ripe strawberry in winter. I wonder if my feint was successful. She will be wondering why I did not avail myself of her tempting offer. I would rather she imagine something untrue, such as, in the way of men my age, the little knight has become capricious about going to war. Yes, let her think this, rather than know the truth.

Yet she is wearing me down, layer by thin layer—a beautiful restoration under loving hands. She has inspired me to compose some verses. It has been too long since I wrote any poetry.

7

A Mighty Pomp of Little Things

Dusk settles over Augsburg after a day of breathless heat. The cloudless sky turns a gentle pink, with undertones of green. Catherine follows a servant to a small audience chamber in the Fugger Palace, where the first cool breezes of the evening drift into the open windows. Servants place chairs in a row in the center of the long rectangular room, flanked by candelabra. Side tables stand heavy with wine and platters of tidbits: fruit, nuts, bite-sized pastries, meats and cheeses, tiny cakes with ripe strawberries pressed on top.

Ludwig looms in the doorway, and sees her. He waves, and when he comes closer, she sees the smudges under his eyes have darkened.

"Evening, Catherine. How nice to see you for once, and not your alter ego."

"Well, I'm allowed to make music here," she looks around, and makes a questioning gesture. "What is going on, Ludovico?" She follows Ludwig past the chairs to the far end of the room. "News from the Hofkapelle never seems to reach me in the ladies' court. They just told me to bring my lute."

"It's time for the emperor's little show. You really must stop missing rehearsals." There would have been no rehearsal for this; she knows that much.

"What do I need to do?" Catherine asks. Ludwig is moving longingly toward the tables with the food, but stops well short of them.

"Don't worry, you don't have to do much," Ludwig turns back to her after a final sigh in the direction of the food, or perhaps the wine. "The trumpets and sackbuts drew the short straws, which means hour after hour of blowing. They really are the whores of the Hofkapelle, poor fellows. The lute is your cue. When you see it, play something grand in honor of the emperor. It's hard to explain, but you'll figure it out when you see the pageant."

'When you see the lute?' It's not much clearer than it was before.

Two trumpet players, four sackbuts, two cornetti and three more singers arrive, and gather against the far wall, chattering like monkeys. No one greets her. Paul Hofhaimer surges into the room, tall and energetic. He doesn't look around but rather stares at the ground. Two deep grooves crease his brow, as though he is following an invisible arithmetic problem on the floor, and is anxious to solve it before reaching his destination. His organ follows him into the room, carried by two strong organ-bearers. She's heard the emperor tell stories of Hofhaimer accompanying him on his peregrinations, even on military campaigns in Italy, so that the emperor could have his beloved organ music at all times. She is shy of him; his presence makes her spine straighten of its own accord.

The guests begin to assemble. Catherine sees the jurist Conrad Peutinger, whom the emperor calls on for everything from legal advice to ideas for names for a new cannon ("We will ask our Peutinger, this is a fitting matter for him."). He is corpulent and majestic as he trundles into the room as though pulled along on little wheels. His wife, the former Margarete Welser, is an appendage, like all the wives. Elector Frederick of Saxony enters, listing like a galleon in peril, favoring his gouty foot, and makes straight for the food. He is followed by Cardinal Matthias Lang, a man of God whose worldly appetites have earned him the nickname 'Whorehunter'. Something in his eyes makes Catherine imagine him trapping an animal solely for the pleasure of watching it die.

The emperor arrives with Jakob and Sibylla Fugger. The wife of Jakob the Rich is insubstantial, not beautiful, and vastly younger than her husband. They have no children. She absorbs everything she sees with a regal weariness as if the opulence surrounding her cannot dissuade her from thinking she is too good for it all.

When Catherine is not watching the people, she admires the room. The beamed ceiling rests on a single central column of pink and white marble. The door frames are hewn from massive pieces of oak crowned with intricate carvings, which look as though they would have taken years to complete. Cozy alcoves with carved tables and chairs covered in brightly painted leather invite intimate conversations. Frescoes of hunting scenes in bright colors adorn the walls. At first, Catherine thinks they are classical scenes, but closer inspection reveals a familiar face in each tableau: a slender figure in a hooded hunting habit following his aquiline nose as he slays bears, boars, stags, and chamois. How curious that the wealthy creditor feels the need to flatter his best customer in this way.

Some instinct, and a prickle at the back of her neck, makes Catherine turn around. The emperor and Fugger are across the room, standing close to one another, conferring. They could be evaluating the value of a work of art. Neither one of them looks in her direction. She sees the emperor's lips move, then Fugger's, then the emperor again. He shakes his head. Fugger speaks again, there is a pause, then Maximilian appears to agree to something. They briefly clasp hands.

Movement near the door drags her attention from Maximilian and Fugger, to a man who has just slipped into the room, moving lightly as though very little binds him to earth. He wears his curly hair longer than the current fashion; it streams from the crown of his head over his shoulders in lustrous brown waves. She senses wiry strength concealed in his leanness, and his lips distract her for a moment. They are pleasing and fleshy in the thin bearded face. After bowing to the emperor and greeting Fugger, the long-haired man ambles about the room, scrutinizing the art on the walls, taking a few morsels of food and eating them out of hand.

Catherine can't stop watching him. He's obviously not a patrician, but he's not out of his element either.

Maximilian seats himself in the center of the row of chairs, and the rest find their way into his orbit. Bulky Elector Frederick makes a surprisingly quick movement, ensuring he occupies the chair on the emperor's right hand. Sibylla Fugger sits on the emperor's left, her slim body angled toward him. She looks straight ahead, heavy-lidded, listlessly waving an ornate fan, which looks like it traveled from the Orient on one of her husband's merchant ships. The long-haired man hovers behind the seated audience.

The chairs face a small stage, level with the floor. A wooden frame, about ten ells long, supports long curtains that fall to the floor on either side.

A herald steps out from behind the curtain. His bright red hose draw attention to his spindly legs, and a hat with a startling plume of peacock feathers balances on his small head. He bows deeply before Emperor Maximilian.

"Imperial Majesty, Herr and Frau Fugger, and honored guests. The mighty Eagle soared over all the world, surveyed his territories, and beheld everything under the sun. He asked himself how he could portray the might, grandeur, power, riches, and splendid culture of his reign, to his praise and eternal memory. The eagle gave the command to his painters, his men of art and skill. They labored over their craft, to produce something worthy of His Imperial Majesty, something that will cause his name to be remembered for all eternity. 'Show my military victories, show my lands and territories, show my family, my ancestors and descendants. Depict coats of arms and flags, show the treasures in my possession, show my artillery, show knights, princes, lords, counts and servants, show the savages of far-off lands, show my artists and musicians. Lastly, show myself, the ruler of all'."

The brass instruments begin playing, and the herald bows and disappears. Two trumpets and four sackbuts overpower the space they are in, and Catherine anticipates ringing ears when it is all over. She imagines Maximilian wishing he had ordered more.

Catherine's eyes must deceive her: she sees pictures moving across the stage, as if held aloft by invisible hands—a stately procession of painted figures on parchment. Painted figures in bright and varied costumes hold banners upon which are depicted scenes from the emperor's life—astonishing in their detail. The colors make Catherine gasp; they are more vivid than anything she has seen in life.

Each standard-bearer wears a different costume, and all are fantastically clothed: some wear sleek, close fitting attire, some wear pleated skirts with contrasting colors, while others are seen in puffy slashed doublets held together by little bows. She wishes she were close enough to examine their faces; she's sure each would be as unique and varied as the faces seen on a busy market day in town.

The herald, now concealed behind the curtain, announces the title of each canvas as it begins its voyage across the stage.

"The War against Naples, and the Swiss War!"

Battle scenes bristle with a thousand painted pikes, flags seem to flap in the breeze, tents are set up in the distance. These campaigns number among the emperor's greatest failures. He was nearly killed on two occasions during the wars in northern Italy. To the viewers of his Triumph, however, they are held up as famous victories, or at the very least, courageous stand-offs.

"Treasures for daily use and devotional treasures!" the herald says.

Wagonloads of precious items pass before them, casks, chalices, table fountains, followed by carts laden with coins and precious stones. While the painted gold and gems wink at her, Catherine wonders where the banner is that announces Maximilian's hundreds of thousands of guilder's worth of debt. She glances at Jakob Fugger, who has the grace to be conversing with Cardinal Lang during this portion of the pageant.

Hofhaimer improvises during this scene, and a distinctive motif of four notes, the beginning of a very familiar song, leaps out at her from the torrent of notes. *Faulte d'argent*… being poor is a great pain, and alas, I know it all too well… The notes come and go so quickly, she's not sure whether she really heard it. She covers her smile and is not surprised to find humor cloaked behind that forbidding face of his.

She watches the emperor as he watches his own life unfold before his eyes, some of it real, some of it fantasy, all of it more glorious than reality. He resembles a child finally given a fantastic toy it has been promised; he can barely sit still. He's constantly twisting in his chair to point things out to Elector Frederick, Peutinger, or Lang, details too small to be seen, which he knows are there since they were included at his instruction. She can't hear much over the brass, and doubts his intended hearers can hear much either, but his gestures speak for him. He is euphoric.

This is all he has, Catherine thinks. This, and the succession of his grandson Charles. His remembrance.

The moving pictures now display familiar things: men playing wind instruments, high up on horseback. The cornetti play in the Fugger's audience chamber while their pictorial doubles move across the stage. She sees Paul Hofhaimer, looking exactly like himself, traveling across the stage in an open cart drawn by a camel. While she watches his painted form, the man himself plays the organ. She doesn't recognize what he is playing, but it sounds like a battle scene, and elicits a spatter of applause from the emperor.

Then come the singers, pulled in another open cart by elk. Ludwig sings a paean to the emperor, accompanied by three viols:

> *The Eagle soars above the earth,*
> *Full of might, none flies higher;*
> *He is praised in all the world*
> *For his strength and mighty empire.*

When he is finished singing, Ludwig gestures to her. There are her painted counterparts on the stage, a cart full of lutenists and viol players, drawn by two stags. It's hard to make a single lute sound magnificent, especially in the wake of Hofhaimer and Senfl, so she doesn't try. Then and there, she creates a new song, which she will later write down and call *Kaiserlied*—Emperor's Song, using the incipit of the tune Ludwig has just sung. She shuts her eyes, and thinks of Maximilian's love of music.

Maximilian's attention wanders from his pageant to the sweet, almost dream-like sounds stroking his ear. Each of his favorite musicians has presented their own personal tribute to him, and each pleased him in its own way. He closes his eyes, and his mind conjures a picture of himself in miniature dangling from the strings of Catherine's lute. Did he doze off? He shifts in his chair to hide his laughter.

Elector Frederick is at his elbow, gesturing at a different array of colorful figures now crossing the stage, held in formation by soldiers holding pikes and halberds horizontally in a kind of moving prison cell.

"Your Majesty has always shown mercy and benevolence to the populations you have conquered—even the Italian chroniclers made note. So it must be true." Frederick lifts his goblet to his mouth and drinks, wiping droplets from his beard with the back of his hand. "In that spirit, if I may have your Majesty's forbearance for a moment to speak about one of my subjects. I would wish to see Doctor Luther spared the fate of the colorful figures before us."

"Do you not think, Frederick, that the future of the empire is a more pressing concern for both of us than a dispute between monks?" Maximilian's voice sounds irritated to his own ears. He has never liked combining work with pleasure, and this pageant is the only pleasure he foresees until the Diet ends.

Frederick is oblivious to his sovereign's mood, or pretends he is. "In my opinion, they are one in the same, Majesty. The pope wants Luther extradited to Rome. He is your subject also, Majesty, deserving of your protection."

"Frederick, I am dancing to a piper on one stilt. If I stop moving, I will topple into the mud. Do you think I would risk angering Leo at this time, by questioning his authority to discipline one of his flock?" The emperor examines the gold goblet in his fingers. He has barely sipped the wine, though it is Ribolla, one of his favorites. "Leo's approval of my successor is vital. I have already written a letter making my position on the question of Luther very plain. As in the matter of the crusade, the empire stands with Rome." Maximilian leans closer to the elector. "Consider Luther's stance on excommunication—you cannot support that. He has swung an ax at the root of God-given hierarchy. If people begin to question the legitimacy of excommunication, what will become of the imperial ban?" Maximilian shakes his head. "He must be brought to heel, Frederick."

"I appreciate your Majesty's position," Frederick makes an effort to sound sympathetic through a mouthful of pastry, "but take a moment to consider mine. I am Luther's ruling prince, and naturally he came to me for help. I cannot prod Rome, but your Majesty can, with your Majesty's infinite talent for walking very fine lines. I would wish to see Luther tried by a German judge before sending my lamb to the pyre in Rome."

Maximilian sips his wine. He is not concerned about Luther, or the Vatican's embarrassment at being rebuked by a 'barbarian'. Germany is considered a cultural wasteland by her neighbor south of the Alps, nothing more than a deep well of jokes from which to draw. He encountered this attitude while in Italy, and in dealing with Italian emissaries. Since no one would openly insult the emperor or the king of Germany, the barbs were wrapped in the cotton wool of jest and courtly wordplay. Maximilian had countered with his charm, his faultless manners, and his mastery of the Italian language. *My soul is German*, he declared, *but my heart and mind are Italian.* Whether or not he had persuaded the officials, he had at least softened the ladies' hearts, among other things, with the passion of his words.

The idea of justice being dispensed to Luther within the empire pleases him, as does the idea of Roman officials operating within his jurisdiction. This way, he can both stand with Rome and distance himself a little. He neither wants to anger the lion, nor reduce himself to the yapping dog at its feet. He wonders if the elector really cannot take a stance against the Vatican, or simply does not wish to. Frederick was recently favored with a highly desired papal award, the Golden Rose, which might have a lot to do with his sudden attitude of cautious submission to the pope.

"We have considered the matter of our subject, Doctor Luther. He will be examined by Cajetan here at the Diet. Let him be summoned—he will receive safe conduct from us." Maximilian says.

"Majesty, your beneficence staggers the imagination," Frederick grasps Maximilian's hand and kisses it. His hand feels sticky now, and he wishes he could wipe it without breaching protocol.

"But we will support the verdict, whatever it is. We take our role as Chief Defender of the Faith very seriously," At least while it suits us to do so, he adds silently. Maximilian enjoys the comfortable feeling of having judged as Solomon might have, and once again turns his attention to the procession. He leans forward. One of his favorite panels is passing before them: the imperial chariot with himself and his family. One of the small figures represents Charles. He takes this opportunity to goad Frederick a little.

"Now that your matter is settled for the moment, we wish to speak about the matter dearest to our heart—the succession. You see Charles there," Maximilian gestures at the tableau. "You have not yet made your choice clear. It almost seems as though you are neglecting your God-given task as an elector."

"I do not neglect it, Majesty. It is ever on my mind. But I do not look at it in terms of succession, but rather finding the correct strong hand to guide the empire. Coming back to Doctor Luther, have you read his writings, Majesty? His special gift is the ability to express complex ideas in simple, colorful language. Lately, he compared Germany to a strong horse that has plenty to eat and fine saddles, is cared for and groomed—"

"That comparison was brought to my attention, along with how he ended the thought: 'but lacks a strong rider to guide it'. Not very loyal, flattering, or correct, as it happens."

"He means no disrespect to your Majesty. In fact, Luther is your very loyal and loving subject, with a high opinion of your Majesty. But the question is, is Charles the strong hand we need? You know I have always said I would never wish the imperial crown onto the head of anyone I liked, and I have always liked Charles,"

"I ask you again for your choice, Frederick."

"I am weighing the matter very carefully, Majesty, as befits a matter of this, er... gravity."

"Perhaps I may help you, Frederick. It would be of interest to you to know who has already promised their vote to Charles." A sudden motion at his elbow assures Maximilian that he has the elector's attention.

"Encouraged by your Majesty's magnanimous gifts, no doubt. Elections should be free, in my humble opinion." Frederick attempts to cover his blunder by singing his favorite refrain.

"We are in complete agreement, Frederick. Unfortunately, another prince was the author of such tactics, and now all of your cohort expect it. What can be done?" The emperor hauls his shoulders up and lets them fall with a sigh. He sips his wine, and watches his chariot roll by. He turns to Sibylla and points out the detailed carvings on the side of the chariot. He knows he has roused Frederick's curiosity, and wants to make him twitch a little.

"Your Majesty is correct; what can be done? But if I may be allowed to know who has pledged their vote already...?"

After the imperial chariot come the coats of arms of the seven prince-electors. Maximilian turns excitedly to the elector. "Look, Frederick, you are not forgotten! There is your house, together with the other princes—" He drains his goblet and raises his finger for more wine,

"—fully behind us, as is proper and fitting!" He hears Lang and Fugger chuckling, but he is not finished. "I bethink myself, and see your point entirely. Free elections are the only way, with each elector making up his own mind, without input from the others. It is far better."

The pageant is rolling on, and the conversation flags. After a moment of silence, Maximilian hears Catherine's voice. Out of the corner of his eye, he sees Frederick turn his head toward the sound, leaving the rest of the food on his plate, apparently forgotten. *Catherine, you sorceress,* Maximilian thinks. *You have made Frederick forget about eating.*

You make me die of desire
to kiss your lovely lips.
I beg you to allow me, some time
in my life, to touch them with a kiss.
You have my desires in your power,
more often than I go to sleep
I am encouraged by your love.
I have been stung by the bug
that so often attacks my heart.
Innermost I have no satisfaction:
You make me die of desire
to kiss your lovely lips.

Maximilian knows Frederick's eye for female beauty. Frederick had once shown him some paintings created by his court artist Cranach for the elector's own private enjoyment—naked nymphs lying in the woods, discovered and seduced by hunters. The images stop short of depicting the act of sex. Maximilian owns similar artwork, in the form of a book of woodcuts. They show naked couples in every position imaginable, including many condemned by the Church. He instructed the artists to uncover for his eyes what is usually hidden. The images are so vivid that when he took possession of them, he briefly considered asking the artist if it had been very inconvenient to work with only one hand.

Frederick releases an audible sigh. "I scarcely know what is more delicious, her lips, or the sound coming out of them. To kiss those lips… I doubt she'd touch old men like us, eh Majesty? Not willingly…"

Maximilian hides his smile as he sips more wine, and is silent. He never boasts about his success with women, or anything that speaks for itself. "She's a member of my Hofkapelle, Frederick, and I treat her as I treat the rest of them."

"Don't tell me you've given up the horizontal joust for good and all!" Frederick sounds baffled.

Maximilian lets this remark pass. He has known Frederick for a long time; together they have stalked four-legged prey, and the kind that goes about on two legs, perfumed and plumy. "Let's just say that her music, and her trust, give me more pleasure than seducing her would."

"You'll not part with her, then?"

"Certainly not. She will sing for me at my deathbed."

"Majesty, you will outlive us all."

"She will be loyal to me, and she will be cared for, even after my death. I have selected a husband for her."

After the imperial chariot and the princes come lords, knights, servants, and a curious group of half-naked figures with feathered headdresses, riding on elephants. After that, the baggage train and the camp followers. Catherine notes that while this would be the place for it, Maximilian has omitted Barbara and her hangers-on in the ladies' coach.

The emperor and the patricians do not see the last panel, since they have already left the room. It depicts two men, the only figures in the whole procession who stand and look at the viewer. One of them holds his head to one side as if to say, 'So, what did you think of that?' The room is silent apart from the invisible hands behind the curtains, so Catherine plays a brief fanfare on her lute to honor the artists. When she turns to leave, motion catches her eye: the long-haired man emerges from one of the alcoves. He looks as though he might speak, but just bows his head to her before she leaves.

8

Night Urges on the Day

"Wake up, Miss. You are wanted." Her servant's voice stirs Catherine from restless dreams. She sits up in bed, rubbing her eyes.

"What time is it?" She asks through a yawn, prying the sleep from her eyes.

Her servant sweeps the bed curtains open. "Late enough that even His Majesty should be asleep, and early enough that I should be, too."

Catherine has a quick wash in her basin and tries to dress while the servant brushes her hair, not very gently. Catherine gargles with her morning measure of wine and water before swallowing it, trying to soothe her throat. Her voice feels strained from overuse, and she'd rather not sing until she's had a chance to rest it. She hopes he'll be content with just hearing her play the lute.

She knows the way by now, but the knowledge is not comfortable. There's no telling what she'll find, or who. Life was so predictable in Mechelen. Duchess Margaret was dependable, regular in her habits, steady in her moods, orderly, prosperous, correct and proper in all things. The opposite of the man she's going to meet now. Life is no longer dull, but neither is it safe.

Except for two candles, the room is dark. He's sitting at his desk, staring at a pamphlet. The curtains have not been drawn, and Catherine thinks she can see the first glow of light in the sky through the open windows.

He doesn't look up, so she looks around for a chair, finds one by the unlit hearth, and pulls it nearer to the desk. She sits, tunes, waits. Then she begins to play quietly. He still hasn't spoken.

She looks at the untidy mass of paper on the desk—she sees letters, printed pages with text and pictures, sealed and unsealed documents. There's a goblet and a pitcher next to him. His face, permanently bronzed from being outside in all weathers, resembles yellowed parchment. The skin under his eyes looks bruised. It is high summer; the room is warm and the air still, but she shivers. Something hangs over him, and she can feel it. She can't bear the silence, and music is not enough. She dares to speak.

"Forgive me, Majesty, but you need sleep."

"I can't sleep, Kathl. I have tried everything."

"Is it your leg?" she asks.

He shakes his head. "It is the thing that is slowly killing me. A sickness of my innards. Collimitius, my physician, was with me just now, and gave me some potion. I have little hope that it will work."

He looks enervated, yet driven on, unable to stop, like the animals she has seen depicted in hunting scenes; stags using the last of their strength to leap into fast-flowing rivers to escape dogs and mounted hunters. She remembers the expression in their rolled-back, painted eyes—too exhausted for terror.

"How is the Diet going, Majesty?"

"Not well at all." He stands unsteadily, with an inhalation that makes his pain more evident than if he had cried out. She moves to help him, but his quick gesture makes her stay where she is. "Do you know what this is?" He asks, indicating the pamphlet.

She shakes her head no.

"It's called a *practica*, a yearly astrological prognostication. Collimitius is my astrologer, as well as my physician. When he was here just now, I asked for his counsel, his insight into the intractability of my subjects. Collimitius reminded me of his predictions, with regard to the eclipse we saw on our way to Augsburg."

He holds the pamphlet up to the light, and reads, *"When the eclipse occurs in the seventh house, it will bring death. Thus the powerful should beware the time between the twenty-fifth of June and the fifth of August.* This is why I wished to hold the Diet earlier in the year, but the princes ignored my summons. Look, that was also foretold! *'What great falseness and baseness there will be in this year! Seldom will anyone defer to his superiors, and the smaller man will wish to raise himself to the level of the greater.'"* Maximilian flings the pamphlet at Catherine. It lands at her feet. "Read for yourself! They do not obey me, and Frederick of Saxony dreams of being elected emperor himself, though his family is from yesterday. I am heir to all the Caesars of Rome, and descended from Noah himself."

Catherine bends to retrieve the pamphlet. As she smoothes the crumpled pages, a sentence catches her eye. *'It should be noted that women and effeminate men such as singers, lutenists, and the unchaste will be smitten with heavy sorrows and deadly illness in this year.'*

She swallows. Her throat feels singed. "But Charles will be elected… how can it be otherwise?" She says.

"Your faith that all will go as it should is as touching as it is naive. The damnable French have promised certain electors pools of gold to swim in, and lakes of milk and honey, and the hand of the king's sister-in-law in marriage." Maximilian stops by the windows, where his birdcages hang on ornate stands. He removes the covers from the cages, and whistles softly to the birds. He opens the door of one cage and gently places his hand inside. A little yellow bird hops onto his finger, and he draws it out into the room. He feeds it a few crumbs from a saucer, whispering to it while it eats. When it has finished eating, he gathers it in his hand and releases it, letting it fly about in the room. It circles the room once, coming to land on the mantelpiece like a tiny sunbeam.

"No one has been made to suffer as I have, Catherine, aside from Jesus Christ. His suffering came at the hands of the Jews; mine at the hands of the French."

"Why do you hate them so much? What did they do to you?"

"That is not for you to know. It is enough that you should know that they are contemptible, false, and capable of the basest betrayal." He whistles again, and the bird flies to his outstretched hand. "They don't sing what is in the music, they don't read what is written on the page, and they don't say what is in their hearts."

The bird is back in its cage, and the rest of the emperor's aviary has been fed. He listens to them chirp for a few moments longer before returning to his chair. "I am bound hand and foot by my lack of resources, and in the meantime, I see the votes tending not toward Spain, but to France. The day that Valois stripling comes anywhere near the imperial throne is the day the Antichrist comes to rule on earth."

The emperor sighs and pours some wine into the golden goblet next to him. "Let us pray it does not come to that, Kathl. Will you sing for me?"

Catherine clears her raw throat, and sings.

From the Emperor's Book of Days
I shall sleep and rest in peace, when you have given a dream to my eyes.

She sang to me of death, but gave me hope. I sat back in my chair, and was asleep before the end of the first phrase. She did not call Kunz to help me to bed, nor did she leave. I think she played for hours, to give my eyes a dream.

My dreams are generally a confused mash of colors and sounds, demons and angels that I cannot untangle upon waking. This was as simple as opening a door.

I dreamed of Mary. She was taking me somewhere, pulling me by the hand, laughing just as she used to when I acted mulish, as she called it. "Come *on*, Maxi!" she said. She was so much herself—I could see, touch, and hear her, yet I was not devastated upon waking, as you might expect. I was happy. I felt her so near, and a lingering sense of closeness remained, as though I might turn a corner any moment and find her there. Spirits usually flee the harshness of daylight.

Forty years have passed, and I've only dreamed of her a few times. Once or twice I sought to contact her spirit. One night, soon after her death, I summoned practitioners of the black arts. My judgment was impaired by drink and many nights without sleep. Conjure her, I said. Bring her back to me. The result was the worst kind of playacting, yet I could not help myself. The lack of blood was so strange, so different from my experience of mortal wounds. Perhaps that is why I have never been fully convinced she is gone.

No painter could capture the charm of her face, at least no Flemish artist could. Her eyes were a mixture of brown and gray, soft-lidded, as though she'd just awakened from a sleep of beautiful dreams. She had a small red mouth, and a smile that transformed her face as sunlight does stained glass. What a pity the artist without limitations came so much later.

Mary and I never met before I arrived in Ghent for our wedding. We exchanged letters and small portraits, that is all. We didn't even share a common language in the beginning, but besotted young people find more immediate ways of communicating. After I learned some French and Mary some German, she admitted that she looked at my portrait some twenty times a day before we met. Habsburg features are not set apart by their beauty, but perhaps she was seeing something else.

9

From the Emperor's Book of Days

Everyone has their secrets at the Diet, and it is fitting that the emperor has more than most.

A large portion of the vital business of the Diet is conducted in secret—the negotiations for the election of the next Roman king, the prelude to the imperial crown.

My grandson Charles. How I despair of him. He seems to have inherited nothing from his father Philip or me, but rather seems to have arrogated his great-grandfather's spirit on its way to the afterlife. I recognize so much of my father Frederick in Charles, and dealing with him inflames the same hot kernel of rage in my innards so familiar from my youth from interacting with Frederick.

I think of my mother, and wonder if she knew how much her words shaped me into the ruler I became. "If I believed you capable of acting like your father, I would regret that you were destined to rule." What would she say if she knew that I am moving heaven and earth to place Frederick's spiritual duplicate on the throne? If only Ferdinand had been the firstborn. He is affable, wise, quick to seize on the heart of a matter and act accordingly, without hesitation. Charles is phlegmatic, dragged down by overthinking and worry, paralyzed into inaction. His mind acts as a trap for him, and he thrashes in it like a wounded animal.

Here is an example: he dithered without end before deciding to put himself forward as a candidate for election as King of the Romans. And his reason? He did not wish to anger the king of France, who made his wishes plain regarding the crown several years ago. Will he consult the king of France every time he wishes to change his shirt?

There are other candidates, naturally. The vultures began circling long ago, smelling blood (mine), anticipating the feast to come. They include my adopted son Louis of Hungary, and François, King of France. All my skills of prevarication are in play as I try to hide my true feelings about *that*. There is Henry, the reckless red-headed king of England. I'm fond of Henry, he reminds me of myself as a young ruler. We shared a famous victory together, on the fields at Guinegate. I have been able to exploit his youthful naiveté, and I will admit to dangling the promise of the imperial crown before his lustful eyes in order to extort money and other favors from him. And he imagines he can hoodwink 'the elderly Austrian' as I heard he called me once.

Henry is so full of his own importance he has all the swagger of a stiff prick. But I wonder about the breeding of the house of Tudor. After our victory at Guinegate, we returned to my daughter's court at Mechelen to celebrate our success. I am known for my courtesy, and when Henry and I approached the door of the dining hall side by side, I stood aside and motioned for him to precede me. Anyone with any notion of courtly protocol would have recognized this for what it was: a gracious gesture. I am, after all, thirty years his senior, and the most formidable ruler in Europe. But Henry took it at face value, and walked ahead of me into the hall! I could not find it in my heart to be affronted by such a puerile misstep. Instead we made a grand joke of it, and laughed at his breach of manners all evening long. I saw him trying to hide his annoyance. I also took my own personal revenge by distracting the attention of his mistress away from him. So I am not young, tall, or handsomely russet like dear Henry. But for the rest of her life, that lady will tell stories of the time old Emperor Maximilian flirted with her for five solid hours.

But let us turn our minds back to the succession. Once Charles announced his candidacy, grudgingly, he began dragging his feet, especially concerning money. I told him to write to his Spanish treasury, to have the equivalent of one hundred thousand Rhenish guilders transferred. He dared to complain to me about his empty coffers. I told him I have pawned and sold everything I have, and ruined my lands in the process. He sent a promissory note, saying he will pay later. I told him the money is needed in advance. Charles replied that the Spanish treasury is mistrustful of the stewardship of the imperial treasury. I finally lost my temper and told him that he'd better not make me regret standing behind him, fighting for him with what little strength remains in me.

Electors don't pledge votes on the strength of a *promissorius*—they want money, gold, goods, and advantageous marriages. I promised one of my own granddaughters to the wretched Joachim von Brandenburg, with a dowry of three hundred thousand, as if the flesh of my flesh bearing his odious children weren't enough. His brother Albrecht, recently elevated to the rank of cardinal thanks to my exertions, required the following items before pledging his vote to Charles: thirty-one thousand Rhenish guilders, a gold table, silverware, tapestries from Burgundy, and a yearly pension of ten thousand guilders. The monk Luther was correct in complaining about Albrecht's thirst for indulgences. At least this was enough to cause Albrecht to dismiss the French emissary, and tell him that the emperor already had all the votes in his purse. That is not yet the case, but steady pressure from me consisting of equal parts bribery, cajoling, and threats will ensure Charles' eventual succession. But by then I will be dead, and I will not see the fruits of my labor. I am almost grateful.

If this weren't enough, the pope has lowered his bullish head, and seems prepared to charge. He declares that he forbids the election of Charles, and that I have no right to campaign for him. What would be his reason? He is a man who can only see the letter of the law, not the spirit. Since I was never crowned in Rome by his predecessor, I have no right to arrange the succession. It would be my dearest wish to finally have the imperial crown on my head, instead of going to the grave calling myself 'elected emperor', but Leo refuses any sort of compromise: no coronation within the empire, and no proxy coronation by Albrecht of Mainz. As long as I have lived, no pope has ever kept faith with me, but Leo's perfidy is the worst.

10

Great is the Injury, and Long the Tale

Catherine is in the sitting room of the ladies' court in the Fugger palace, replacing a string on her viol. A cool cross breeze makes the room pleasant, as does the absence of any other ladies. She had a few female friends in Mechelen, but those friendships had been based on mutual interests, like music, hunting, or whether one preferred reading Horace or Virgil. Duchess Margaret had never allowed the ladies of her court to idle their hours away with gossip and cards, which is all she could discover Barbara and her cohort ever did.

She should have known better than to think about Barbara; now it seems she has summoned her. Barbara sweeps into the room, and suddenly the sitting room is full of chatter and other noises: chairs scraping on the floor, tables being arranged, and giggling. Catherine gathers her courtesy and greets Barbara.

Barbara walks over and stands above her, watching her span the string and increase the tension to the desired tautness.

"Why don't you get someone else to do that?" Barbara asks. "It looks so dull and menial. Aren't there workmen who do that sort of thing?"

"I prefer to do it myself," Catherine says. "Instruments are like people; they all have their quirks and oddities. I know this one better than anyone else could."

"But look at your hands!" Barbara gasps as though three fingers have just fallen off for no discernible reason. She takes Catherine's hand and examines it. Barbara's skin is like that of a young doe, and Catherine knows that hers isn't. "My dear girl, you must let me help you. Francesca, please fetch a small bowl and some of that new Italian ointment Herr Fugger procured for me. And a file." Francesca is a Milanese, one of the ladies who had served the late Empress Bianca.

Catherine sifts her mind for a way to politely decline. She can't make up the excuse that the emperor has called for her; he will be sequestered in meetings until late afternoon. She could invent a rehearsal of the Hofkapelle, but she realizes this might be a way of healing the breach between Barbara and herself. If not peace, at least détente. She allows herself to be led away from the table with her viol, which still needs a few treatments to be playable again. Barbara sits her down at a table. Francesca sways in sedately with the materials, and scoops a small amount of ointment in a bowl, adding water from a nearby pitcher.

"Soak your hands in that, my dear," Barbara says. Catherine can smell the delicate perfume. "You poor thing, your hands are nearly as rough as a servant's!"

Catherine laughs. "Oh it's not that bad, surely. My hands are tools; they work hard, and I don't have much time to pamper them." Or much interest in doing so, she thinks.

Barbara clicks her tongue. "Men like soft hands on a woman. The emperor says mine feel as good on his skin as a favorite garment!" A chorus of giggles resounds from all sides of the room. Francesca plays cards with someone, and a third lady works on embroidery by the window.

Bathing her hands in the cool liquid, Catherine strains to think of a topic of conversation. There's always gossip, but she doesn't want to hear about who has been seen conversing together in the shadows at a patrician dance, or which lady wore something in flagrant violation of the sumptuary laws. She wants something useful, or at least interesting. At last she thinks of something Barbara might know, and she knows how to get it out of her.

"You've been with the emperor for many years, haven't you?" she asks.

Barbara nods, giving her own nails a quick swipe with the file, even though they are perfect, shining ovals already. "Yes, more than twenty years. We have three sons, Cornelius, Georg, and Dietrich. Of course, you must know Dietrich."

"Yes, I know Dietrich," Catherine rushes the words, looking down at the scar on her finger. "How did you meet the emperor?"

"My husband was one of his most trusted captains. But he died fighting the Hungarians," Barbara says.

"I thought he was meant to be King Saul, not King David," Catherine murmurs.

"What?"

"Oh, nothing. Just a little story he told me once. So, after your husband died...?"

"The emperor...took care of me, and the children I had with my husband. They are with his family in Carinthia. I've been with him nearly everywhere since then, except when he's on one of his military campaigns, of course."

"You probably know him better than anyone."

Barbara laughs. "He's not hard to know. He's like a kettle on a high flame. Left alone, the contents eventually spew out of their own accord. If he's happy, the whole world knows, if he's sad or angry, same thing. And he sulks. When he does that, I pack him off hunting, and he is happy again when he returns."

"So you probably know why he hates the French," Catherine prods gently.

Barbara takes one of Catherine's hands from the bowl, and begins to massage the ointment into her fingertips. "I thought everyone knew that! It was the talk of Europe when it happened, and your duchess was at the heart of it. Though I don't suppose she'd want to talk about it, any more than he does. He forbids anyone to speak of it."

But I know you are dying to tell me, Catherine thinks. She takes a gamble. "Oh, if it's a confidence, then you must keep it to yourself." Nothing makes gossips more inclined to talk than the realization they really shouldn't.

Barbara lowers her voice. "Well, if you're his privy musician, you must be trustworthy. I will tell you, but you must never reveal it." She scoots forward and sits on the very edge of her chair, the top of her head nearly touching Catherine's. She can smell the morning wine on Barbara's breath.

"This happened many years ago, before you were born. The emperor had been a widower for several years, and had an eye out for an acceptable match." And a large dowry, Catherine thinks. Barbara goes on. "The old duke of Brittany died, leaving his daughter Anne as his sole heir. Her position was precarious, especially with France. The French king really wanted to absorb Brittany into his territory. So, she needed to marry someone with enough military might to keep Brittany independent. She wrote to the emperor, and they were married by proxy." Barbara takes a cloth and dries Catherine's left hand, then buffs her nails. She sighs, shaking her head at the state of Catherine's nails. She takes up her file.

"The problem was, he was off fighting some war or other, and couldn't travel to Brittany," she giggles, "to lawfully fulfill the marriage contract. Though I don't see why Anne couldn't have traveled to where he was…"

"Probably because France was threatening to besiege her land, and her leaving would have been their cue to march in," Catherine tries to sound patient.

"Oh, something like that. Who can make any sense of these military games men play? Anyway, the marriage was not consummated, and Charles, King of France, stepped in. His excuse was that Anne had violated a treaty by marrying Maximilian, and he wrote to Rome to have the marriage annulled, on the grounds of non-consummation." Barbara lowers her voice to a whisper. "The scandalous thing was, he didn't even wait for the pope's ruling. He marched to Rennes with an army, had a private meeting with Anne, and married her that very day."

"And probably dragged her off to bed with 'Ite missa est' still hanging in the air," Catherine says.

Barbara laughs harder at this than it deserves. "Oh that's very good." She stops filing Catherine's nails and admires her work. "Better. So, my dear, that would have been bad enough, just stealing Maximilian's bride, even though everyone knows a proxy marriage is legal and binding in the eyes of God. But he betrayed the emperor in another way, and Duchess Margaret also. Can you not guess?" Catherine shakes her head. The duchess had never told her of any painful experience at the hands of the French. She had always spoken highly of her years at the French court, and the education she received there. "Charles had been betrothed to Margaret, as the terms of some treaty or other. She went to France when she was just a little thing, two or three, and was promised to the Dauphin."

"I heard they were legally married," Francesca says from the card table. "To be consummated later, of course. The dowry! Remember, Barbara?"

"Oh yes, I forgot! Little Margaret had taken her dowry to France as well. All those years, growing up, being educated to become the queen of France, to be thrown over in that humiliating way. And King Charles kept the dowry, and kept Margaret at court to use as a pawn in another marriage game. That was another outrage!" She sighs. "Maximilian endured being the butt of jokes all over Europe. It was one of the lowest periods of his life. But he likes to say the Almighty avenged him upon the death of Charles, King of France, who died from hitting his own head. 'Can you think of anything less befitting a sovereign?' he says. 'I have hit my own head from being unhorsed in tournaments more times than I can count, with no noticeable damage.'" This time Catherine laughs along with the ladies.

Two servants enter the room with platters of fruit, and Barbara waits until they have placed them on the tables and departed again.

"So there you have it—the whole story. It would put anyone off interfering with an established couple, wouldn't you say?" Barbara says with a quick upward glance at Catherine. "Before his health took a bad turn, I'd been seeing more of him. That pleases me. I love him, you know."

Catherine's feet begin to tingle, and her shoulders tense like drumheads. Have less faith in your fellow men, the emperor said. He didn't mention women, but Catherine should have known.

"I love him," Barbara repeats, "and I will not let anything come between me and a situation I've enjoyed for twenty years. He doesn't like fair-haired women, you know." Catherine bites her tongue to keep from smiling. The idea of the emperor having such a preference is absurd. It's like a hawk expressing a preference for prey.

"Madam, you are mistaken. As you said before, I am his majesty's servant." Catherine removes her hand from Barbara's and reaches for a cloth. Barbara grabs her wrist; not cruelly, not even violently, but with enough strength that Catherine relents for the moment. She may be on the defensive, but she arms herself nonetheless, like bringing out the cannon when the arquebus has failed.

"He tells me things, you know. Things he never tells anyone else. I've been with him for so long, I have his complete trust," Barbara resumes her care of Catherine's hands.

"He has not given any indication that he is interested in me." Catherine says, knowing that nothing she says will have any effect.

Barbara reaches out her hand and lifts Catherine's chin, so that their eyes meet. "He is not the source of my worries." She dries Catherine's left hand, and begins to massage her right.

He never would have told Barbara about the kiss. Catherine can't believe it.

"You're so young and stupid," Barbara whispers, "You have no idea what you've stumbled into. I know something that would have you in custody sooner than you can tune your wretched instruments. And I'm thinking of using it."

Catherine stands suddenly, grabs the cloth, and walks away from the table, wiping her hands. "In that case, I'll see it coming. I seem to spend half my life tuning." Catherine gathers her viol and tools from the table and walks out.

11

Discordant Harmony of Circumstance

A few days after her conversation with Barbara, Catherine stands in the Fugger music room. She has already spent many hours here, playing the collection of well-made instruments, and perusing the enviable collection of music manuscripts. There are some curiosities here: Arab music, and Italian treasures collected during Jakob Fugger's years in Venice, such as a unique instrument that makes it possible to hear the sound of plucked strings and organ pipes simultaneously. Usually these wonders absorb her attention, but today she stands frowning at a patch of empty air where something valuable of hers should be. She had come especially to play her table organ, the one the emperor had given her so many years ago.

One day when she was about twelve, her teacher, Hendrik Bredemers was giving her a clavichord lesson in Duchess Margaret's library. She remembers Bredemers' fluffy head, which made him look like a dark sheep in need of shearing, and his eyeglasses, without which he could see nothing. He was kind, nervous, and capable of coaxing music out of the most intractable instrument or student. Catherine recalled the wonder of hearing him play the big organ in Antwerp cathedral, and the swell of excitement when she decided then and there to become an organist herself, only to be told later that girls couldn't play the organ. At lessons after that, she looked at her hands, and his, wondering what it was about female hands that made it impossible. They looked the same, only a little smaller. Maybe that was the problem.

At that lesson in the library, they were sitting near the open windows. Sometimes she would glance out, and see the flowering trees in the garden below. Behind them, half a dozen scribes were working at various tables. Catherine always hoped what she considered her clumsy playing wouldn't distract or annoy them; at that age she had no way of knowing how much pleasure hearing a pretty girl making music gave them, in all sorts of ways.

She was improvising on *Een vrolic wesen*, when the door behind her opened, and all the chairs in the room seemed to scuff across the stone floor at the same time. Bredemers jerked out of his seat like his chair had just turned into a razor blade, gesturing wildly to Catherine for her to stand.

"Majesty!" Bredemers gasped.

Before Catherine could stand, she heard the emperor's voice, and felt his hands on her shoulders. She couldn't really have felt heat from his hands on her skin; not through her shawl, woolen dress, and linen chemise. She must have imagined it.

"You may all be seated, and continue with what you were doing. We are merely here to conduct our yearly perusal of our daughter's library—" Catherine smiled at his phrasing, after hearing the duchess sigh about this or that book, which was suddenly missing, only to receive a letter from her father in which he praised the book, thanking her for giving it to him. "—and we would enjoy some music while we are doing this, if Kathl would do us this favor."

"With pleasure, Majesty," The warm hands were removed, and she strained her eyes to the side to watch his shape move toward the shelves.

Bredemers took his chair again, and shuffled through the pages on his lap. He held one briefly in front of Catherine, and she noticed his hand was shaking. She hoped he would not infect her with his nerves. She played through several intabulations, then improvised on *Christus surrexit*, since it was still Easter season, and finally, played a short preludium.

"Paumann," said the emperor from his station by the bookshelves. Catherine stopped playing and turned to him. He was holding a volume in each hand, and had tucked a third under his arm. "Do you like Paumann, Kathl?"

"Very much, Majesty. But it doesn't sound right on a clavichord; it should be played on an organ," Catherine glared at Bredemers.

"You are right, of course. Why aren't you playing an organ?" the emperor turned back to the shelves.

"Duchess Margaret says that girls can't play the organ."

"Cannot or should not?" the emperor asked.

Catherine glanced at her teacher, but Bredemers appeared to have lost the power of speech.

"I think she believes it is improper, Majesty," Catherine replied. The emperor was silent, so Catherine assumed the conversation was over, and turned back to her instrument.

"I heard Paumann himself play the organ when I was about your age. At Regensburg. At that time, he was the best organist in the world. From that day, it was my favorite instrument, and still is. I have never forgotten it," the emperor said.

She wanted to tell him it's her favorite too, but then wondered why he would care.

"My friend Paul Hofhaimer was with me," the emperor went on. "I took him with me especially so that he could study with Paumann. And now he's the best organist in the world."

"What did it sound like when Paumann played, Majesty?" Catherine asked, realizing even as she spoke what an impossible question it was.

Maximilian had collected a stack of five books, which he handed to one of the scribes. He walked back to the clavichord by the window. Bredemers stood and offered his chair, and the emperor sat. He leaned his elbows on his knees, which somehow didn't stop him from gesturing continually with his tanned hands.

"One piece in particular I remember. I can still hear the shape of it in my mind, if not the substance. But I remember the effect it had on me. He improvised on a chant melody, as you have just done. His ornaments were so quick and dazzling they reminded me of standing in the forest on a windy day, and looking up, and seeing the sun play between the shaking leaves." Maximilian smiled at Catherine, and his look was so infectious that she smiled back, without knowing why. "I was a twelve-year-old boy, remember. Getting me to pay attention to anything that had nothing to do with war, hunting, or jousting was akin to seeing dry land amid the Red Sea."

His pleasure in music was so genuine, and she was so drawn out by his affability, the words formed before she could think. "It is as though you can feel it under your skin, and it breaks through, but gently—"

"—like a warm spring seeping from a rock. You have felt this phenomenon too, I see. In all my years of listening to music nearly every day, it has only happened a few times. Paumann at the organ was the first."

The bells of St. Rumbold's church began to ring, and the emperor stood up and turned away to collect his books. Catherine stood and curtsied as he approached the door. He turned to her one more time, offering her his hand. His palm felt rough, almost like the hand of a laborer. She bowed her head, but it was not a gesture of deference. She was suffused with an ache that felt like pleasure, and must hide her face from him, otherwise he would see it, and know.

She didn't see him again on that visit. The organ arrived in a rough wooden crate about eight weeks later, along with a formal note, no doubt written by a secretary, but the emperor had signed it himself. Even as excited as she was by her new instrument, Catherine took a moment to admire the signature: exuberant, barely controlled chaos. Literally, Maximilian on paper. Then she opened the simple wooden case, and found a beautiful little table organ, with bellows to be pumped by an assistant. She tested the feel of the silent keys, and examined the pipes that she could see: it would be perfect for playing Paumann's music, plus the newer German music she loved, the works by Schlick and Hofhaimer.

Her organ had been carefully packed and pulled in a cart from Mechelen to Augsburg, and she had unpacked it once it became clear their stay would be one of months, not weeks or days. It had weathered its return journey to its homeland very well, needing only tuning and a few minor adjustments. At home, she had bribed children to pump the bellows for her. Maximilian's granddaughter Mary was always keen, since she needed only to be bribed with the promise of being allowed to play it. Here, Catherine would bribe a choirboy with sweets or, failing that, one of the Fugger's servants.

Catherine sets her music down on the table where her organ was yesterday when she came to make sure it had been tuned properly. The table is now empty. She stares at the empty space for a moment, trying to think. Could someone from the Hofkapelle have come to borrow it? It didn't seem likely. Hofhaimer and Buchner have their choice of all the organs in Augsburg, most of them much finer than this one; what would they want with her little table instrument? She wonders if Ludwig is playing a joke on her, or Kunz. This seems more likely, and Kunz would have the run of the palace, aside from the ladies' wing. She's not worried about encountering Kunz dressed as a woman. Some ideas defeat even the richest imagination.

She goes back to her room. A strange feeling nips at her: she feels watched, or exposed in some other way. She feels certain someone has been here. She opens the wooden chest that holds her belongings. All of her dresses are there, but two valuable parting gifts from Duchess Margaret are gone: a book by Christine de Pizan, copied and illustrated by hand before the days of printing, and her heavy wool cloak with the ermine collar. She turns around and at once her innards feel cold and liquid. She had been so wrapped up in thinking of her organ she had not noticed the gaping absence next to the door: her lute and viol are gone.

How can her valuables have been taken from the Fugger Palace, more closely guarded, she's sure, than any besieged fortress? More importantly, who has done this? Her first thought is Barbara. She can imagine Maximilian's jealous courtesan taking her things (though the book of verse would be pointless—she doubts the Salzburgerin can read French). But her instruments? Barbara wants to stay in the emperor's good graces, not irritate him by removing the source of his favorite pleasure. Catherine can hardly go ringing the alarm and accusing the Fugger servants of theft. She thinks for another long moment, then decides what to do. She needs advice from someone who knows his way around the circus in which she now finds herself. She calls her maid back in, and dresses herself as Hannes.

All afternoon, she fruitlessly hunts for Ludwig. She looks at Holy Cross, at the emperor's residence, even at the Cathedral, the monastery of St. Anne, and St. Ulrich. Then she starts looking in taverns. When she returns to the Fugger Palace, she looks for Kunz and Hofmeister Firmian, to see if they have any information for her. She can find no one.

She returns to her room, defeated. She hurls her hat into the empty corner where her lute and viol were supposed to be, and hurls herself on her bed, hot, thirsty, and unhappy. She dozes. After sleeping heavily for some time, she opens her eyes, and finds her maid standing next to her bed.

"Forgive me, Madam, but there are three different men looking for you. They are all in the small audience chamber."

Catherine gets up in a rush, rinses her mouth, retrieves her hat, dusts it off, and runs down the corridor, across the courtyard, to the small chamber near the main entrance. Ludwig, Kunz, and Firmian all stop talking when she enters the room.

"What is going on?" Ludwig asks, looking none too happy about being interrupted.

Kunz says, "I knew it—you're a Turkish spy, aren't you? Come to pack us off to Constantinople, and demand a ransom? Well, we're doomed, if that's the case. But maybe they'll let us guard the harem." Catherine wants to remove her shoes and hurl them at his head, one at a time, just to make him stop talking.

Firmian catches Catherine's eye, looking like he's seen an execution, or is on his way to one. He takes a folded sheet of paper from his cloak, and walks toward her without meeting her eye again. She takes the paper from him. It is a list of goods—her goods, with sums of money next to each item, and a total at the bottom, with a signature and a seal. She stares at it, uncomprehending, then at Ludwig, long-time juggler in the *circus maximilianus*.

He walks to her, takes the paper from her fingers, and looks at it.

"It's a receipt." He understands at once, and he glares at Firmian. "Mary's crown, Firmian. Is this the state of things now? There was nothing else?"

The Hofmeister shrugs.

"Oh naturally, you just did as you were told. I hope you may sleep very well tonight."

Catherine swallows and tests her voice. "Ludwig… he pawned my instruments? Under the roof of the richest man in the empire?" If this is supposed to make sense, she fears for her sanity.

Ludwig takes her arm and moves her away from Kunz and the Hofmeister, as though he is afraid she might cry, and embarrass them both. She wants to tell him there's no fear of that: the shock has numbed her; she feels deadened like a limb that was slept on at an odd angle. They stand together under the marble portico, looking out into a tiny piece of Italian paradise: the sunshine in the courtyard, blooming plants, pools, and fountains. Ordinarily, the sight would have made Catherine stop and stare, though she has seen it dozens of times. Today, she sags on a bench and stares at her shoes. They already look a bit worn.

"Look at it this way," Ludwig says. "You're really one of us now. You probably thought it happened at Mass, but it didn't. You have now been used by the emperor. You're real." He's trying to cheer her up, and she wants to hit him.

"Ludwig, help me to understand. I am his privy musician, who he calls to his room nearly every night to help him sleep. With music!" she adds savagely, seeing Ludwig's face about to break into something of which she wants no part. "Why would he take away my instruments, from which he himself derives so much pleasure?"

"I tried to tell you that day in the tavern. He fills the need of the moment. He needed some coin for something, and looked around for what was to hand. Do you think he relishes begging Jakob Fugger every time he needs this or that trifle? For something small, he goes elsewhere."

Like rubbing a numbed arm or leg, the deadness wears off eventually. The hot prickle in her eyes makes her turn from Ludwig. He turns her back to face him, sliding her easily with his big hands over the surface of the smooth marble bench.

"The next time you think you are something special, remember this: he used to leave his own wife, the late Empress Bianca, behind as collateral when he couldn't pay his bills. She pawned her linens to pay for food for her people. Even the caged songbird must go without in this company."

"You've made yourself clear, Ludwig" Catherine extracts a linen handkerchief from her sleeve and blows her nose. "The question is, what are we going to do about it?"

"Not a whole lot to do, without money," Ludwig shrugs.

"Do you know where this pawnshop is?" Catherine asks, still dabbing at her nose with the handkerchief.

"Yes, I think so." Ludwig unfolds the receipt and studies the seal again. "What do you have in mind, theft by night?"

Catherine reaches into her tunic. A small pouch is hidden under the wrappings, between her breasts. She looks up at Ludwig, who resembles a greyhound who has sniffed prey. "Your mouth is open, Ludovico."

"Sorry," he shakes his head, reminding her even more strongly of a dog.

She extracts the pouch, and holds it in front of him, shaking it gently, so he can hear the coins rattling. "It's all I have. It will cover the sum on that receipt, with a little left over." Her mouth twists into something between a smile and a grimace. "This is the money that Duchess Margaret gave me for my journey. She said, 'Don't loan anything to the emperor; you'll never see it again.'"

"Well, she is his daughter. Come on, let's go buy your darlings back," Ludwig makes a move to stand. Catherine puts out her hand.

"Wait a moment. I'll be right back." She springs up and walks quickly back to the ladies' wing, and gives her servant instructions. "Whoever it is, no one is allowed to see me. I am unwell, and need to be left in peace. Understood? Not even if the pope himself is at the door."

Catherine and Ludwig cross the Weinmarkt toward St. Ulrich's, then toward the Red Gate over the *Stadtgraben*, the city moat. He points to a cluster of buildings just inside the gate. "Don't want to be seen there, although plenty of important people are, I'm told." Seeing her look of confusion, he explains. "Pox hospital." He shudders visibly. "I've seen what it does to people: pustules all over the body, agonizing pain, sores so deep they reach the bone. Sometimes, they lose their eyes, their nose, or limbs…Everyone knew how it spread from the beginning, but it didn't prevent certain people from sticking their *Schwänze* into any available holes." Ludwig looks at Catherine, a bit of red visible in his pale cheeks. "Sorry. Sometimes I forget who you are."

"I'm surprised you're not afraid of getting it from whores," Catherine hears the tone of a nagging older sister in her voice, but doesn't care.

"I've never been to a whore!" He looks incredulous. "Have you not been listening to me?"

"That day in the library you said—"

Ludwig laughs. "Catherine, the male mind is a perverse thing. The more we like you, the more repellent we act, at least in the beginning. I have no excuse for it."

"I like you too, Ludovico," She flushes, and can't look at him while saying it. The art of flirtation is as foreign to her as the language of the Turks, and about as easy to counterfeit.

She imagines Duchess Margaret's horror at the life her protégé now leads: dressing up in male clothing, spending time alone in male company, and walking around in the neighborhood of a pox hospital, discussing prostitution. And, of course, the pawnshop is nearby. She follows Ludwig inside. It is everything she imagined it would be: small, dark, dank, and under the proprietorship of someone with whom she'd rather not be in the same room. Her fears about the state of her treasures gnaw at her (The wood! The strings!) Her lute and viol had been built by two of Flanders' most revered instrument builders, and are finer than anything played by the Hofkapelle.

Ludwig produces the receipt, negotiates, haggles, shouts, using every measure of his size to intimidate the shopkeeper. In the end, he is successful. He buys her items back, at a small win.

Outside again, he whistles for a carter, and they load her instruments onto a wagon. Catherine turns the cloak inside out, and folds it so that the fur collar is hidden, so no one will be tempted to steal it from her. On the other hand, there are so many armed soldiers engaged during the Diet to keep the delegates safe, only a true madman would attempt a robbery of that sort in broad daylight.

They follow the carter back to Holy Cross and stow the instrument cases in Ludwig's chamber. "Do you really think I'm going to let the emperor have another go at them?" Catherine says. "As Kunz would say, 'Fools deserve to be deloused with clubs'." Back out on the street, Catherine does some arithmetic in her head. After paying the carter, she has very little left. But it's enough for what she has in mind. She turns to Ludwig, and says a few words. She wants to reward him for helping her, and make herself feel better at the same time. But his grin is already reward enough, and she can't imagine feeling better than she does at that moment.

Greetings to you, you noble drop!
If you've found our throat,
You bring us joy, courage, and strength!
He puts the goblet to his lips,
He drinks it down to the last drop.
It comforts when the going gets rough.
The goblet, let it make the rounds!
In the end, one fell under the bench,
Another's tongue was a tad too long...

Ludwig Senfl, Schweizer

12

The Cup of Lethean Slumber

Catherine huddles near the surface of consciousness for some time, but refuses to push herself forward into daylight. There is a vague feeling of wrongness about everything: herself, her surroundings. At last reality will not be rebuffed any longer, and she opens her eyes. The light makes her brain revolt, so she closes them again.

She's aware of the worst pain she has ever felt. It takes her a moment to locate it. Yes, it is in her head: like two miners are trying to burrow out of her temples using pickaxes. She opens her eyes again, and takes in the narrow room: a utilitarian but comfortable bedroom. She has never seen it before. It's not very tidy—clothing and papers are strewn about, and all the bedclothes are on the floor. She tries to raise her head, but the miners increase the rate of the blows to her temples, and she flops back onto the pillow with a low moan, holding her head. She gets a brief glimpse of her body on the way up: she's wearing stained breeches and chemise, but no tunic, and no shoes. She wonders where her tunic went.

She turns onto her side, in the vague hope that the pain will not follow her, but it does. Her vision has a blurry, smudgy quality, but she can see the man in the room clearly enough. Ludwig is asleep in a chair about three ells from her. The back of the chair is wedged against the only door in the room. His head rests on the door, his long legs are stretched in front of him, arms folded across his chest. His soft breathing tells her he's asleep. She feels well enough to enjoy the sight of the solid bulk of his thighs under the close fabric of his breeches.

Her mouth tastes foul. A Landsknecht using her tongue to scour his linens after a six-month campaign could not have tasted worse. She also feels a ravening thirst. Her eyes flick back to the only table in the room, and she sees a pitcher and a cup. For a moment, she lies there, mentally preparing herself to sit up. Then she swings herself upward. The motion and the blur in her eyes make her nauseous, but she remains upright. Her head explodes in pain. "*Verdomme*," she whispers, while hauling herself to her feet and shuffling across the room, holding onto the wall for support. She reaches the table, grips the edge to keep from teetering over, and grasps the handle of the pitcher. Her hand shakes like she's become an eighty-year-old woman overnight. *Gloria*, there is clean water in the pitcher. She raises the cup to her lips, drinks, then slumps into the chair behind her.

She hears the sounds of movement from Ludwig's side of the room. She opens her eyes to see him stretch, yawn, and rub his neck. He looks at her and laughs.

"You poor lamb. If you feel as bad as you look, you have my deepest pity."

"I'm going to die, Ludwig."

"You're not going to die. You're just hung over. *Kätterlin hat einen Kater.*" She can't even smile at his German wordplay. She watches him through slitted eyes. He springs out of his chair and walks across the room to a wooden chest. He rummages in it, and takes out a small flask.

"Here, drink this, it will make you feel somewhat human again."

"I am never drinking again, Ludwig."

"It's a harmless herbal remedy. It will help your headache and cure your dragon breath. Come on, drink up." Ludwig holds the flask to her lips, and gently helps her to take a sip.

The liquid makes its way down. The question is, will it stay? She sits very still, and all seems well. A few moments pass, and she opens one eye, then the other. Ludwig is perched on the edge of the desk, looking down at her. The concern in his face makes her smile a little, and it doesn't even hurt.

"I can't remember much about last night," Catherine whispers. It's all the volume she can muster.

"That's probably for the best. I have all the fodder I need if I ever need to blackmail you," He's smiling, but he's not joking.

"What did I *do*?"

"You drank six cups of wine in less than an hour on a completely empty stomach. Then you got ravenous, you said, and ate the most disreputable stew I have ever seen. And then you spewed. Then you went outside and spewed some more. Then you wandered up and down the street singing this crazy Flemish song, while I tried to steer you back home without attracting attention. Then you tried to piss on someone. Standing up. At least you stayed in character," Ludwig grins.

With each word Catherine slumps lower and lower until she is doubled over, with her arms over her head. "Oh God, Ludwig. How mortifying!" Her headache stands no chance against her humiliation.

"For you maybe. I haven't had such a good time in ages. You're very entertaining."

Catherine slowly sits upright again. She braces for the pounding to start back up in her head again, but it has subsided. She looks back into Ludwig's face, and sees that he doesn't really think badly of her.

"You're a good *Kerl*, Ludwig. Thanks for not dumping me on Jakob Fugger's doorstep."

Catherine stands up, and walks across the room, feeling much less shaky than before. She peers into the mirror, reassured that she doesn't look as bad as she feels. Her hair is still braided, and her face is clean.

"Did you clean me up?" she asks.

"A little. Your tunic may only be fit for burning; we'll see when it gets back from the laundry. I'll go find something for you to put on in a minute. Really, you don't look bad at all. If you're going to go out drinking with a colleague, make it the kind that turns into a beautiful woman by morning, that's what I always say," Ludwig says.

Catherine laughs and feels her face grow warm.

"Where are we?"

"Guest quarters at Holy Cross monastery. I rank high enough that I don't have to sleep with the monks. I doubt you're the first woman to have slept here. I stayed at quite a few monasteries in Italy. *Kruzi*, those fellows got up to all sorts of tricks." Ludwig gets up and crosses in front of her on his way to the door. She turns as he passes, wanting to say something, but not knowing what.

"Ludovico..."

He half-turns, one hand on the door handle.

She lifts her hand, an unsure, fluttering movement. Then she decides what to do. "Ludovico, thank you for not—"

"Do you think I would have taken advantage of you in that state?"

"No, I know you wouldn't have—that's the point." She places her hand on his arm.

"Besides, you weren't so tempting covered in vomit. Funny, that stew looked the same as it did when you were eating it." He shudders. "Don't go away. I'll be back with a robe for you." He winks at her and shuts the door behind him.

High up in the mountains
There is a tall house
Every morning, three pretty girls come out.
The first one is my sister
The second is my friend...

Ludwig Senfl, Schweizer

AUGSBURG, *1518*

13

Chained Fast to the Bird of Prey

Like most courts, the ladies' wing of the Fugger Palace is locked at night, and guarded by two armed soldiers who are under orders only to open up in case of emergency. The doors are unlocked in the morning before breakfast, which most of the ladies eat privately in their rooms. Shortly after nine o'clock, Catherine arrives dressed as Hannes. She crosses the courtyard, intent on regaining her room and taking a long bath. Ludwig's cleaning job had been rudimentary; she feels clammy, as though her own cloud of stink is clinging to her, and leaving a trail.

She's about to cross the threshold into the ladies' court when a male voice shouts behind her.

"Hold on, you!" One of the guards pounds up to her. "What are you up to, young fellow?"

Catherine swallows. "I'm a member of the Hofkapelle."

"Then the ladies' court is no place for you, is it? What's your business here?" The guard's hand is pinching her upper arm. She tries to think, but her mind is blank.

"The emperor called me here to sing for him during his breakfast. I don't know the way."

The guard observes Catherine through narrowed eyes, then yanks her arm, swinging her around.

"We'll see. Move it."

The guard forces her to walk in front of him with the butt end of his halberd jabbing right between her shoulder blades. He marches her through the corridors. They stop outside the emperor's door. The guard confers with Maximilian's doorkeeper, who disappears inside. When he returns, he motions her inside, looking at her as though she were some strange species of animal recently found in a distant jungle and brought back to Augsburg to be displayed in a cage.

The emperor sits at his writing table, which looks, as always, as though the contents of a small library had exploded and settled on and around it in no order whatsoever. A tray of food sits untouched on a small table at his elbow. Catherine looks around for Kunz, who is nowhere to be seen. The room is deserted, so she removes her hat.

"Where have you been?" the emperor asks without looking up from the document he is writing. "I summoned you last night, only to be told you were nowhere to be found."

Catherine expects to feel ashamed, standing there unwashed in a borrowed clerical robe, but another emotion rules her at that moment.

"Making friends with the Hofkapelle." She tries to anger him in return.

"All of them? Are you, like Phryne, not content with just one man?" His voice is even. Her eyes follow his pen on the page, willing him to look up at her. She can't see much of his face; he is bare-headed, and his hair partially obscures his expression.

"Majesty, may I speak?" Catherine takes a step nearer to his desk.

"Of course. You need not ask," He dips his pen in his inkwell, and continues with his document.

"Then I choose to ignore that you just compared me to a prostitute, Majesty." The blaze of anger under her skin makes her reckless. She steps right up to his desk, and leans on it. "If you must know, what I really did was go to a foul part of town to purchase my own instruments back." The swell of heat results as it always does in water to cool it, a weakness she despises in herself. Her voice wavers, impossible to control, and breaks as she speaks. "Why did you do it? The organ you gave me—you have no idea how I prized it."

"I needed the money, Kathl. You have no idea what I am facing here." The emperor's voice betrays no emotion.

"How was I supposed to do my job without my instruments? I thought I was here to give you enjoyment, and for you to show off." His apparent unconcern makes her hands clench into fists on the desk.

"There are several instruments in Fugger's music room you could have used instead. But you said you bought them back, so this conversation serves no purpose. I wish I had known you had such a sum, I would have asked you directly."

"And I would have refused." Her throat feels tight, but at least she has mastered her voice.

"What a meager thing your loyalty is," the emperor sighs. "You are dismissed. I have much to do today."

Does something actually snap in her head? Her flat hands slam his desk.

"You sold the things I love most in this world. Would you at least look at me?" She doesn't raise her voice, but her words have the force of a shout.

He looks up at her. She sees surprise in his face at her appearance, and she feels her features draw back into a look of shock before she can check them. How can someone change so noticeably in so short a time? His skin hangs from the bones of his face, and his neck shrinks away from the collar of his robe.

"I have also sold the things I love most in this world," he says quietly.

"I'm sorry…" she whispers. Shame bathes her head, and her voice gives way entirely.

"Neither of us is at our best at the moment." His voice is dry and flat.

"Are you in pain?"

"It is with me all the time now. The rich food here has not helped. I need simple, plain food as much as I need air, movement, and mountains.

I need Tyrol, which is where we shall go when our business here is complete. I wish for you to see Innsbruck." He reaches for her hand, and her will deserts her. He pulls her to his side, and stands unsteadily. "Please forgive me, sweetheart. If there had been another way, I would have sought it. Your music has brought me nothing but pleasure. And that organ was given to you out of affection and respect, and because only Paumann himself ever pleased me more with his music. Say that you forgive me."

What choice do I have, she thinks. Without speaking, she lifts his hand and turns it over, resting her face in the cup of his palm. Her head grows heavy as Maximilian presses his face into her hair. His breath feels hot on her scalp. She stands, open and wanting, sword in the dust.

"You will not fail me," he says. An assertion or a command? She can't tell.

Movement across the room makes Catherine lift her eyes. Kunz has appeared as if from a trapdoor, but in reality he has just risen from a chair near the window. He had been covered from head to toe with a blanket, and so had been utterly unseen. He stretches and yawns dramatically.

"Peace restored among warring factions? So early? That's a first at the Diet." He worms his feet into his boots and clomps toward the desk. He hovers over the tray of food and helps himself, pulling open a roll and stuffing roasted meat into it. He pours himself a measure of wine and water, which he drinks in a gulp. He presents himself, breakfast in hand, in front of Catherine.

"My lady, may I have the honor of escorting you to your quarters?" He leans close to Catherine, and she flinches. He sniffs at her like a curious hound. "And may I recommend a bath?"

They cross the courtyard, and Kunz stops suddenly by the large fountain.

"There's something you should know," Kunz speaks in a low voice, through a mouthful of meat and bread. A few flaky crumbs explode from his lips and land on her.

"Kunz, you should know that I don't believe anything you say," Catherine says.

"Fine by me," the jester begins walking again. Despite his jerky and bowlegged gait, he can still walk very quickly.

Catherine realizes her error immediately, and trots to catch up to him. He stops walking so abruptly that she careens into his broad back. Anyone watching from the arcade would have thought they were performing a comedy.

Catherine rubs her nose, sore from where it impacted his shoulder blade, as Kunz grabs her arm and pulls her back to the fountain.

"You're attracting attention in very high places, my dear," Kunz says. His grin makes Catherine shiver. "You have a new admirer, who is eager to meet you. Very eager. In fact, I've heard he's not even going to issue an invitation, rather something more, er... arresting."

All her blood settles in her temples again, trying to pound its way out. "Who are you talking about, Kunz?"

"I bet you can guess. You have something in common. Of course, he is a music-loving prince of the church, but you're both named after birds."

"Cardinal...Cajetan? Oh God," Catherine feels for the side of the fountain with her hand, then sinks down and sits on it.

"To the latter I would direct my prayers." Kunz pats the top of her head.

"What should I do?" She looks up at him.

The jester creases his brow and rests his chin on his hand in a parody of deep thought. Then he grins again. "I'd go take a bath."

How someone his age can move so quickly remains a mystery to Catherine, but the next thing she knows her entire upper body lands in the fountain, with her legs sprawling in the air. She struggles out of the water, gasping. Kunz is nowhere to be seen, but a row of servants has gathered in the upper gallery, laughing and clapping.

14

Beware of Straying Too Far; Don't Trust the Riverbanks Too Much

The day is one of searing sun and baking heat. The sky is a dangerous blue, with no clouds to offer respite. Catherine visits the baths in the Damenhof in the morning, but all the good of her bath is gone by the time she dresses. Barbara lounges in the bath, fanning herself, not even bothering to keep up the pleasant banter with her ladies.

"I don't envy you, having to go out in this wretched heat," she says. "And stand up and perform! Really, it's no life for anyone who was brought up well."

Ignoring Barbara and her caustic mouth is the only way to cope with her, and so far silence has served Catherine well. Yet she can't keep her eyes from Barbara's torso as she lounges in the tub. The tips of Barbara's breasts droop into the water like someone filled two skins by a river and then left them hanging there. Barbara sees her looking. She stands up and moves to the other end of the tub, under the pretext of having one of her ladies refill her cup. Her body is still pleasing; she has a long neck and graceful shoulders. Her slender shape contrasts with the high roundedness of her belly. A little posthumous twig for the emperor's other family tree, Catherine thinks, which has more branches and leaves than the official one. She is not really surprised.

She thinks I envy her, Catherine thinks. How absurd that is, when I have been that child.

The evening brings another party at a patrician house. Too many to count: the days, the parties, the broken strings, and the mornings spent gargling with warm salt water to soothe her throat.

The musicians are positioned in a small alcove in the Welser's dining hall. Catherine feels surprise at how similar all the houses are. The Fugger palace outpaces the rest in terms of grandeur, gilding, and finery, but the rest blend together. There is nothing to set one dining room apart from another. The ladies all dress alike, as though they are afraid of distinguishing themselves, afraid to stick out too much. Catherine is dressed as Hannes, and has surprised herself with how easily she now assumes his identity. With the exception of Senfl, the members of the Hofkapelle still largely ignore her, but at least it feels like a benevolent disregard now.

Hans Buchner is playing a solo piece on a small organ, after which Catherine and Ludwig will sing a duet. Buchner's face is as fine-boned and delicate as Catherine's, and his mouth might be described as pretty. Looking at him, she doesn't feel quite so conspicuously female. Buchner is pictured in Weiß-Kunig, in the woodcut with the emperor standing among his musicians. At first glance, Catherine thought he might have been a woman.

A half-open curtain separates the alcove from the dining room. She peeks around the curtain, trying to find Maximilian in the crowd. She can't see him. The quiet duet she and Ludwig have planned will be lost in the noisy chatter of the room. But she forgets the sway the music-loving emperor holds over each person in that room. Suddenly, he's standing in front of the alcove, flanked by their hosts, Bartholomeus Welser and his wife. Matthias Lang and Dr. Peutinger are there, and Kunz, of course. Kunz winks at Catherine and makes some quick gesture she is unable to decipher.

"Herr Senfl, and my latest acquisition from Flanders, whose name I can never remember. If you are quite ready, we would like to hear one of the duets you have prepared for us," Maximilian says.

The room is now as silent as a chapel before matins, and a chair is brought for the emperor. He sits with his elbows propped on the armrests, arms tented, hands folded in front of his mouth. Catherine looks at him once while preparing to tune her viol. The emperor stares at her with an expression that is hard to read; she can't see whether he is smiling. His eyes glitter at her, and even when she looks away, she imagines she can feel his gaze. It does not bore in, but alights and spreads over her skin. Her mind goes blank—she pretends her instrument is hard to tune to give herself a chance to gather her thoughts again. She looks up at Senfl. His bulky presence and perpetual indifference give her the foothold she needs. She angles her body toward Senfl, away from the silken trap of the emperor's stare.

Catherine learned the song from the composer himself, an Englishman named William Cornysh who visited Mechelen on his way to the French court. He explained the words to her in his excellent French: two men are discussing their lovers. The song is in three parts, and Cornysh himself suggested performing it with two singers and a viol.

She sings the refrain on her own, without the viol. The room is warm and welcoming to her voice. The refrain repeats, and Ludwig joins her. The parts don't seem to blend so much as pace together; two friends taking a walk, not touching, but never straying more than a hand-breadth apart.

Ah, Robin, gentle, Robin,
Tell me how thy leman doth
and thou shalt know of mine.

Catherine plays harmony for Senfl on the viol as he takes up the repeated underlying melody, while she sings the verse in counterpoint:

My lady is unkind I wis,
Alack why is she so?
She lov'th another better than me,
and yet she will say no.

Ludwig takes up his part of the dialogue, singing the second verse:

I cannot think such doubleness
for I find women true,
In faith my lady lov'th me well
she will change for no new.

They sing the refrain together twice more, the homophonic texture and tightly-knit intervals lulling the listeners. Catherine can sense that they are drawing the attention of the audience almost against their will, as though they were being stupefied by an elixir with no taste or smell.

There is a long moment of silence after the last note. Then Maximilian speaks from behind his folded hands.

"What a lovely song. You brought that with you from my daughter's court, did you not, young man?"

Catherine swallows hard. "Yes, Majesty. I learned it from the composer himself, William Cornysh."

"Please remind me of your name once more."

"Johann Flamme, Majesty." She dares not look at Ludwig.

"And what do you think it means, Johann? Not many here have the command of English that you and I do." Maximilian drops his hands suddenly. His palms curve against the arms of his chair. Catherine sees something hard about his mouth, though his smile seems kindly enough.

"I think the two men are discussing their lovers, Majesty." She is surprised at how calm her voice sounds; her heart is hammering hard.

"Are they? What say you, Lang?" the emperor leans his head just slightly in the direction of his chancellor. Catherine feels a small river of sweat race down her back into her breeches.

"If it's about women, you can bet there's treachery." Lang grins like the skirt-chasing priest he is.

Maximilian faces Catherine again. His upturned lips seem brittle like steel in a freeze.

"I have consulted my chancellor, and I must say I agree with him. I think the two men are singing about the same woman, with no idea they are doing so. Not only will she 'change for new', she has already done so."

The summer night is nothing to the oppression of the heat on Catherine's face. She bows her head, and remains silent.

"But you and Senfl were made to sing together, that is clear. You will give us another duet, when we are sketched by our court artist for our final portrait. Now we wish to hear something lively. Let the city pipers come in."

The imperial musicians gather outside the Welser house, in a vain attempt to find a breath of cool air. It's well after midnight, but the heat is still rising from the baked stones of the houses. Their host follows custom, and hands Ludwig a handsome tip to be divided among the musicians. Catherine reflects on the appropriateness of the German word for tip: *Trinkgeld*, drinking money. She's certain all the coins Ludwig is doling out will be pissed away by morning.

Catherine stands awaiting her pay-off, looking around at the sharp shadows cast by the full moon. Suddenly, Ludwig is at her elbow, a cloth bag slung over his shoulder.

"Are you tired?" Ludwig asks, taking her hand and depositing a few coins in it.

"Not at all. Wide awake and too hot to even think of sleep." She wishes she could fan herself with her hat, but the hat is keeping a vital secret, and mustn't be disturbed.

"Good. Come with me; I have a surprise for you."

"What if we're wanted again?"

"Oh, I wouldn't worry about that. We are dismissed." He gestures down the street with his head. "Let's go."

"Where are we going?" Catherine asks. She has difficulty keeping up with Senfl's long strides.

"Hush, it's a surprise." He walks on for a bit, then says, "What was the emperor grumbling about, I wonder."

Catherine shakes her head, wanting to stay far from the subject with Ludwig.

"I suppose it would help if I actually knew what the song was about," Ludwig says, turning a corner suddenly. Catherine swerves to follow him.

"What happened to asking your colleague who spent time at the English court?" she says.

Ludwig shrugs. "We were in a hurry. He just told me how to pronounce the stuff. We didn't have time to parse the meaning of every word."

Catherine stops walking and puts her hand on Ludwig's arm. "So you have no idea what you were just standing there singing?"

"Not really, no." Ludwig laughs like a boy who just liberated a bag of candied almonds from the meanest shopkeeper in town.

"Then how did you *do* that? It sounded like it was written on your heart."

"Well, I took my cue from you, for one thing. But the notes were fairly eloquent themselves, don't you think?"

Catherine shakes her head, struggling between admiration and the urge to reproach him.

They walk down a narrow street. In keeping with the festive atmosphere of the Diet, many houses keep fire pans burning in front to guide partygoers home. Between the fires and the full moon, they can see reasonably well. Catherine is grateful that the streets are still clean; during the Diet all the excrement and other garbage is cleared away several times a day. The city council wants to avoid prince-electors grumbling about filthy streets, and Maximilian's nose is not only famous for its unique shape. He's been known to cancel meetings because he walked through a cloud of reeking vapors on his way to the council chamber.

Catherine sees the city wall looming ahead, and another dark shape she can't identify.

"We can't leave the city, Ludwig. The gates are all closed until dawn," she whispers.

He makes a shadowy gesture. "*Porta nocturna*. Follow me." He takes her hand. Their fingers interlock, and when she grips, the pressure is returned. She hopes Ludwig doesn't mind how sweaty her hand is. They enter a door and walk up a dank staircase. A narrow passageway is lit by a few torches, and Catherine sees an immense iron portal. Ludwig raps loudly on it with his free hand.

"Peter, it's Senfl. Open up."

A small peephole opens, and she sees a pair of eyes surrounded by a network of wrinkles.

"Evening, Herr Hofkomponist." The eyes veer from Ludwig to Catherine and back again.

"Important imperial business. Put it on the emperor's slate, will you, Peter?"

"A token, if you please, Herr Hofkomponist, in the usual manner." The eyes slant down to a narrow gap in the ironwork of the door.

"Christ's crown, Peter, I am broke. But if you insist..." Ludwig roots around for his coin purse, finds a pfennig, and presses it into the slot.

"Thank you," the eyes say. "Have a most pleasant evening."

Catherine hears a loud clanking sound, like metal wheels grinding together, and the door opens just wide enough to allow one person to pass. Ludwig has to turn sideways to fit his shoulders through the gap.

"Don't overexert yourself, Peter, by any means!" He shouts after he and Catherine pass through the gate. Once they exit into the milky light of the full moon, Ludwig takes her hand again.

She has never been outside at night like this. Duchess Margaret had followed Burgundian custom, and had not locked the ladies' wing at night in Mechelen, but that did not mean any sort of free movement was allowed. Despite feeling safe with her companion, stories of marauding bands of robbers raise themselves in her mind.

"Is it safe out here, Ludwig?" Catherine whispers.

"Safer now than it usually is, I should think. All the mercenaries are locked up in town, robbing people as they leave the taverns."

"How did you know about the night exit?"

"It's the emperor's private gate. He had it built so that he could enter the town after the gates close. After hunting, you know. Animals or women," Ludwig says.

"You sound envious." Catherine looks down at her feet, now swishing through calf-high grass.

"God, not me. I get exhausted just thinking of half of what he gets up to. Anyway, as a high-ranking court official, I can get away with using the gate. Not that Kaiser Max knows. Hofhaimer told me about it."

A small breeze is discernible outside the walls, and Catherine sees moonlight reflecting on water.

"Welcome to the Wertach, a source of blessed coolness," Ludwig stops walking, tosses the bag he's been carrying into the grass, and starts undressing. Catherine laughs and turns her back.

"Life below the tree line has affected your mind, Ludovico!"

She hears Ludwig grappling with various articles of clothing as he speaks.

"Can't—stand—this God-blasted heat." A flung shoe flies past her and lands in the grass, "—was having fantasies about a swim all day." The sounds of struggle with sweaty clothing cease, and Catherine hears a splash. She turns around.

Ludwig's dark head skims the surface of the river. "Fantastic!" he shouts. "Aren't you coming in?"

"I can't swim, Ludwig!"

"Neither can I. Just paddle around and it takes care of itself. Come on, would I let you drown?"

Without contemplating that question for too long, Catherine turns her back to him again, as though that would keep him from seeing her undress.

"Don't look!" She calls over her shoulder, just to make her point. She kicks off her shoes, and peels off her tunic, but decides to keep her breeches and linen shirt on, to say nothing of the wrappings, which she can't remove without help anyway. She tiptoes to the water's edge and stands for a moment, then sits on the brink and dips her feet in. It is deliciously cool, just skirting the narrow edge of being too cold.

Ludwig's floating head comes nearer. "Well, come on, I'm not going to ravish you."

"As if I'd worry about that! You probably wouldn't know what to do with a woman, priest," Catherine says with more confidence than she feels. The way he moves tells her he knows exactly what goes where and when. Or maybe she learned it from his songs.

"I'm only in minor orders," Ludwig's teeth show themselves in the moonlight. "No chastity required."

She pushes herself away from the edge, and submerges. A momentary panic jabs her gut, but it fades as her head bobs to the surface. She thinks of how hunting dogs leap into water with abandon, and how their limbs work underneath to keep their heads up. She does that, and the rest takes care of itself, as he said.

"Well done. I thought you'd sit on the edge all night. If you get tired, just lay on your back, and relax all of your muscles, like you've just fallen into bed. The water will hold you. Watch."

She waits for his demonstration of this marvel, moving her limbs underwater. He seems to be having trouble with something, and doesn't show her how it's done. Eventually, he paddles away from her saying, "Never mind. You get the idea."

Catherine tries lying on her back, perfectly still and straight. She's so excited to discover she can float that she moves around too much and starts to sink. Then she calms her limbs again, straightens her back, and lets the water carry her. She stares up at the sky. The moon is so radiant that only a few of the brightest stars can be seen. A bat flits and swerves overhead. The muffled hollowness of the water in her ears is a strange sound, but it soothes her.

After too short a time, she starts to feel cold, so she struggles up the bank, pressing with her arms, weighed down by her waterlogged clothing. Finally, she achieves dry ground, and stands there, a little out of breath, wringing out her hair. She strips off her linen shirt, knowing her breasts are safely out of sight under the wrappings. Her skin thrills with the sudden shift from cool water to warm air.

Ludwig's bag spilled a few of its contents when he tossed it into the grass; she sees some bread and cheese, and what looks like a flask of wine. He's still paddling around in the water, so she helps herself to the food. She lays back in the grass, her heart as buoyant as her body had been in the water. It is not a feeling she is accustomed to.

She hears splashing and the sound of water rushing from Ludwig's limbs as he clambers up the riverbank.

"I think I'm going to live the rest of my life as a man, Ludwig," she calls to him without sitting up. She hears him mumble something.

"What?" She sits up suddenly, and sees him kneeling in the grass, rooted to the spot; his outstretched arm reaching for a piece of clothing to hold in front of him. She stares at the upright length of what he wants to conceal, thinking of Horace's line about the young tree firmly planted in the hills.

"I said, don't get up!" He is surly to cover his embarrassment.

She quickly turns from him, hoping to make him less uncomfortable. "Don't be ashamed, Ludwig. I grew up around boys, not to mention dogs. It happens sometimes." She pauses, smiling to herself. "Besides, you'll make some woman very happy with that thing someday."

The grass rustles as he pads up and kneels behind her.

"Why not right now? You like me a little, don't you?" He doesn't touch her, but she feels him as solidly as though he were pressed against her, like some inner force of hers is rising up to meet the corresponding vitality in him, drawn together by their own magnetic weight.

His fingers graze her neck. Her skin ripples, but not from cold. He must be able to hear the thumping of her heart from where he's kneeling.

Catherine gulps for air. "I like you more than a little."

Ludwig leans near to her. He doesn't take her in his arms, just dips his face into her hair, and takes a deep breath.

"Come here," He scrambles up and lifts her by her hands. With the dexterity of a tailor, he finds the tied end of the wrappings, extracts the knot, and pulls. Instead of removing the wrapping from her, he twirls her out of it, until he's holding a damp pile of rags in one hand, and a dizzy, laughing girl in the other.

He gathers her up; she tucks her face into the hollow at the base of his neck, smelling their skin together. Ludwig lifts her chin and finds her mouth; she tastes fresh river water, and his own taste, sweet and sharp, like a peppercorn in honey. She takes his prick in her hand, feeling the heft of it, the astonishing hardness covered in softness; silk over stone. She blazes inside, and he is the cause: his kiss, and his hands on her body. The only way to extinguish this fire is to let it burn.

Yet a thought seeps out from somewhere in her brain, a thought she hates, because it forces her to master her sensing, driven flesh. As much as she wants her flesh to carry her, like the water had, she cannot ignore it.

She takes her mouth from him, puts one hand on each side of his chest, and presses gently.

"Ludwig, I can't. You don't know how much I want to. But I can't." Now we find out what you are made of, she thinks. We are all alone, and you are like an ox. If you believe you have the right to help yourself regardless, I am lost.

He's silent, and motionless. She lets his mind rejoin his body, as she had done.

Another long moment. "Why?" He says at last. His arms are still around her.

A picture of the emperor's *Schlafweib* standing up in the bath rises behind her eyes. "Because I want something other than my mother's fate, or Barbara's. She's pregnant again." Catherine wishes Ludwig would drop her in disgust, as Adam must have done to Eve. She feels like Eve, not ashamed to be naked. But she's the Serpent too, destroying their little paradise.

"I'll take care of you. In fact, I'll marry you. We can enter into a clandestine marriage, here and now." Ludwig says. Far from dropping her, he holds her closer—cupping her head with one hand, pressing her cheek against his chest.

Catherine knows all about such marriages. When both parties are sincere, they are wonderful things: a contract between a couple who respect each other, are well matched, and have physical affection for one another. Any couple who are both of age can speak vows to one another, and then seal the union with their bodies. Marriages are made by God, not parents, guardians, or the church.

But an insincere man, and it is always a man who thinks he can afford to be generous with other people's valuables, makes hollow promises and then denies them once his wick is dry and he's thinking clearly again.

"I'm not saying that just to get what I want from you. I know that's what you're thinking. I'm thinking about Isaac and Bartolomea. They were married, and both were members of the Hofkapelle. That is what I want, Kätterlin, and I want you. I will take care of you," Ludwig says again.

She thinks of his worn clothes and endless cups of wine. You can't take care of yourself, she thinks, but some of that is not your fault.

"Herr and Frau Isaac didn't have children, if I remember correctly. Babies need a home, not Augsburg this month and Innsbruck the next," Catherine says.

"I know, Kätterlin." He shrugs his big shoulders. "Maybe the next emperor will have a real court."

"And maybe he won't."

Ludwig lets her go, and turns away to pull on his breeches. Catherine hunts around in the dim light for the strips of cloth Ludwig had discarded, and tries to wrap herself up again.

"Give me that," Ludwig says at last, taking the cloth and swathing her body, carefully avoiding touching her skin. When they are both dressed again, they sit down in the grass, well out of reach of one another.

After a long moment of silence, Ludwig finds his bag of food. He stares down at it, then starts eating as though he can think of nothing better to do.

"So if you don't want to get married, what do you want to do? What is your grand fate?" he asks, uncorking the flask of wine and offering it to her.

She takes the flask from him. "I do want to get married," she says after taking a long drink.

"Oh, just not to me. I see. Not quite up to your ladyship's standards, I suppose." He's chewing savagely, and she worries he will bite his tongue. "You have such a close bond with the House of Habsburg, perhaps you are crushed that Charles and Ferdinand were already married by proxy. Poor Kätterlin."

"Don't be absurd. They are like my younger brothers." Catherine watches her fingers pull a piece of grass into tiny pieces.

"Then maybe you can give the emperor some comfort, and enjoy being empress during his final weeks of—" Ludwig stops chewing and stares at her. He finally swallows, with the help of a swig of wine.

"That song. That's what he was firing warning shots about. God's breath, Catherine."

She shakes her head. "You're wrong. I'm his daughter's ward, practically his granddaughter."

Ludwig sets his bread and cheese down in his lap, like he's lost his taste for them. "From what I know, that wouldn't deter him at all. We're a long way from Mechelen. Has he—?" He cuts off his own sentence.

"Would it matter so much if he had? I don't remember giving you any promises." Her inner mule is doing the driving now.

"Of course, it would matter, what do you think?" The revulsion in his face outshines the moonlight.

"I think I've heard stories that he gives his former lovers to his lieutenants for them to marry, kind of like prizes," Catherine has no idea why she is saying this. She doesn't want to hurt Ludwig, but there's a cold lump in her stomach, and fighting with him makes it easier to ignore. She looks down and sees that her arms are hugging her chest, and her hands are fists. She forces herself to relax.

Ludwig is not relaxed. He stands so suddenly that the food in his lap bounces to the ground, and the rest of the roll he'd been eating tumbles down the bank and into the river. He takes her arms and yanks her to her feet.

"I don't want any prizes of that kind from the emperor," Ludwig shoves her away. The force makes her stumble, but she doesn't fall. She watches him stalk to the water's edge, where he stands with his back to her, arms folded to his chest. He mutters something that sounds like "Sorry." She doesn't reply.

She sees the first glow of dawn, and knows the city gates will open soon. She stares at Ludwig's back for another moment, then turns away and walks to the nearest gate alone.

*

Day is dawning by the river
Stand up, Kätterlin!
Dearest love, show yourself!
Stand up, Kätterlin!
I am yours and you are mine,
Stand up, Kätterlin!

Ludwig Senfl, Schweizer

15

By the Aid of Art

One hundred and forty seven steps. Catherine stands at the top of the tower of the bishop's palace, dizzy from the narrow steps and the continuous turn of the stairwell. It's early, and the June day promises endless heat, but the stone stairwell is still cool.

She hears Ludwig lumbering up behind her, and she steps aside to make room for him on the landing. This is their first encounter since their night by the river.

The two singers pause on the landing to catch their breath. Catherine doesn't really want to go in. She whispers a question, just to stall, although she hears faint plodding footsteps lower down on the stairs. They will have to move soon.

"Why on earth is the emperor using this room, high up in a tower? What about his leg?"

Ludwig shrugs, leaning back against the wall. He doesn't seem inclined to move on, either. "God's ways are completely transparent compared to his majesty's." That little smile of his, barely more than a twitch of his lips, always makes Catherine pay it back in full.

"Ludovico, I'm sorry about what happened by the river," She shifts her lute case awkwardly from one shoulder to the other.

"You don't have to—" Ludwig says.

"I know I don't have to, but I want to. I told you the truth when I said I'm not his *Schlafweib*. He hasn't touched me. Can we be friends again?"

Ludwig looks down and brushes some invisible dirt from his breeches. "Is that what we were?"

Catherine shakes her head. "I don't know…"

The plodding footsteps she heard before are louder now. She hears the emperor talking to Kunz. Ludwig leans past her, brushing her shoulder with his arm. He raps on the door.

They hear a voice from inside, and Ludwig pushes the door open, allowing Catherine to pass in front of him. As soon as she steps inside, she understands why the emperor chose this room to sit for his final portrait. The small paneled room at the top of the tower is lined with crown glass windows, and is full of diffuse midsummer light, without the intrusion of a single sunbeam at this early hour. The shadows are clearly defined, but not too dark. Each item in the room which has color sings with it: the red cushions on the window seats, small portraits hanging between the banks of windows, and the painted wood of an hourglass hanging near the door.

An easel stands in front of a wooden chair with elaborate carvings on the arms and back. Catherine sees a figure leaning out of an open window. He's very slim, and dressed like a high-level craftsman. She can't see his head or shoulders. She hears a muffled voice; the man appears to be speaking softly to himself.

Ludwig pulls a chair across the floor for Catherine to sit on while she plays the lute. The man at the window seems to realize that he is no longer alone, draws his head inside, and turns to them. Catherine recognizes the long-haired man who had been present at the emperor's showing of the procession paintings. His hair swings about his shoulders as he walks toward them.

"Albrecht Dürer, artist of Nuremberg," he nods in greeting. "Have you seen the view? You must come and look."

Dürer veers across the room again. His movements remind Catherine of a dragonfly, darting and unpredictable. She follows him, casting an inquiring glance at Ludwig over her shoulder.

"It is exactly how a bird sees the world, is it not, madam? I love to paint landscapes in watercolor while perched on a peak, looking out and over the world. Look at that sky: blue like the Virgin's robe. If eternity had a color that would be it."

"Ludwig, come and look! The colors—the green of the trees and the baked orange of the roof tiles! I can even see the river!" Catherine calls over her shoulder from the window.

"No thank you, I can imagine it very well." Ludwig says.

Catherine peeks back into the room. "Are you afraid of heights, Ludwig?" She hadn't intended to mock him, but her mouth curves of its own accord.

"Of course not. I was raised on the side of a mountain, for God's sake. I'm not afraid of heights, I'm afraid of depths."

The door opens, and Maximilian arrives with Kunz. The emperor walks with visible effort, and Catherine wonders if they abandoned all pretense, and Kunz carried him bodily up the stairs. If he negotiated those stairs on his own, he must be inured to pain, and harder than granite.

"Herr Dürer," Maximilian gives the artist his hand. Catherine sees astonishment flit across the man's face, which he hides by bowing low over his patron's hand. "Your art has been my joy for so many years, it is difficult for me to believe that we have never met face to face. We cannot attempt to catalog all you have done for us, but we will mention our special favorites: the Arch of Honor, the drawings in our prayer book, and your designs of statues which will guard our tomb." The emperor finds his chair and sinks into it. "Not to mention our little message to the Doge. The crowning with roses. Our friend Pirckheimer showed us the sketches, and we have asked him many times to tell us the story of how it was received in Venice. How we would enjoy hearing it again. Catherine, you will delight in this."

Dürer steps back so that he faces all of his listeners. "In 1506, I paid a visit to Augsburg, on my way to Venice. My home city of Nuremberg was in the grip of plague, which I was anxious to escape, and I chose Venice as my destination with the intent of studying the new styles being cultivated there, and learn from the artists. I only intended to stay in Augsburg for two days, but I found myself with the offer of a large commission, via a letter from Herr Peutinger."

"We needed something which would create a stir, and our Dürer got all of Venice talking. The Doge was incensed, wasn't he?" A light passes across the emperor's face; a pale ray of winter sun triumphing over an overcast sky.

"Yes, Majesty, but he was also seduced; the colors... he could not stop talking about the colors. He even offered me a respectable sum to stay in Venice and paint for him! I will admit that I was tempted... not only by his offer, but also by the reception I enjoyed there. At the time, in Germany I felt like a parasite, whereas in Italy I was a gentleman. And the sun and warmth. But despite all these joys, I could not stay, and your Majesty's patronage has allowed me to be a gentleman at home." Dürer bows to the emperor. "But, returning to your Majesty's story, I spent several days in Augsburg sketching members of the Fugger family, and then made my way to Venice."

"The concept was mine, and Fugger provided the capital and the pretext: a new altarpiece for the church of the German merchant community in Venice. The Feast of the Rose Garlands," Maximilian says.

Dürer bobs his head, his eyes vague, as though he were picturing it before him again. "The Virgin Mary, enthroned, holding the Christ Child, surrounded by kneeling figures. I was able to work more rapidly than normal. I almost felt that someone was guiding my hand. After the Virgin, the two most important figures were kneeling in the foreground: the pope and his Majesty the emperor. I used an existing sketch by an Italian artist as a model for the emperor."

Maximilian begins to fidget, leaning forward in his chair, as if awaiting the climax of a favorite joke which never loses its flavor.

"The viewer catches the scene precisely as two putti are preparing to crown the Virgin. She, in turn, has just placed a wreath of roses upon his majesty's head. He is portrayed kneeling before the pope, with the imperial crown on a cushion in the grass before him. There is a lute-playing angel with rainbow wings in between them," Dürer says.

"What a pity, Herr Dürer, that you have only just now seen our Songbird, or her face would have graced the scene."

"Majesty, as ever, you are too kind to me. But I still don't understand. What was the message to the Doge?" Catherine asks.

"What would you imagine the theme of the painting was, from this description?"

"Well, a coronation, I suppose."

"Exactly! My coronation, in Rome, by Pope Julius, which was being obstructed by the Doge, that *Hurensohn*, due to his tiresome feud with Julius. We would not be allowed to pass through the territories of the state of Venice with our retinue. At that time, the empire was allied with the Papal State, hence an enemy of Venice. But the Doge always did conduct politics on a level more suited to the schoolroom…but unlike a fractious child, you cannot turn the Doge over your knee to teach him a lesson—"

"—though something tells me such a thing might be counted among his secret desires—" says Kunz from behind a book.

"—but he would allow us to pass through as a private gentleman. Such munificence," Maximilian says. "Can you imagine the heir of all the Caesars tiptoeing through Italy on his way to his own coronation? The message was, Catherine, that heaven itself ordained my coronation, and the Fuggers, those pillars of industry, whose business paves the streets of Venice with gold, are literally behind me!" The emperor laughs aloud.

"Indeed, Majesty. The crowd surrounding the Virgin is made up of members of the Fugger family, and high-ranking officials in his Majesty's service, like Eric von Braunschweig. I even took the liberty of including Pirckheimer and myself," Dürer says.

"What a pity we will never see your altarpiece, Dürer. I heard it was nothing short of wondrous. But we will never set foot in that wretched swamp called Venice after their affronts to us." He settles himself in his chair. Catherine sees it's time for the serious business of the day.

"Herr Dürer, you wish to sketch our profile? From which side?"

"If it pleases you, Majesty, please make just a slight turn to your right. I would like a three-quarter view of your majesty's face."

"A wise choice. There have been enough representations of the fearsome Habsburg profile." Kunz is no longer barricaded behind a volume of Virgil, but now circles the room like a humorous hawk. "Anyone who can render the Imperial *Schnauze* will get a commission from his Majesty."

Maximilian turns in his chair, and Dürer begins his work.

"Take no notice of my fool. I have tried to teach him the importance of art and representation in the life of a sovereign, but his head is as thick as the walls of this tower, and about as receptive to new ideas," Maximilian says.

There are a few moments of quiet. The only sounds are the artist's chalk moving over the paper, and faint noises of city life far below them drifting through the open window. Catherine begins to play a solo lute arrangement of a song by Dufay: *If my face looks pale, the cause is love*. Portrait music. She wonders if the emperor will catch her joke.

"Do you prefer silence while you work, Dürer? Does it hinder you or disrupt your concentration if we speak, or if my musicians entertain us?" the emperor asks.

"Your Majesty is very thoughtful. But I could stand on top of the Ulmer Münster at high noon on Easter Sunday, drawing and painting, and not be distracted."

From time to time, Catherine glances at the easel. She can see Maximilian's head and shoulders taking shape on Dürer's paper. His art is a skilled kind of sorcery at which she marvels.

What appear to be a few simple lines define the structure of his face; the planes and angles of his cheekbones and nose, and the strong lines around his mouth and the deep grooves around his eyes caused by years of squinting into the sun, or through the slit of a helmet visor. She knows that laughter helped to form those lines too. In life, his presence fills a room, though he is neither large nor loud. Dürer brings this impression across to the viewer by filling the width of the page with his shoulders. He looks every bit as imposing as he is in life.

It is as yet a black and white sketch, so no impression is given of the deep chestnut brown of his eyes. She wonders if Dürer is close enough to see the contrasting color in them, like little flakes of gold. Dürer renders the strife-weariness and resignation in the emperor's face. But Catherine sees nothing like defeat. And something else is lacking: regret. How is he able to portray emotion in such a simple sketch? She notes with approval that the artist has perceived and depicted the only tender thing on that face: his mouth.

Kunz is watching too, and gives voice to his ridiculous thoughts at intervals. "Do you know when his Majesty picked you to paint his final portrait, Herr Dürer? When he saw your rhinoceros print. 'Here is the man who will render our face for the ages!' he said." Kunz's imitation of the emperor's speech is uncanny. Catherine bows her head over her lute to hide her smile.

"Oh you may well laugh, Catherine, if you find it worth your while," Maximilian does not sound the least perturbed. "The rhinoceros was a marvel. Just imagine, the Almighty gave the creature a hide I have to pay armorers a small fortune to produce for me! But that was not the reason we requested the talents of Dürer. We have long appreciated the work of Strigel, and still do. He has a way with faces, but his portraits of us are remote and removed from the viewer. There is little life in them. But for the image that will represent us on earth after our death, for years or centuries, if God wills it, we desire a more immediate engagement with the viewer. We wish to confront the viewer with who we are. We know

Dürer can do that, since we ourself have seen the portrait you created of Frederick the Wise. I know the man well. The look in his eyes in your portrait gave him away: sober, shrewd, and spoiling for a fight. You captured him completely, gave him up to be known. This is what I would wish for my final portrait."

Though worms destroy the body, some part of you will survive, Catherine thinks.

Ludwig nudges her shoulder with his elbow, and she realizes that she has been staring, and not playing for who knows how long. He whispers to her, and she nods without looking up.

They sing a duet by Dufay. The two parts are written like an embrace, the voices entwine like sinuous creatures, pacing together, before Ludwig's voice serves as a platform for her flight. Catherine hears their precision on the phrases ending in unison: they sound like one being.

"Remind me what you said about the Ulmer Münster again, Herr Dürer?" the emperor says.

"Forgive me, Majesty. I've rarely heard anything so astonishing." Dürer's right hand still holds the chalk, but he has stopped sketching. He stands and listens.

The emperor's face resembles an alpine sunrise; a sudden, blinding brightness from behind black rock. "It pleases me to hear you say so. I do not trust people who are not moved by music. What do you imagine this song is about?"

"My knowledge of French is sadly lacking, Majesty, but from the contour of the music and how the voices relate, I would say it's a love song. It reminds me of a partner dance—each voice using the other as a point of reference, despite being in constant motion."

"You heard the skillful legerdemain of these two singers. They can make the driest Kyrie sound like a passionate declaration of love. The source of that alchemy is best left a mystery between them. However, they have led you astray in this case: it is a song about death. Catherine, would you translate the first verse for our artist, please?"

*My dear Friend, why have you decided
to remain so melancholy
if God has taken a good friend
and parted him from your company?
Do not give up all life,
pray for him and forsake mourning,
for one day we shall all have to take that road.*

Before Dürer can respond, his restless subject is on his feet. "May we see your sketch?"

The emperor stands slightly behind Dürer, looking over the artist's shoulder. Dürer makes a slight move, as if to give way, but the emperor places his hand on his arm.

"No, stay," he says, "continue. We have no wish to impede you."

The emperor removes his hand from Dürer's arm, and Dürer continues shading his drawing. Catherine might be imagining it, but the artist's hand looks slightly less steady than before.

The bells of the cathedral begin to ring. Catherine hears the sound of centuries passing, and the resonance of time itself.

"Do you have any special wishes regarding your portrait, Majesty?" Dürer asks.

Kunz laughs aloud. "I thought you said you've done work for him before. When does the emperor *not* have special wishes? Sometimes he has them on an hourly basis, sometimes he has new ones once the work in question is already finished, from the artist's point of view."

"I will send you a detailed list of requests as soon as may be," Maximilian says. "For now, I simply ask you to erase the signs of sickness from our face. Make us look robust. Retain the marks of our age, by all means, but we do not wish to be remembered as an ailing monarch."

"It will be as you wish, Majesty," Dürer says.

"The Diet is waiting, and everyone knows the estates are incapable of action without the guiding hand of their emperor." Emperor Maximilian beckons to Kunz von der Rosen before turning to face Dürer again. "Farewell, Herr Dürer. You will be rewarded for your invaluable service to us, as far as is in our power."

Dürer bows to the emperor.

Maximilian and Kunz make their way across the room, and disappear down the stairwell. Catherine and Ludwig prepare to follow them. Dürer seems content where he is.

"Madam," he says, not looking at Catherine, but continuing to work on his sketch, "I wonder if you would allow me the pleasure of sketching you as well."

Catherine looks at Ludwig, feeling bashful and flattered all at once. Ludwig sweeps his eyes heavenward, puts down his music, and goes to the desk near the window, and picks up the volume of Virgil that Kunz had been looking at. He folds his enormous body onto a small stool, and settles in to read.

"I'd be delighted, Herr Dürer. I'm sorry I can't seem to encourage my fellow singer to entertain us while you work."

Catherine sits in the chair Maximilian recently vacated. "How would you like me to sit?"

Dürer doesn't answer, but stands watching her. "What an enviable structure your bones have, Madam," he says at last. "Your cheekbones are high, yet they do not jut in the way one so often sees. You look as though you just thought of something incredible, and are waiting for the right person to tell." Dürer crosses the room, carefully picks up Catherine's lute, and hands it to her.

"Please sit just as you were, with your head inclined to the side, looking down." The artist retreats behind his easel again.

Catherine hears the hiss of his chalk moving across the paper. Her eyes are lowered like he asked, but she can feel his gaze like a ray of light intensified by a mirror. It has an observable, palpable power. It seems she can feel it penetrating cloth, skin, muscle, sinew and bone, seeking out her essence. She has no doubt that he has found her out, and will lay her inner self bare on canvas. Heat wells up, and sweat glazes her skin.

Dürer seems to sense what she is feeling. After a few more almost intolerably exposed seconds, he says, "It is over, madam. I hope you were not too uncomfortable. Thank you for your forbearance."

Catherine forces her eyes up, and looks at him. It is over. His gaze is upon her, but the power is gone from it. She rises from the chair, sways a little, feeling faintly foolish. She walks toward Ludwig, and places her lute on the table in front of him.

"Now *your* face has gone pale, Catherine. I hope you're not ill," Ludwig says.

"I'm afraid sitting for me has proved to be a trial for his majesty's lutenist," Dürer says.

"What a load of nonsense," Ludwig says, "She's overwrought, probably needs to be bled."

"You may scoff," Dürer says, keeping his eyes on his sketch, "but it is a very real thing. I have painted and sketched myself several times, and must avoid my own eye in the mirror for days sometimes afterwards." He smiles briefly at Catherine. "Herr Senfl is simply carved from harder stuff than we are, madam."

Ludwig unfurls himself from the stool, briefly touches Catherine's arm on his way by, then goes to inspect the artist's work. He doesn't ask, just stands behind the artist as though it were his right.

"How does it look?" Catherine is curious in spite of herself.

"Come look for yourself," Ludwig says.

She shakes her head emphatically. She doesn't want to see what the artist unearthed inside of her.

"It's remarkable... how do you capture someone's essence so completely with such simple means?" Ludwig says.

"There is no simple answer to that question, Herr Senfl. Can you explain to me how you make someone hear emotion in words that they cannot understand, simply using your voice?" Dürer asks.

"I see your point," Ludwig has that dry little upturn in his lips. "May I ask you, Herr Dürer, how you can bear that the emperor is so proprietary about your work? How can you bear that he tells you how to paint?"

"I see it as a privilege to work for a patron with such a clear artistic vision. His designs for the Arch of Honor and his concept for the Venice painting were truly inspired. It is my challenge to realize his ambitions on paper and canvas." The artist stands back and regards the sketch. "Have you ever felt a presence while looking at a painting? If all you see is the art of the maker, the artist has missed his mark. To touch a mind, slow the step, capture the eye and the imagination: that is what his Majesty wishes, and what I will endeavor to create for him."

Dürer lays the sketch of Catherine aside, and takes up the sketch of Maximilian again. Catherine leaves her lute and walks to the easel, where she and Ludwig stand, watching the artist as he writes a note at the top in meticulous script:

This is Emperor Maximilian, whom I, Albrecht Dürer, portrayed way up high in a small chamber in the tower at Augsburg on Monday after the feast day of St. John the Baptist in the year 1518.

16

A Poet of Dual Form

"Bath, bread, bed," Ludwig yawns to himself. He is alone in the library, lazily paging through a volume of Horace odes, looking for a text. His friend, the humanist Minervius, had asked him to set to music some classical poetry for his circle in Munich.

It had been a rare day of rest during the Diet for the imperial court composer, no Masses where the Hofkapelle had been required to sing, no dinners or parties where his voice was in demand. No doubt the emperor was sequestered in council chambers listening to a philippic by the electors, or delivering one of his own. Just imagining the tedium makes Ludwig yawn again. Who cares who the next emperor is, he thinks, as long as he hires me.

He hears a knock at the door, and his friend Wagenrieder pokes his head in the room.

"Come in, Lukas. I'm about to put up my spurs for the day," Ludwig says.

Wagenrieder plods into the library, looking as drained of life as Ludwig feels. Not only has there been a lot of music at the Diet, there has been a lot of drinking, and the Hofkapelle is as ragged around the edges as their cloaks.

"Imperial messenger just came and left this for you," Lukas hands Ludwig a letter, marked with the emperor's seal. "I'm off to the refectory. Are you coming?"

"I'd better see what Himself wants from me first. I'll see you down there," Ludwig says.

"You hope…" Wagenrieder waves to him and disappears.

Ludwig breaks the seal on the letter, and recognizes Treitz's handwriting.

Please set these verses which his Majesty has recently composed at your earliest convenience. He requests a simple setting for voice and a few instruments, which will bring out the words with force and clarity, as is your custom. He wishes to hear your creation privately in a day or two.

Senfl's eyes roam over the verses without much interest. Nothing new here—the poem is yet another overblown paean of devotion to some unfortunate young woman. Kaiser Max considers himself quite a skilled poet, but his verse form and use of language are so unmusical, it's a challenge to set them artfully.

When Senfl's eyes reach the bottom of the page, he reads the dedication. He reads it again and again, and each time, his soul takes a battering.

To Catherine von ?

It can't be her, Senfl thinks. She's not from a noble German house. She told me she wasn't a lady, not in any real sense.

Senfl shoots out of his chair, and takes the verses over to the window. He reads them over again, this time, his eyes dissect each word and phrase, while his gut churns. This morning's hangover revisits him with force.

No eagle soars so fine, my lady,
Be it even with a crown adorned,
As you with noble grace display
The beauty in you born.
Stay, stay with me!

He can't mean Kätterlin. Each time he reads the first verse, Senfl reassures himself of this. Then he reads the second verse, and the reality of the situation pounds him with renewed pain.

Misfortune and woe be far from you!
Your music and song delight my ear.
You paragon of virtue and honor,
are wise beyond your years.
   Stay, stay with me!
You who grace art beyond all measure,
Do now my prayer accept,
If you will grace me with your treasures,
Never will you feel regret.
   Stay, stay with me!
With longing heart I pledge to you,
My lady, note and mark my word,

You shall have all you ask of me,
I will your pleasure serve.
   Stay, stay with me!

Senfl hasn't cried since he was ten, but the hot pain in his eyes still feels familiar. He knows she bears some strange affection for Maximilian. She is loyal and steadfast, and will do whatever the emperor asks of her, with an eager heart. How can the emperor misuse that innocent love? She must find it repellent, Ludwig thinks. An infirm old man must be repulsive to a beauty like her...

Ludwig's angry words to her on the riverbank prey on his mind. Why did he lash out at her, when love makes her pain his too? His thoughts skip over time, like a pebble over water. He sees her walking, softly swaying, heavy with his child. He sees himself bending over her mountainous belly, singing softly to his son or daughter inside. A hunger gnaws at him. It is not physical, and not easily stilled.

Senfl moves the back of his hand across his eyes; it comes away wet. He looks at his other hand and finds the emperor's verses mangled and creased as though trampled by cows. He knows the emperor—his whims, his oceanic self-love, his need for adoration that surpasses even the normal royal craving for worship. These verses are the prelude. She has caught his eye. Next comes pursuit, coaxing, persuasion, little gifts and expressions of devotion. The legendary hunter seldom misses. Senfl has seen it happen so many times, and even understands, to an extent. To find yourself the focal point of that charm, with its full strength brought to bear... men can scarcely withstand it, and women rarely try.

Ludwig paces back to his desk, lays the emperor's verses down and smoothes the crumpled paper with his large hands. He's a composer, and he will give his patron his best work. He finds a wax tablet, jots down a few preliminary intervals, a turn of melody, an ornament or two. He's a composer, and knows the way to bring the words out, make the notes the servant of the text, so that his songs sound as natural as speech.

But he's also a man with an aching heart, and he will not give the emperor the simple setting he asked for. Senfl chooses to forget those instructions. He knows who else will be at the emperor's private audience, and he knows her sharp ear. A keen listener will hear a message. The emperor might hear it too. A heart in pain is rarely a wise counselor, and Senfl does not let the thought of consequences deter him. A month ago, all he wanted from life was to be imperial court composer, to serve one emperor or another until the end of his days. He still wants that, but he wants her with him. Maximilian may cast him out, so be it. He's dying anyway. Ludwig plans to petition Charles, or whoever the new emperor ends up being, and has no doubt he'll be hired. Why wouldn't he be? Who is a better composer? Only Josquin, and he's not young anymore, either.

Ludwig sits at his desk, and immerses himself in the work. This type of composition is a puzzle, and he loves puzzles. When it becomes too dark to see, he lights a candle. Wagenrieder comes back, bringing bread, cheese, and wine from the refectory of Holy Cross. Ludwig barely notices him come or go.

He wakes up slumped over his music, unaware of having gone to sleep. The day is bright outside, and he hears the bells of Holy Cross. He counts them—it is nine o'clock. He has had nothing to eat since yesterday morning, and is ravenous and thirsty. He devours the food Wagenrieder left him last night, goes in search of a chamber pot, returns to his desk, and writes and writes, oblivious to everything, until he is finished. Then he counts the bells again. Six o'clock in the evening.

His fingers and shoulders are cramped, and his rump protests the long hours of sitting. But there's still work to be done. He sends his assistant to round up two other singers, and three instrumentalists: he wants a lute, a cornetto, and a recorder. There's no time to have all the parts copied, so the participants will just have to stand atop one another to read the music during rehearsal. The instrumentalists will just play through the melodies a couple of times anyway, to commit them to memory, in order to improvise. Ludwig will be singing the emperor's text himself. Some part of him does not want this to be easy—not for him, and also not for Catherine. He loves her, and does not wish for her to suffer pain, but he does want her to know what he's enduring.

At last, they are ready. He sends a message to his majesty at the Fugger Palace, and they are summoned soon afterwards, as he suspected. When Maximilian anticipates a pleasure of his own devising, he does not like to be kept waiting. Senfl drains the last of the brandy in his flask. There's scarcely a mouthful, not enough to warm him, let alone allay the crawling anxiety in his innards. At this moment, losing his position is the least of his fears.

Catherine has been called to the emperor's sitting room, but told not to bring her lute. The room is empty, and she stands off to the side, unsure of what to do. There are books strewn here and there, but it feels presumptuous even to page through them. Finally, boredom drives her to reach for one of them, but the sound of a door opening makes her jerk her hand away. She turns to find Kunz half-carrying the emperor, who waves him off as soon as he sees Catherine. He hobbles up to her under his own power, takes both of her hands, and kisses her cheek.

"Dearest, this is a great day. I have a surprise for you. Please, be seated, and we will wait for it to arrive. Kunz, the items from my desk, please," Maximilian says, beckoning to his fool.

Kunz hands Maximilian a letter with a broken seal. Then he hands Catherine a large scroll tied with ribbon. Her curiosity is wide awake, and she restrains herself with difficulty from opening it. Maximilian is watching—she can feel his eyes on her. She looks up, and sees a new light in them. What does she see? Pride, triumph, vindication? He has been proved right about something, and is beside himself.

"Open the scroll," the emperor says. She unties the ribbon with difficulty; nerves make her fingers clumsy, unless she's performing. Finally, she unrolls the parchment. She sees a coat of arms, with many familiar elements she remembers from her childhood. Lion, ermines, blue background, decorated with the collar of the Order of the Golden Fleece.

"Do you recognize the house to which it belongs?" Maximilian asks.

"It looks like the house of Burgundy," Catherine says. The outer door opens, and six men enter the room. She turns her head, attention drawn by the noise and movement, and the first person she sees is Ludwig. He is not looking at her. There's a lutenist, a recorder player, a cornettist, and two other singers.

Maximilian is also distracted. The musicians bow to him, then retire across the room to arrange themselves and await the signal to begin.

"Herr Senfl," the emperor says, "this is a larger contingent than we were expecting. More is not necessarily better."

"I was inspired by your Majesty's moving verses, and my hand was guided to create something very special. I hope your Majesty will not be offended that I chose to embellish a little."

"We have the highest faith in your abilities, Senfl. Please improvise a little while we finish our business here. We will give you the signal when we desire you to begin our piece." The three instrumentalists confer briefly, then begin to play on the lutenist's signal. Catherine's curiosity has turned to bafflement—she feels like a cork bobbing in a gray and stormy sea. Ludwig will not look at her, and now she must turn back to Maximilian and this coat of arms. She'd rather be standing with the musicians. At least her role would be clear, and all would make sense.

"The House of Burgundy," she repeats, looking from the colored parchment in her hands to the emperor's face. Just then the recorder player makes a clumsy error, and tries to hide it with an even clumsier ornament. She blushes on his behalf.

"The noblest house of Europe after my own," Maximilian says. "The lineage of Philip the Good, and Charles the Bold, Dukes of Burgundy—the grandfather and father of my beloved Mary. Your lineage, Catherine."

"What?" Her whisper is no match for the cornetto. It drowns her out, as she drowns in Maximilian's words.

He holds up the letter. "This letter is from the Bishop of Utrecht: Philip of Burgundy, one of Philip the Good's favored natural sons. He acknowledges the affair he had with Ghislaine de Croÿ in 1494, and claims you as his daughter. He gives you his name. I give you this coat of arms."

Thoughts crowd her mind like bold beggar children, all clamoring for her attention. Here is revenge on her childhood tormentors; she is now the recognized natural daughter of a nobleman. In her veins flows the same blood as the woman who Maximilian loved like his own soul. The thought that crowds them all, however, forcing itself to the front of her mind like the ringleader: Now I can't marry Ludwig. She turns her head. He's leaning against the wall behind the musicians, arms crossed, each hand tucked under the opposite arm. He stares at the floor.

She turns back to the emperor. "Sir, I don't mean to sound ungrateful, but are you sure? Isn't it suspect that he ignores me all my life, and now that I am in your service, at your right hand, so to speak, suddenly he makes his claim on me?"

"Dearest, I have never been more sure of anything. I saw Mary in you from the very first, but did not recognize what I was seeing. You are both granddaughters of Philip the Good! When you know nobility as I do, you cannot help but see it and respond to it. I can elevate any tradesman, call him a duke or a prince, but true nobility is God's alone to bestow."

He takes her hand as he turns to face the musicians, and motions to Senfl. While the instrumentalists hurriedly wind up the piece they were playing, Maximilian leans to Catherine. "You inspired me to take up my poet's pen again. I wrote these verses for you, and asked Senfl to set them. He must have worked day and night, for I sent them just yesterday."

Oh no, Ludovico, Catherine thinks. What hurts worse: setting these words to music, or singing them? She wishes she could spare him the latter. She briefly considers standing, walking to Ludwig, taking his hand and leading him from the room, from the palace, from the city. Away from

Maximilian. But where could they go, and how would they live? She keeps her seat.

Catherine forces herself to breathe calmly. If she can just keep the tears from forming, and keep a clear head, and not make it worse than it is. A month ago, all she would have wanted was this: a miracle from heaven, her origins explained, the emperor's hand in hers, a poem, the hope that he might love her. These wishes have been uprooted one by one, gradually washed away like the tide creeping in, wave by tiny wave. A look, a smile, a friendly cup of wine, kindness, the bond of common history they share: two parentless children growing up at court, unmoored from ties of family, finding salvation in music.

Her eyes focus on Ludwig; if she can't touch him, as she wishes to, at least her eyes may rest on him. He gives her a look, long enough for her to read his eyes. She sits up straighter. She curbs her roiling thoughts and concentrates on the music.

For a moment, she thinks her efforts have been inadequate; she can barely process what she is hearing: three melodies, a confusion of texts. Her ears are pulled from line to line: one catches the attention only to be overwhelmed by another. Maximilian's carefully wrought verses are almost completely obscured. She feels like she's undergoing an emotional quartering: she wants to weep, laugh, shout at Ludwig to stop it, and kiss him for his ingenuity all at the same time.

A strange coded message emerges, sung by three different singers:

Kätterlin, my dear love
a maid fair and fine
I hear you want to leave me
I am yours and you are mine
Listen, my fair love,
listen to what I am saying.

Stand up, Kätterlin!
In all your days, you will never regret it.
Hear and mark my words!

Each verse ends with an unadorned minor third, which speaks of mournful and lonesome thoughts with more eloquence than a thousand verses. The phrase 'Stand up, Kätterlin!' is repeated so many times, with such clarity, that she begins to squirm in her seat. She comes back to herself and realizes that Maximilian has let go of her hand.

Her jaw aches from clenching it, and she tries to relax. Even so, she worries about the emperor. Will he rage? Will he throw things? Will he take it as a good joke? Will he ennoble Ludwig on the spot for his ingenuity, and allow them to be married? Catherine realizes the improbability of that last option, but what if…? What if she could appeal to him, use his affection for her? Remind him of his love for Mary? Tempt him with the thought that if he allows them to be married, he will have created another great alliance, not linking two noble houses, but rather two musical servants, who will create a musical dynasty to serve the House of Austria until the Day of Judgment.

In the end, he does nothing. He dismisses them all without a word. Kunz is at his side, he looks at no one.

This is worse than an outburst.

Catherine follows the musicians out. Ludwig is already halfway down the corridor, so she calls after him. He turns unwillingly, it seems to her. The recorder player makes a crude gesture using two fingers and his tongue on his way by. Ludwig allows him to pass in silence.

"Ludovico… what made you do that?" He is standing farther from her than she would like.

"If you have to ask that, then we are not singing off the same sheet, you and I." His voice strains with weariness.

"No, I mean, why run the risk of angering Maximilian in that way?"

"As if I thought of him at all! I can work anywhere, Kätterlin. Italy, France, Burgundy…"

"But you want to work for the imperial court!"

Ludwig half-turns from her, and stares down the corridor. She can't imagine what he's thinking. He turns back, takes one long step, and stands so near to her that she can clearly see two days' worth of stubble on his neck and chin. She notices for the first time that his beard is much lighter in color than his hair. He keeps a small distance, two finger-breadths, but touch doesn't seem to be required for him to kindle her. Ludwig's arm crosses in front of her; he takes hold of her right forearm with his right hand, pulls her hand up, and plants it on his chest, against his heart.

"You are not stupid, so why do you overlook the point?" He says quietly. "I did it for you. Did you hear the message?" He strengthens his grip on her arm, pressing her hand against his chest until her wrist aches. "I love you, and I'm prepared to wait. But not forever." He drops her hand and walks off.

17

Rumor Flies

"Please come in. Thank you for arriving so promptly. You are kept rather busy, I believe. I hope your rest, when it comes, is comfortable in the Damenhof."

It's just after morning prayer, and Catherine has been summoned to Jacob Fugger's office. She's surprised at how simple and unadorned it is, for the richest man in the empire. She wonders whether this is deliberate. Perhaps the austerity here spurs him on to earn more money.

The merchant banker sits at his desk: a rough table with a writing stand, pens, neat stacks of papers and scrolls tidied in baskets. She contrasts this with Maximilian's desk, which always resembles the result of a destructive storm. A large cabinet stands in the corner, with drawers upon which are written the names of cities: Innsbruck, Milan, Nuremberg...

Fugger watches her enter the room, and is on his feet in an instant.

"Please sit. Would you like some wine?" He strides across the room without waiting for an answer. He pours wine and water into a goblet, and hands it to Catherine. He doesn't return to his side of the desk, but paces around a bit before perching on the edge of the desk. He is nearly touching her.

"I enjoyed your performance in the cathedral so much, Catherine. Don't worry—it never occurred to me that you were singing. The emperor told me. He knows I can keep a secret—it's a necessity in my line of work. He likes to get his jabs in at the church where and when he can. Who can blame him? Rome has rarely been a friend or ally to the emperor." Fugger picks up a discarded bit of sealing wax and rolls it between his fingers. His voice is soothing and monotonous, but his eyes disturb her—not what she sees in them, but what she doesn't see. Whatever light or spark animates a person from within is missing from him.

"You are aware of how much is at stake for the emperor here at the Diet? The succession? The Spanish are not forthcoming with their funds, so in the end, yet again, it all depends on my capital."

Catherine doesn't know where this line of questioning is going, but the crawling feeling at the base of her skull tells her it is somewhere she'd rather not be.

"In the end, I will make Charles emperor, not Maximilian by championing him, and not the pope by putting the crown on his head. I know you don't care about Charles. I know who you care about, God knows why. That way he has with women. He has nothing to offer them, but they fall at his feet. Even my wife. I asked her about it once, and she expressed astonishment that I still thought that money can buy anything. In my view, it can."

Fugger's arm resembles a puppet as he reaches out—it seems to be happening outside of his control. Catherine makes a quick, sharp movement. He must not touch her. This startles Fugger. He jerks his hand back, then stands and moves as rapidly as a desk-bound scribbler is able to, away from her. He stands behind his desk, gripping the back of his chair.

"Forgive me, I have also had little rest. The negotiations go on and on, even in my own mind when I lay down and try to sleep."

"What do you want, Herr Fugger?" She thinks she knows. She's already encountered this attitude, even at Duchess Margaret's court. The belief of visiting noblemen, primarily, that female musician is synonymous with whore.

"Briefly stated, I want you to work for me. Now. I don't want to wait until Maximilian is dead."

Catherine forgets to be contained. The words bite at her lips until she releases them. "No. I won't leave him."

Fugger moves around to the back of her chair. She sees the glint of gold from his round Venetian hat in her side vision. His breath smells like meat and wine. "I think you will."

"I've reached the pinnacle of my profession, Herr Fugger. Imperial court musician. If there's been a woman in my place before, her name has been lost to history. Why would I take such a large step back?"

Fugger turns to face her again. He stares at her, and nothing reaches back when she looks into his eyes. "The answer is the same as it is to all of life's questions: money and power. And my desire to squeeze the emperor any way I can. It amuses me to see how little it takes to make him jump."

"He has my loyalty," Catherine says. "Do you really think hearing you talk this way is some kind of inducement?" Fugger is altogether too close to her, so Catherine springs up and moves to the windows.

"Do you know how much Maximilian owes me? I don't either—it's all in here," He opens a drawer and hauls out a thick, leather-bound ledger. "Do you think I'll ever see a *Kreuzer* of it again? I know I won't. He'll charge his heirs with repayment, but they won't do it. They'll be as strapped as he is. Charles may have a little more, due to his holdings in the New World."

Catherine can't help being curious. "Then why continue to loan him money?"

Fugger walks toward the cabinet with the names printed on the drawers. From the drawer marked 'Tyrol', he hauls an armload of papers. "What do you imagine these are?"

Catherine shakes her head.

"The deeds to silver, copper, and salt mines in Tyrol. The emperor pawned them to me for cash, with full mining rights. I have already made enough from those mines to make the endeavor quite worthwhile. I am a nobleman, thanks to the emperor. He made me a count of the empire—I'm the first merchant to have achieved that status." Fugger replaces the documents and closes the drawer smoothly. "I'm financing Charles' election in order to expand my enterprises in Iberia and the New World."

Fugger sits down behind his desk again. "I have the emperor in my purse, so to speak. Once there was a dispute about transporting Hungarian copper, sold by my firm, on the Baltic Sea. The Hanseatic League balked, saying I was monopolizing copper trade. What I was really doing was upsetting *their* monopoly. I called on the emperor, and he immediately threatened the city of Lübeck with the imperial ban. They backed down, and I continued shipping copper all over the Baltic."

Catherine sips her wine, growing curious about something else. "What will you do for me, if I agree?"

"You'll receive fifty per cent more salary than the highest paid musician at the imperial court. More importantly, the money will actually find its way to your purse. In fact…," Fugger opens another drawer and removes a small wooden chest, which he unlocks with a key worn on a chain around his neck. He extracts several coins from the chest, counts them, makes a note in his ledger, and hands them to her. "An advance."

Catherine shakes her head. "I can't accept that, Herr Fugger."

"I insist. If not an advance, then consider it repayment for the unfortunate business with your instruments. I will also help your lover attain the position he wants at the new imperial court, and make it possible for you to marry."

Catherine gapes, astonished. How does he know? Then she remembers Maximilian's words: *Fugger is like a bad smell—he gets in everywhere.*

"And if I refuse?"

Fugger's smile is so faint it could be the beginnings of a sneeze. "I'll tell Cardinal Cajetan who the remarkable singer was he's so anxious to get to know. My understanding is that he wants to take the boy back to Rome with him." Fugger plants the coins in her hand, then walks to the door and opens it, motioning for Catherine to leave. "Take some time to think about it, and let me know what you decide." As she passes him, Fugger takes her hand and kisses it, holding it to his lips with both hands. The prolonged, damp contact makes Catherine queasy.

The door closes behind her, and she stands in the hall for a moment, wiping her hand on her dress and making sure none of her emotions show on her face. What had the emperor said? 'I have also sold the things I love most in this world'. Her hands feel like she dipped them in the Wertach mid-winter, and she holds them against her fevered cheeks and forehead.

She steps away from Fugger's office door, eyes on the ground. Her mind works furiously, and she nearly collides with a small figure in a bright red silk dress. Catherine and Barbara stare at one another for a long moment, before Barbara hurries away. She enters Fugger's office without bothering to knock.

Stalemate, Catherine thinks.

18

He Tells Truth as He Laughs

Market day. The square in front of the Rathaus resembles an anthill in the sheer number of people and the pace of activity. Stalls of food: butcher boys waving flies away from the meat, farmers selling their fruits and vegetables, bakers, fruiterers with exotic imported goods, roasted nuts and dried fruit, knife sharpeners, leather workers, printers selling pamphlets, woodblock prints, and propaganda about what's going on at the Diet. Jugglers and conjurers perform here and there, gathering crowds around them, especially knots of little ragged children.

Catherine is tired of sitting around in the Damenhof, so she puts on her male clothing, slips out of the Fugger Palace and makes for the marketplace. She feels hungry, so she buys a roasted sausage for a few pfennigs, and eats it while wandering around, enjoying the spectacle. The sun is high and hot, but the air feels cool.

Someone bumps into her, and her hand moves instinctively to feel for the purse around her neck.

"I think you dropped this," A familiar voice. Catherine turns and sees Kunz von der Rosen holding her money pouch.

"Did you just rob me, Kunz?" Catherine tries to retrieve the pouch, but Kunz yanks it away.

"I insist upon a finder's fee. A beer, if you please. I'm feeling generous—you can buy yourself one, too." The fool leads the way to a small *Bierstube*. Musician and jester stand at the counter together sipping their warm, flat beer.

"Have you ever seen one of these?" Kunz produces an apple from somewhere, Catherine can't quite see where.

"An apple? Yes, a time or two…" Kunz places the apple on the bar, and takes his hand away. Catherine watches, along with the tavern landlady. Slowly, the apple begins to wobble a bit, then rock back and forth. Catherine glances at Kunz, who holds up his hands. "Nothing up my sleeve." The apple topples over, then begins to roll itself toward the edge of the counter. When it falls, Kunz catches it neatly.

"An old trick," the landlady sniffs.

"Something you would know all about, turning old tricks," Kunz grins and raises his glass. The landlady begins cursing him loudly, so Kunz and Catherine retire to a far table.

"How does that work?" she asks, looking around for the apple. It has vanished, and she sees no place the fool could have concealed it.

"I'm not about to divulge my secrets. And I have many. Even about you. Well, your 'other self', shall we say." The jester's smile is maddening to Catherine, who fights to conceal her reaction. "Ah, so you both share that trait—you are as good at obscuring your emotions as a baby. Even open books can close, but your face is as private as a painting on permanent display. But your blush is very fetching, whichever guise you are in." Kunz laughs. "I'd be on my guard if I were you—artists and humanists are notorious sodomites, and Augsburg is swarming with them during the Diet. How amusing it would be to see the fellow get the surprise of his life!"

"Perhaps I might do the opposite," Catherine says, determined not to let Kunz get the better of her. "Perhaps I might deceive some innocent girl. A sort of modern-day Tiresias." She notices that she no longer has

139

Kunz's attention. The jester's eyes have gone glassy, and he appears to be watching some invisible scene unfold in the far corner of the room.

Kunz focuses on his companion again, with a faint smile on his wind-battered face. "All this talk is not very chivalrous, of course, but I forget that you are not who you purport to be." Kunz takes another long sip of beer.

"Kunz, can I ask your advice, as someone who has known the emperor for a long time?"

"If I am a fool, what do you call someone who asks a fool's advice?"

"Can you not be serious for even one moment?" Catherine says, exasperated.

"No, I cannot. That is how I have lived so long. But ask your question regardless."

Catherine turns and leans against the wall, straddling the bench.

"My alter ego wants to marry Herr Senfl. What she learned about her origins makes it unlikely that the emperor would consider it a favorable match."

"You don't need the emperor's permission to marry, certainly," Kunz says. "You are both of age."

"No, but Senfl needs the emperor's continued good will if he is to work for the next emperor. He needs the pension that Maximilian promised him, and a reference."

"Yes, I see your problem. Erm, Catherine's problem." Kunz makes a deft movement, and a coin appears in his hand. He plays with it, spins it around on the table, then appears to swallow it. Catherine realizes that he's doing these things mechanically, to stimulate his thoughts, the way a normal person might drum their fingers on the table, or scratch their head.

"The emperor ennobled you, didn't he? And Herr Hofhaimer?" Catherine says.

"Yes..." The fool makes a heaving sound, like he's about to bring up his beer, but the coin reappears instead. He passes it back and forth between his hands, making it disappear and reappear each time.

"You are hoping he will agree to elevate Herr Senfl, so that he and Catherine can marry?"

"Yes, that's it exactly!" She exhales, stupidly imagining that hearing the words spoken aloud equals success. "Would you say it is possible?"

"It's possible."

Catherine grins and suddenly feels like she might just be able to fly.

"It's also possible that tomorrow morning, we'll all wake up with our legs growing out of our heads, so that we have to walk around upside down."

Catherine feels so heavy, she might not even be able to rise from the bench, let alone fly.

Kunz swivels on the bench and looks her in the eye, and she can see that the fool has departed, at least momentarily. "I have served Maximilian since he was a humble Archduke who didn't know how to behave at high table at the Burgundian court. He has my undying loyalty and love. He trusts me like he trusts no one else, and I would never break faith with him." Kunz dips his jutting chin once, as if to say: there, now you know. "The emperor is very covetous. He doesn't like anyone else playing with his pretty things."

There goes the rug, right out from under her. "I'm not his pretty thing," Catherine studies what's left of her beer.

"Oh but you are," Kunz says, singsongy.

"But he rejected me! Catherine, I mean."

Kunz stands up. "The only reliable thing about his majesty is his unpredictability. Seek patterns at your peril. Didn't it occur to you, dear infant, that his majesty might want something else from you?"

"Men usually don't."

"Fair enough. You know, there are few things more important to his majesty than kith and kinship. Genealogy. Antecedents are as vital as descendants are, as long as they're the right kind. If you're a monarch with a less-than-ideal family tree, you search far afield until you've found the roots you want, then call them your own. You engage a respected historian to research your heritage, and *vide*! He discovers Noah is your ancestor, and yours is suddenly the oldest ruling family in Europe."

Catherine only realizes she's been holding her breath when she tries to speak. "Are you telling me he made it all up about my Burgundian heritage? It's not true?"

Kunz shrugs and stands up. "What is truth to one who believes?" He thumps Catherine's money pouch down on the table in front of her, and walks away.

Catherine watches his back as he leaves. The people in the tavern part before him like rows of grain before a strong wind. Then she picks up her money pouch. Without quite knowing why, she opens it and roots around in the coins with her finger. She finds an extra one: the coin Kunz was playing with. It's a *Kreuzer* from Tyrol. For a long time, Catherine stares at the crowned figure, shown in armor, holding a scepter in his left hand, and a sword in his right. The angle of the aquiline nose and the forceful set of the chin are very realistically rendered—the emperor must have been pleased with the design.

She holds the coin on its edge on the table, flicks it, and closes her eyes as it spins itself out and comes to rest on the table. Heads I go to the emperor, tails I try to sort this out on my own. She peeps warily at the side facing up, and sighs before downing the rest of her beer and leaving the tavern.

19

All Are Wrong, but Wrong in Different Ways

The problem with the Swiss Guard, the soldiers who guard the pope and his cardinals, is that they resemble Landsknechten in almost every regard. Same gaudy clothing, same plumy berets, same pikes. On her way past the cloister of St. Anne, Catherine is passed by three figures in red and green striped satin, breeches with bows, and pleated skirts. They do not even register with her, until one of them shouts something she can't understand. Suddenly her arms are seized by two men who are so strong that they lift her off the ground and carry her along.

"What are you doing?" Catherine tries to flail her arms, but can't budge their superior strength. "Where are you taking me? I'm a member of the imperial Hofkapelle! I'm the emperor's personal musician!" She's yelling all this at the top of her lungs in German. The guardsman behind her responds very calmly in a language Catherine can't interpret, which sounds like Italian.

She's been abducted by the Swiss Guard, who are undoubtedly taking her to meet Cardinal Cajetan. Dragged along by her arms, Catherine thinks back to the story of the sculptor in Nuremberg, wondering whether there might be worse things in the world than having your hands cut off.

It's a short walk to the bishop's residence, where Cardinal Cajetan is staying during the Diet. Catherine can't help tossing a desperate glance and a silent cry for help over her shoulder at the tower of Holy Cross, where she imagines Ludwig is.

The bishop's palace is a long, square residence situated around a large green walled garden. Catherine's captors leave her in a small, comfortable room. The door is locked, but at least she is not in a dungeon, yet.

All the popular modes of torture parade behind her eyes, like a gory variation on the emperor's procession. Holy Mother Church, one of the most fanatical exercisers of the art of torture. No doubt Catherine's secret will be uncovered, and she will be found to be a witch. Which form of torture will they start with? Thumb screws? The Spanish horse? Perhaps being basted with simmering oil, while lying stripped and bound on a board. The company of men has filled her in on all the ingenious ways men have of torturing women sexually, and witches are a favorite target. She's heard rumors of an ingenious, devilish device, which wrenches the victim's jaw painfully open. The suggestion was that torturers liked to stick it other places, too.

Catherine counts the chimes of the cathedral next door. Four hours elapse before she is collected by a guard and marched to another part of the residence. The guard opens a door to a sumptuous apartment full of carved furniture, Flemish tapestries, Italian paintings, and brocaded draperies. The cardinal sits at a massive oak desk, spread with pamphlets and broadsheets.

"Come in, dear boy. You don't know how glad I am to see you! You've been hard to trace lately," Cardinal Cajetan dismisses the guard with a quick jerk of his bony wrist, and guides Catherine to an alcove, where a table has been set with a small snack: wine, pastries, bits of cheese and meat, and a large plate of berries.

"Be seated, please. What shall I call you?" the cardinal's voice is rough and papery. He pours wine for Catherine, then himself.

"Johann, Eminence," Catherine is desperate to find something to do with her hands, but when she reaches for her wine, the tremor makes her wish she hadn't.

"Please don't be afraid, Johann. You are here because of my admiration for your voice. Do you know that I wrote to the pope as soon as Mass was over? Everyone marveled over your voice. I wish only to get to know you, and make you an offer." The cardinal reaches for the plate of fruit with his thin fingers. "My digestion has been in a state of near revolt since I arrived. The food here is wretched, don't you agree? Of course, you wouldn't. You are from Flanders, are you not?"

"Yes, Eminence," Catherine sends up a prayer of thanks to Duchess Margaret for allowing her to study Latin; this disguise would have been useless without mastery of the language of scholars. She also had a lot of practice puzzling out the myriad accents of strange lands. Every foreigner speaks Latin with his own particular melody and rhythm, and Catherine delights in deciphering them, the way others delight in magic squares and other puzzles. She could understand Cajetan's Italian Latin reasonably well.

"Food not much better there, I expect. I hope to introduce you to delicacies you probably never imagined," the cardinal bites into a strawberry with his front teeth, holding it by the hull with this thumb and middle finger. The rest of his fingers splay out in a way that puts Catherine off the idea of food entirely. Her roiling stomach wouldn't take any, anyway. She manages to guide the shaky glass to her lips and take a sip, at least partially resolving the lack of moisture in her mouth.

She sees the cardinal observing her nervous state of mind, and he seems intent upon calming her. The cardinal, a slim older man with layers of pouches under his eyes, stands and walks back to his desk, taking another strawberry as he leaves the alcove.

"What do you imagine I'm doing, Johann? Have you heard of this monk from Wittenberg, Luther?" The cardinal pronounces it 'Veetenberge' with a little 'eh' at the end.

"Everyone at the Diet is talking about him, Eminence," Catherine says.

"Have you read his writings yourself?"

Catherine replies that she has not, not wanting to be tortured for heresy along with witchcraft.

"They are all the same, these men who seek to overthrow the church. Hus and Wycliffe were stopped, and so will Luther be. The pope has asked me to interview him when he arrives, so I am making myself familiar with his writings," the cardinal takes up a letter from his desk, and waves it in Catherine's direction. "The pope says, 'to accomplish this, secure the support of the most beloved of our sons in Christ, Maximilian, elected emperor of the Romans.' Do you know why the pope addresses Maximilian in that way?"

"Because he has not been crowned in Rome by the pope, Eminence."

"Very good, you've been paying attention. You know a lot for the short time you've been with the imperial chapel," the cardinal says.

Catherine's heart rate had slowed to nearly normal, but with these words it begins to skip like a goatling again. How does he know that?

"His Holiness was correct, of course. The elected emperor Maximilian was only too glad to deliver Luther up to us. My task is not to debate with him, though now that I have read his ravings, I find myself unable to resist the temptation. I may indulge in a little debate, just for intellectual sport. But my task is actually to get Luther to retract, and bring him to repentance. As the pope says here, 'Holy Mother Church never closes her bosom to one who returns to her.' If Luther does not, I will await further orders from his Holiness. I will return to Rome, with or without Luther." The cardinal moves back toward the alcove, and sits across from Catherine.

"I would like you to accompany me to Rome, and join the papal choir. We do not want a talent like yours languishing among the *barbari*. Rome is the center of the world."

Catherine sits very still, mind whirring like a mill without grain. Her thoughts grind over one another, but none are lucid enough to help her. How can she give Cajetan enough hope for him to let her go, without actually saying yes? She imagines trying to maintain this disguise among the clerics of Rome, without people like Ludwig and the emperor behind her.

Negotiate.

Catherine remembers Ludwig telling stories about how star singers are feted in Italy. They can name their price while being courted for service by a prince, duke, or pope: whatever they want can be theirs: houses, money, jewels, horses, men, women. Top singers are also lured away by princes from rival courts in spectacular poaching activities.

She is about to open her mouth, when the cardinal speaks. "What do you imagine the elected emperor would require from his Holiness to release you? You are quite a jewel, as I'm sure you are aware. I do not say 'jewel in the emperor's crown', you notice." The cardinal winks.

Catherine clears her throat. "I think the elected emperor would like to travel to Rome himself. Perhaps I might accompany him, and sing for the pope while he places the crown on Maximilian's head." Her fingertips pound painfully, and she glances down to make sure blood is not spurting from them.

Cajetan smiles. "You ask a lot, young man. Do you really think your voice is worth the imperial crown?"

"With respect, Eminence, it doesn't matter what I think. What would the pope think?"

"His Holiness loves music more than most, is talented in that arena himself. He sings, composes, plays the lute, and was trained by Maximilian's former court composer, Isaac, while he worked for his ' father, Lorenzo de' Medici."

The cardinal smiles again. "Think about it. In turn, I will put your interesting request before him. You would delight his Holiness. I imagine you'd create more stir than we've seen since the days of the pope they called John VIII." The cardinal puts out his hand, Catherine kneels and kisses his ring. "You are dismissed, for now. Please don't disappear again."

CATHERINE runs straight to Holy Cross after leaving Cardinal Cajetan. She goes to Ludwig's room, and is disappointed to find him gone. She sits down at the table, pushes her hat away from her forehead, and rests her head on her arms, trying to calm herself.

The sound of the door banging open awakens her. Wagenrieder and Hoffmann enter the room, each of them supporting half of Ludwig Senfl. Hoffmann is so short he staggers under the composer's weight, and looks like he needs someone to support him. Catherine jumps in alarm, swearing in Flemish.

The two singers dump Ludwig onto the bed. His head lolls on his chest.

"Is he drunk, at this hour?" Catherine asks, then gasps when Ludwig raises his head. A large bruise is emerging on his right cheekbone. He's bleeding from his mouth and a gash over his right eye. His clothing is bloody, dusty, and spotted with some suspicious-smelling stains.

"Should we get a doctor?" Hoffmann sounds unsure. Wagenrieder just stands mute.

"No doctors," Ludwig mumbles. He appears to be having trouble speaking. "Get out, you two. I'll be fine." He stands unsteadily, moves toward his wooden chest, and finds a flask without too much searching. He takes a large sip, then curses. "I bit my tongue during the...incident," he says to Catherine.

"We'll be right across the street, if you need anything," Wagenrieder says.

Catherine looks at Ludwig, and decides what he needs. "Sit down. I'm going for some water and something to bandage up your head."

She returns in a few minutes with a basin of cold water, and some rags. Ludwig sits with his head resting against the wall, eyes closed. Catherine dips a rag in the water, and starts dabbing the cut over Ludwig's eye. "I should probably clean this with some brandy. There's dirt and God knows what else in it," she says, glancing back at the stinking stains on Ludwig's cloak.

"Don't you dare," Ludwig says without opening his eyes.

Catherine does it anyway, and Ludwig winces when the alcohol hits the wound, uttering a stream of unintelligible Swiss-German.

"Are you going to tell me what happened?" she says.

"Do you know what a *Backpfeifengesicht* is? A face in need of a fist. Really, I did him a favor. Now he's missing some teeth, has a split lip, and can only see out of one of his eyes." Ludwig sounds smug.

"Who was it?" Catherine sighs.

"Cornetto player from the Saxon court."

"Ludwig! Will he be able to play again?"

"What do I care? Ow! What are you putting in there now, acid?"

"Stop whining. Why were you fighting with the cornetto player from the Saxon court?"

"Because he's a hedge-born *Hurensohn*."

Catherine laughs in spite of herself. "Did he say something?"

"Well, first he insulted the emperor, which doesn't bother me. Then he said the imperial Hofkapelle sounds like a bunch of eunuchs, which I suppose we have you to thank for. I let that pass also. I was feeling generous."

"What finally pushed you to your limit?"

"He said he saw me with Matthias Lang's balls halfway down my throat. He was this weaselly little…" Ludwig gropes for a word, gesturing with his hand.

"*Backpfeifengesicht*," says Catherine.

"Indeed. You have to teach people like that to respect their betters. He may have a dislocated shoulder, too, by the way."

"Well, I hope you are deeply pleased with yourself." Catherine soaks a cloth in water and lays it against Ludwig's cheekbone.

"I am." He lets his head fall against her hip with a little sigh. Something sinuous curls in her core; she smiles down at him, and strokes his head with her free hand. His hair feels coarse, which surprises her. His curls had always looked so soft.

"Thank you," His face is partially obscured by her tunic, and she can barely hear him.

"It's nothing. You clean me up after drinking, I patch you up after brawling. A bit of blood, a bit of vomit... what are friends for?" She refreshes the water in the cloth; Ludwig doesn't move his head.

"Is that what we are?" he says.

She shrugs, but then her curiosity begins to work on her. "What did this weaselly cornettist say about the emperor?"

Ludwig laughs, then grimaces in pain. "I wouldn't offend your dainty ears with language like that. Besides, if I want to have any hope of future employment at the imperial court, I shouldn't be a teller of tales. Certainly not to the emperor's little songbird."

"Why are you so bitter, Ludwig?" Catherine moves away from him, wringing the cloth in her hand again and again, though no liquid comes out.

"Why am I so bitter? Not only do I not get paid, none of the perquisites ever seem to come my way. I mean, besides the knighthood, Hofhaimer received a house from Maximilian, as well as extras for wine, assistants, and even horses. Treitz was given not just a house but a castle, if you can believe it, while I get the occasional bonus. And not much, at that." He pauses, and seems to be weighing his words. "And now he's taken you from me too, like the poor man's lamb."

"He hasn't taken me from you. I can't imagine Kaiser Max having anything against you, Ludwig. I mean, he loves your voice!"

"You can't imagine anything bad about him; that's your trouble for a start," Ludwig sits up and pulls Catherine down next to him, so close she's nearly sitting on top of him. She stares at the floor. "Look Catherine, I like the emperor. Maybe you can't tell right now, but I do. He doesn't pay his bills, and sometimes the conditions are hell, but for an ambitious musician, there's nowhere else you'd rather be. But he's not much of a ruler, and he's not any kind of hero. He's not the White King. He's a paper monarch. He can't afford to create real monuments, buildings and gates and statues, so he builds them out of paper. And they are as flimsy and unconvincing as he is."

Ludwig stands and stretches his back. "I may have strained something in there," he says, taking another swig from his flask. "I do have some news for you. I doubt your hero will have told you—you are off to Innsbruck with him very soon."

Catherine knows more is coming. "And you, Herr Hofkomponist?"

Ludwig settles heavily back down on the bed. "I also have my orders. I'm staying here."

Catherine's stomach lurches. "What?"

"Oh, don't pretend to be surprised. We all know why. Ostensibly I'm to remain here to continue to work with the publisher on *Liber Selectarum*. But I'm being punished for writing that song. He wants me out of the way, and he wants you all to himself."

Catherine is silent. She stands up, and takes a long strip of cloth from the table. She moves to stand next to Ludwig, and wraps the cloth around his forehead, to cover the cut over his eye. "Do you know what I thought when the emperor gave me the coat of arms of Burgundy? I thought, 'Now I can't marry Ludwig'." She tucks in the end of the bandage with gentle hands.

She tilts his face up and kisses him, tasting her own salty tears and the mineral tang of his blood. He pulls her down onto his lap, and she clings to him with a fierce little sigh. She hears him whispering, "You can, and we will. Tomorrow."

Catherine pulls away and looks into his face. "Aren't you worried about the emperor? Getting married to me right under his nose, so to speak?"

"A lot can happen under that nose," Ludwig says, pulling her close again.

"I wish we could do it now," Catherine says.

Ludwig smiles. "You are full of surprises, aren't you? Now I'm the one hanging back, and you're forging ahead. I'm not stalling—something needs to happen first, and I'm going to take care of it. Then we can ratify it right away." He gives her a little squeeze.

"What about your orders?" Catherine says.

"Minor orders don't bind one to chastity. And my position in life already binds me to poverty, apparently, so that vow would have been superfluous, anyway," Ludwig says.

"Speaking of those in holy orders, I have some news for you, too." She gives him a summary of her meeting with Cajetan, while Ludwig rests his head in her lap. "He said something odd before I left. Something about the pope they called John VIII, who created a stir. What could he have meant?"

Ludwig doesn't look up. "The woman. The female pope. Apparently she fooled them for a couple of years, and then was discovered when she gave birth right in the middle of a procession."

Catherine just stares at him, waiting for the pfennig to drop. He sits up slowly and faces her.

"Jesus, Joseph, and Mary..." Ludwig whispers.

Catherine clamps her hands in front of her mouth.

Ludwig stares at her. "What are you going to do when he comes to his senses and realizes you've bewitched him, which is the only explanation?"

"I'm not a witch, Ludwig," Catherine says, sounding unconvinced even to herself.

"So you say," Ludwig says. "Can I at least come with you?"

"I'm not going to the papal chapel!"

"Oh, very well. I guess they wouldn't look with benevolence upon married chapel members, anyway," Ludwig says.

*

High up in the mountains
There is a tall house
Every morning, three pretty girls come out.
The first one is my sister
The second is my friend
The third one has no name
She will be mine.

Ludwig Senfl, Schweizer
AUGSBURG, 1518

20

A New Maecenas

Ludwig Senfl stands in the Fugger Chapel in St. Anne's, watching stonemasons at work for a moment before climbing to the organ loft. The masons are working on epitaphs for the Fugger family, placed in the wall under the organ. He tips his head back to look at the instrument above him, built and installed just few years ago at the specifications of the man who is upstairs playing at the moment. Ludwig stands and listens. Hofhaimer is improvising on *Salve Regina*. The work is broken up into segments, which correspond to motives of the chant. He varies each one in endless ways: changing the number of voices, the stops he uses, and employing an unending variety of ornaments.

Like Senfl, Hofhaimer has more than one job, though he somehow manages to be well compensated for both of them. Besides bearing the title of *obrister Organist*, chief organist to his majesty the emperor, since 1517, he has also been private organist to the Fugger family. Kaiser Max allows him the latitude to stay in Augsburg for months at a time to perform his duties for the Fuggers. As Hofhaimer himself said, he's getting a bit too old to be traveling around like a gypsy.

Ludwig stands there for a few more moments, staring up at the painted panels on either side of the organ. He himself is depicted on one of the smaller *Rückwerk* panels along with Isaac and other members of the Hofkapelle, but the panel is too high for him to see his own face.

Against his will, he glances higher to a larger panel on the right side of the *Hauptwerk*, where Kaiser Max and Jakob Fugger are shown watching the Blessed Virgin ascend into heaven. Their faces are large enough to be seen, of course. It's a good likeness of both of them; the emperor is shown in his habitual hunting garb, gesturing with his hands, which he can't keep still in life, either. Fugger points to the miraculous scene happening above their heads. The third man in their little group comically gapes at the sky in the wrong direction.

Senfl turns away and walks to a small door around the corner from where the stonemasons are tapping out their work. He walks up a staircase, and comes to a landing where he sees the bellows-blowers: two men standing on the large air supplies, using the weight of their bodies to provide Hofhaimer with the wind he needs to work his magic. The movement of their bodies as they work makes it seem as though they are ascending an invisible stairway leading nowhere. They greet him and he nods to them in return. The organ has never been a favorite of his. He doesn't want all those mechanisms between him and the music: levers, pulleys, and rollers. It's too distant; too impersonal. He continues upward, and emerges in the organ loft, standing to the side until Hofhaimer plays the final chord.

Senfl comes forward, bowing slightly to his older colleague. Hofhaimer insists upon formality, but he almost doesn't need to. Something in his personality puts you on your best behavior whether you want to be or not. Students who are flippant or coarse are dismissed and not accepted back again. Ludwig had never been his student, but after Isaac died, Hofhaimer became an important figure in his life. Isaac had been warm and friendly, with an appetite for life, which is why he felt so at home in Italy. He was a man who loved to laugh. If Isaac had been Ludwig's adopted father, then Hofhaimer was a stern, distant grandfather, who by his very remoteness made you want to please him.

"Herr Senfl, thank you for coming today." Hofhaimer half-turns on the organ bench to face his younger colleague. The deep grooves between his dark eyebrows make him look forbidding, while his long, very straight nose gives his face an air to match the noble title given to him by Maximilian. Hofhaimer is the same age as Kaiser Max, but seems much younger, no doubt because he has not lived as hard as the emperor.

"I was glad to receive your note, Ritter von Hofhaimer," The organist waves his hand.

"Please don't bother with the title. Address me as you always have." Senfl bows again. "How is your wife?"

"She's well, thank you. Glad to have me home in Augsburg for this length of time."

"And your own health, sir?"

"My hands are stiff in the mornings; it takes me some time to get them limber, which is why I'm here practicing. I will be playing for the emperor and electors in a few minutes; they are in session here in the cloister. But otherwise, I can't complain for someone who will be sixty before he cares to think of it." After a brief smile, Hofhaimer turns away from Ludwig, and takes a few papers from a shelf next to the keyboard. He taps them in front of him on the organ bench, though they are in a tidy stack already.

"Senfl, word has gone round about you and Fräulein Croÿ, and especially about your song for the emperor, and his reaction to it." Hofhaimer continues tapping, choosing his words.

Ludwig takes a step forward, but the words tumbling from his lips die in the air as Hofhaimer holds up one elegant hand. "No doubt you realize that this is a very foolish juncture to antagonize the one man who can ensure your future employment. Especially you, Senfl." Hofhaimer fixes his sharp gray eyes on Senfl, who fights not to squirm.

"You are right, sir. But it was not done idly. I meant it, and I'm prepared for the consequences," Senfl says.

"That is what I wanted to know. You intend to marry Fräulein Croÿ?"

"I do intend to. I've already asked her."

"And?"

"And she is concerned about how we would live." Senfl can't help squirming a little now.

"Sensible young lady. That is her only objection?" Hofhaimer asks.

"Yes, sir."

"I'm glad to hear it. You have waited far too long to marry, in my opinion, Senfl, but I realize you have had little choice." Hofhaimer adjusts the sleeve of his robe with one hand. It is the same kind as rich gentlemen wear: satin, with a fur collar. His doublet is brocaded, and the linen visible above it is flawlessly white. Senfl clasps his hands behind his back to hide his frayed sleeves, but not before realizing the rest of his clothes are just as shabby.

"Hofhaimer, do you have any idea why the emperor—"

The organist interrupts him. "No, I do not, and I will not ask, even given our long association and friendly relationship. But I have appealed to him on your behalf many times, and I have given my opinion of your worth and how you should be treated as Isaac and I have been."

Senfl drops his eyes. "Thank you, sir."

"But as you can see, it yielded no results. I continue to receive gifts of money and goods from the emperor,"

"—Whereas I can't remember the last time I received a salary. If it weren't for the money we receive from guests at private performances—"

"—You would have no drinking money. You should watch that, you know." Hofhaimer says severely, but Senfl refuses to hang his head like a choirboy caught stealing raisins from the kitchen. "At any rate, I'm sure your wife will cure you of that. They have their ways, you know." The glint in Hofhaimer's eye catches Senfl off guard, and he grins. Hofhaimer has been married three times, no doubt he's seen every female maneuver on the face of the earth.

"I wished to understand your motivations before giving you this," Hofhaimer takes one of the pages from the thin stack in front of him and hands it to Ludwig.

Senfl stares at the parchment in his hand, feeling hot suddenly, though it's eternally cool in the church. He swipes at his eyes with the back of his hand before looking back up at Hofhaimer. The older man hands him the rest of the documents. "These pages authenticate it, and certify that I authorize you to use them."

"Thank you, Hofhaimer, I—" Senfl says,

The organist waves his words away, looking almost irritated. "This will not give you anything to live on if you marry, of course, but it may help, especially in light of the new information about Fräulein Croÿ's heritage."

Senfl shakes his head. "I don't believe any of it, sir."

"Who gave you the liberty to doubt his Majesty, Senfl?" Hofhaimer narrows his eyes.

"You've known him longer than any of us. Have you always known him to be rigorously honest?" Hofhaimer is honest to a fault, and Senfl knows he can't truthfully answer in the affirmative.

Hofhaimer's lips become a thin line. "In politics, everything is negotiable. Especially the truth." Hofhaimer continues. "The emperor's financial situation is precarious, as you know, and paying off debts and honoring contracts may not be at the top of his successor's immediate list of tasks. I will continue to petition for you, but you will need to do the same. In the meantime, I stand ready to loan you money, so that the two of you can marry." His lips arc into a minute smile. For Hofhaimer, it is the equivalent of a laugh. "I have no doubt the two of you will raise an entire choir's worth of children."

Senfl risks irritating Hofhaimer further by thanking him again when he hears voices in the chapel below. Hofhaimer turns to the keyboard without another word, and adjusts the stop knobs. Senfl bows to him and descends the stairs, past the bellows-blowers into the chapel. He hurries out via a side aisle to avoid the group of electors, and prays he won't encounter the emperor on his way out.

21

Losing Thyself and Me

No doubt many couples got married during the months the imperial Diet was taking place in Augsburg, but only two weddings made their mark on Catherine: her own, and the marriage of Susanna of Bavaria and Casimir von Brandenburg. Catherine's wedding took place during the celebration of the other. Susanna's festivities lasted three days; Catherine's approximately an hour.

The bride's uncle, Emperor Maximilian, always the cunning matchmaker, arranged the marriage of Susanna and Casimir. Casimir was a valued friend and ally, and to marry the emperor's niece was nothing less than a prize and token of respect, and a way to bind the groom more closely to the House of Habsburg. The bride and groom were accompanied by a glittering procession of three thousand knights in armor, and his imperial majesty was well enough that day to mount a horse once more. The emperor led his niece to the altar himself, where the ceremony was performed by Cardinal Albrecht of Mainz.

Catherine and Ludwig sing with the Hofkapelle at Susanna and Casimir's ceremony in the morning, then arrange to meet later in the day. During the ceremony, she and Ludwig stand next to one another among the singers, outwardly nothing more than colleagues. The Hofkapelle is packed in close, as always, and Ludwig takes her hand and squeezes it, unseen by any of their fellow singers, while the couple at the altar recites their vows.

After the ceremony, there is a tournament on the Weinmarkt, and before Catherine departs she watches a round of combat.

The Fugger Palace is practically empty; all the servants are clustered around the periphery of the lists, and Fugger, the emperor, and the bridal pair are seated in the prime vantage point under a pavilion. Ladies crowd the windows on the second story of the palace to watch the action.

Catherine arrives just as a round of *Rennen* has been announced— mounted combat with pointed lances. The knights seem to blaze in their armor in the brilliant sunlight. They wear fanciful decorations on their helmets: one is shaped like a wheel, the other looks as though a bright arrangement of flowers is growing out of his head. The horses are decked out in colorful draperies, and wear armor on their heads. This doesn't just protect them; it also deprives them of their sight so they will rely entirely on the spurs and reins of their riders for guidance.

The knights take their places on opposite ends of the Weinmarkt. The emperor himself gives the signal to begin. The shouts of the crowd dwindle to a murmur as the knights gallop toward one another, lances poised. They clash, and both are unseated. At the moment of impact, to a deafening roar by the crowd, the knights' shields fly up into the air, and seem to shatter into many pieces.

Catherine knows how this is done, thanks to the tournament-obsessed boys with whom she grew up. The shields are catapulted into the air when hit dead center thanks to a mechanism on the knights' breastplates. Furthermore, they are fitted with metal triangles which loosen upon impact, giving the impression that the entire shield has broken apart.

From her vantage point she has a good view of the emperor, the most exalted jouster of his day. He sits on the bride's right hand, talking and gesturing ceaselessly, no doubt informing his niece of every technical deficiency he sees, and what he would have done better.

Catherine meets Ludwig on the steps of St. Steffan's just as the bells chime two o'clock. He waves and walks toward her, and she stares. He is transformed, but it takes her a moment to register the change. His face is still bruised and his head bandaged, but his clothes are different. He's no longer wearing clerical garb, but rather looks like an up-and-coming member of the middle class. Once she's standing in front of him, she sees that the clothes are not new, but they are well-made and in good condition.

"Ludwig... you look astonishing!" She can't help laughing at his metamorphosis.

"*Kruzi*, this is nothing. Just wait," he scoffs, but she can see the pleasure in his eyes.

Catherine touches his bruised face gently. "We had this old nurse back in Mechelen who was always dishing out strange bits of folk wisdom. For every skinned elbow or broken finger, she would say, 'That'll get better before you get married'. But that's not true in your case, is it?"

Ludwig takes her elbow and guides her across the street to a narrow, three-story house. He knocks, and a young girl opens the door. Inside, a joyous din and delicious smells greet them. Three children of various sizes tumble about, shouting. Frau Rehling, the wife of the leader of the city pipers greets them, with a fourth child attached to her breast. She looks a few years older than Catherine. Herr Rehling is not at home, since he and his musicians are playing at the tournament on the Weinmarkt. The air is scented with roasting meat and something delicious baking in the oven.

Frau Rehling finishes feeding her child, and hands the infant to her eldest daughter, who bounces it and pats its back vigorously. Frau Rehling kisses Catherine on both cheeks, tired eyes shining.

"Congratulations, my dear. You both are very welcome here. My husband has known Herr Senfl since the first time he came to Augsburg with the emperor, almost twenty years ago." At this moment, one of the tumbling children slips and falls at Ludwig's feet, smacking his head on the wooden floorboards. Ludwig and Catherine stoop at the same time: Catherine scoops the child up, and Ludwig finds a discarded toy, a wooden knight on horseback, which he causes to gallop in front of the child's face. Together they manage to distract the child, and forestall the wailing.

Frau Rehling continues, "My husband is disappointed that he was called away, but wishes you to know that you are welcome to stay as long as you like. When you are finished, please come down and celebrate with me. There will be a little supper, with wine and cake."

Catherine thanks her, mortified and grateful. Well, we're not the first, she thinks. Not Adam and Eve.

Frau Rehling shows them upstairs, and promises to keep the children quiet. Catherine rather wishes they'd be as loud as they can, and that Herr Rehling was there to play the bagpipes as well.

Ludwig shuts the door, gives Catherine a quick kiss, then sits down on the bed. He opens the leather satchel hooked to his belt and takes out several folded documents. He pats the space next to him, and Catherine sits.

"I know you have no faith in my ability to provide for you, but I hope these will change your mind." He hands her a page. "Benefices from Constance and Verona, and I have been promised one hundred and fifty Rhenish guilders per year upon the emperor's death. We won't be rich, but it will be enough."

He hands her another page. "The lease to a house not far from here, in the Lang Gaß. Hofhaimer owns it, and will rent it to us cheap. Room for our little choir to grow up. And finally…" He extracts a parchment from the back of the stack of pages, turns it over, and hands it to her. "Just to prove I'm not a Swiss boor, or whatever you call me in the deep vaults of your mind, I present you with this."

Catherine takes it from him. It's a coat of arms with a Latin motto: *Psallam Deo meo quamdiu fuero*. I will praise Thy name forever and ever. The shield is simple: blue bars divided *per pale* on a white background, with feathered mantling, supported by elaborate vines.

"I know it's nothing to the arms of Burgundy, but at the very least: if you marry me, you will marry a gentleman," Ludwig says.

"I didn't know you had a coat of arms," Catherine says.

"See, now I've impressed you! Women, always grubbing for money and status—Ow!" He rubs his side where Catherine's elbow scored a direct hit. "Hofhaimer gave it to me. After he was knighted, he was given two coats of arms: one to keep and one to give away. He kept the one with the German motto, and gave me the Latin one." Ludwig holds up his empty hands. "That's it, I'm afraid. I wanted you to know what you are getting into before we do this."

Catherine admires the arms for a few moments longer. "Despite this, or any title you might be conferred, you will always be a Swiss boor. Who I would love to marry." She stands up and carefully lays the pages on the windowsill, then returns to her seat by Ludwig. Her chest feels tight, and her breath is coming in shallow waves. "What do we do now, exactly?"

"We give our hands and our hearts to each other, and speak vows of faithfulness before God. Then we become husband and wife of the flesh, and it's done." Ludwig says.

"And it's legal?"

"Entirely. We are both of age, and there are no impediments. On my side, at least." Catherine shakes her head, indicating there are none on her side either. "So it's a legal bond that can't be dissolved by any man, not even the emperor."

He stands up, and takes her hands. He pauses. There are no sounds from downstairs, and somehow the silence makes it seem solemn and real. "I, Ludwig Senfl, take you, Catherine de Croÿ, to be my wife before God." He nods to her, the beginnings of a smile on his face.

"I, Catherine de Croÿ, take you, Ludwig Senfl, to be my husband before God." She can't curb her smile; it becomes a laugh of pure joy. He pulls her to him and kisses her, even though she's still laughing.

"Now for the fun part," Ludwig says, stripping off his cloak and tunic. He kicks off his shoes. Catherine unlaces her gown and slides it over her head, laying it carefully over the back of the only chair in the room. She allows him to lead her back to the bed and remove her chemise.

She lays back against the bolster, and studies the beams in the ceiling while Ludwig surveys the landscape of her body with his hands, starting at her shoulders. His fingers play over her ribs, dipping softly into the hollows between them. "They're not overfeeding you, are they? Never mind, 'the sweetest meat is closest to the bone,' as they say." He nibbles on her side, then kisses her mouth, pressing his tongue between her lips.

The feeling of lightness from the riverside is entirely gone. She tries to summon it again, tries to remember the fire on her skin when he touched her, but the only thing that burns in her is fear. It makes her body tight, unyielding, and unharmonious in the way of an overstrung instrument.

She turns her face away, mind racing for something to say to stall him, to buy time to get the feeling back. "Doesn't your tongue hurt where you bit it?"

"Not in the least."

Just my luck, Catherine thinks.

Ludwig lays above her, maneuvers between her legs, and starts pushing himself into her.

"Stop clenching," Ludwig says after a few fumbling stabs.

"You're hurting me!" An anguished whisper. She hears nothing but the silence on the ground floor.

"It's supposed to hurt a little the first time, but it gets better after that," She feels his fingers between the folds of her flesh, gentle and soft. Now that he's not trying to plant that tree trunk in her, she relaxes a little, and feels a small warmth trying to rise. "Ah, there's the problem. You're drier than a cask after carnival. Luckily, there's a solution," He rolls slightly to one side, raises his hand, and spits into it. He deposits this with a brief swipe in her slit, and then resumes what he was doing.

With her physical pain comes a torment of confusion. She feels rent in two by a paralyzing inaction brought on by shock and a violent urge to flee. A primitive, fragmented memory surfaces: being held by force on a lap she didn't want to be on. There were hands where they shouldn't be, and pain. She was small; far too small for that type of game. Her captor tried to get her out of her dress. She struggled with him. She doesn't remember how she got away, or what happened in the meantime, but she remembers finding the duchess later, kneeling beside her, pressing her hot face into the duchess' cool silken lap, and crying. The duchess asked her repeatedly what was wrong. Catherine refused to answer.

Catherine tries to push Ludwig away. She may as well be pushing against a fortified wall. Ludwig conversely battles with something which will yield, one way or another. He obtains victory in three sharp jabs, each one more agonizing than the last. Her perceptions dwindle to the state of the field of conquest: tearing, burning, pain upon pain.

She hates him most for the sounds he makes at the end, a shuddering yelp like a felled animal. His entire weight compresses her chest. He's finished.

This is what drowning feels like.

"Get—off—me," she gasps, flopping under Ludwig's inert bulk like a fish in a net.

"What—?" Ludwig rolls off of her.

Catherine looks down. The sheet is red, stained and glossy, and her first thought is shame and remorse toward the sweet, weary housewife who will have to clean it with her own hands. Catherine doesn't raise her head, but her eyes creep up to her husband's face.

"Oh my God, Catherine, I—I had no idea. I'm so sorry," Ludwig says. He stares at the bloody sheet with wide eyes.

She looks at Ludwig, at the shock and sorrow in his face. Her hand moves down between her legs. It comes away wet, crimson and streaked with whitish slime. He makes a move, as though to reach for her, and she watches her hand swing out in an arc. It catches the side of his face, and his head jerks toward the window as if startled by a strange noise.

Catherine barely registers the smear on his flaring cheek before climbing painfully out of bed. Ludwig may be speaking, but she can't hear him—a dull noise roars in her ears, and her head feels stuffed with cotton wool.

Frau Rehling thoughtfully set out a basin and cloths for washing. Catherine stuffs one of the cloths between her legs, pulls on her chemise and dress, and leaves Ludwig to deal with the mess. She stops in the open door, facing the hallway when she speaks to him. She can't bear to look at his face.

"Please tell her how sorry I am," Catherine says. Her voice is steady and calm. She closes the door gently, then tiptoes down the stairs and out the door. She couldn't have borne seeing the housewife's expectant face. It would have broken her.

When she regains her room in the Damenhof, she washes her wounds with water and vinegar. The sting of the vinegar finally summons her tears. The bleeding has mostly stopped, but she still uses a rag, like she would for her monthly course of blood.

She has her cry, and feels calm, and more importantly, numb. She must sing for the other bride and groom, Susanna and Casimir von Brandenburg. She must sing Ludwig's music while standing by his side.

A few days before the wedding, Catherine had searched through her collection of music, then Ludwig's, and the Fugger's, and finally, the imperial library. She sat, bleary and bewildered. Ludwig came to her, distracted her with kisses, seated her on his lap, and asked her what she was doing.

"I'm looking for something to sing for the bride and groom: Susanna and Casimir. I never realized how few happy love songs there are. They are all about pain and longing and disappointment, and any songs which mention married couples are full of bad jokes and reproaches. Like this one:

THE EAGLE AND THE SONGBIRD

Whining, scolding man, how does this suit you?
I will sit with you at table
And kiss your wife on the mouth,
How does that suit you?

Or

A beautiful girl called out:
'O God, if it came to dying this year,
Then my old husband should die,
Who can give no joy at all.
Hey-ho! How long must I suffer this
All the time, from the old man?
God bring him pain and torment!'

Or your song of a cunning wife hoodwinking her unwitting husband. I can hardly sing any of those at a wedding celebration!" Catherine says.

Ludwig didn't seem to be listening. His mouth was busy kissing the back of her neck.

"I'll write you a song as a wedding present. It will be ours, but you can share it with them. How does that suit you?" He teases her by repeating the words of the song about the scolding husband.

Catherine swivels on his lap and hugs him tight. "For a Swiss boor, you are a real gentleman. Which text will you use?"

"The most beautiful love poetry in the world, of course: the Song of Songs."

Catherine stands on a dais in her best dress, made of dark red silk, the bodice trimmed with embroidery. Ludwig had written a four-part setting, and he stands with her, along with a tenor and a bass. The first verse combines all four voices, but was obviously written to bring her voice to the fore. The superius part is very high, and cascades in little ornamental scales, like gentle breezes bringing the scents of an oriental garden.

Awake, O north wind; and come, thou south;
blow upon my garden, that the spices thereof may flow out.
Let my beloved come into his garden, and eat his pleasant fruits.

The next part of the text is exchanged between her voice and Ludwig's, as though two lovers are passing a goblet between them, sharing the delights mentioned in the text:

I am come into my garden, my sister, my spouse:
I have gathered my myrrh with my spice;
I have eaten my honeycomb with my honey;
I have drunk my wine with my milk:
eat, O friends; drink, yea, drink abundantly, O beloved.

In the last verse, all four voices emphasize the text by singing the syllables at the same time, though on different notes. The last two lines showcase Ludwig's voice, the beloved singing to his bride. The last word is sung in perfect unison; the two at last have become one.

I sleep, but my heart waketh:

it is the voice of my beloved that knocketh, saying,
Open to me, my sister, my love, my dove, my undefiled:
for my head is filled with dew, and my locks with the drops of the night.

She does not think or feel; she reads notes, and she sings. Her voice rings from every corner, a tone struck with a golden hammer, not dying out, only waxing in sweetness and intensity.

When it is over, she hurries back to the Damenhof, desperate to avoid Ludwig, whatever happens. She is halfway across the courtyard when he catches up to her.

"Catherine, wait," Ludwig is out of breath. "I'm supposed to be singing again, but this could be my last chance to talk to you."

They come to stand under the portico, away from any inquiring eyes. He's very close when she turns around, and she tries not to flinch away from him. She's not entirely successful, and he sees. He takes a step backward, well out of reach of her.

"You don't have to say anything, just listen to me," Ludwig rushes the words. "I'm sorry. I honestly didn't know how bad it was." He takes a step nearer, palms up in a gesture of supplication. "Do you think I would have done that had I known? To you, who I love like my own self? I'm not a brute."

Catherine is silent, thinking of the Saxon cornetto player, whose livelihood was lost to Ludwig's fists.

"I am sorry, Catherine. All I ask is that you forgive me. I know you have to leave with the emperor. I won't ask you the question that's on my heart, because I don't think I can bear the answer."

His face is open, and she sees everything. He speaks in a low, clear voice, forming each word carefully, as though his remorse were a language he wasn't sure she could understand.

"I told Frau Rehling what you said. I wish you could have heard the tongue-lashing she gave me," Ludwig says. He looks away from her. "Catherine, I—I thought you wanted me, by the river that night."

She catches his meaning. "I did."

Ludwig whispers. "I felt the same. I thought you did too." He lifts his hand, and she lets his fingers graze a pleat of her skirt.

"You didn't give me a chance," she says this out loud, with force. She has not forgiven him, and is not sure she can. The raw pain she feels in the core of her body must heal, and even then, how can she let him close to her again? But how can she not? She is bound to him in the eyes of God and man.

Wagenrieder pounds up to them, urgently gesturing to Ludwig that he needs to come back to the dining hall.

"Please, at least let me write to you?" Ludwig says.

Catherine nods briefly.

He turns away, but not before she sees the relief in his face.

*

Of pain and distress my innermost heart!
I cannot complain to you that
My heart, spirit and soul are hurting
For you alone, sole heart of my heart.
Do you know how much I would love you,
What I would desire, you are giving me.
It seems like a thousand years
Since I have seen you.
Wherever I go, my heart hurts;
it desires you, My Heart; help me!

THE EAGLE AND THE SONGBIRD

I mourn that I cannot see you.
Remain constant and pious, I beg you!
Whatever I do, my heart knows no rest
Believe me, it feels pain and distress.
I sleep, I wake, it cries out for you.
It wants to be with you: please, help me!
still, my desire is nothing more than this:
Fear God, remain pious, safeguard your honor!

Ludwig Senfl, Schweizer

22

From the Emperor's Book of Days

I am weary. Once I secured the majority of the votes from the electors, it was as though a strong vessel that has been knocked about for years with no visible injury has finally been breached. Now I watch my life force drain away.

Frederick was the first of the electors to take leave—actually, he bolted from Augsburg like a frightened animal. His ambitions were not realized, so he had no further use for the whole charade. When his secretary, Spalatin, approached me to take leave, I could see the shock in his face. I must look very poor indeed.

Though I am weakened, I am also delighted, for we are on our way to Innsbruck. Tyrol, the first territory I ruled, that I love like a wife, like a child of my heart. Through the years, it has been my first refuge; any defeat, any illness or injury, any disappointment—Tyrol soothed, healed, made me whole again. The mines could be counted on to provide capital, or bargaining tools, or collateral. Silver, copper, salt. I could trade castles or land for money and services. My Tyrol warms like a good, heavy peasant coat.

In some ways we are on parallel courses, my land and I. Tyrol is as exhausted as I am. Both are my doing. She is now bankrupt, due to the money I poured into Charles' candidacy. I received word in the waning weeks of the Diet that the treasury there unanimously resigned, with many harsh words for their sovereign for his mismanagement of the monies. I deserve no less. When I arrive there, with my remaining strength I will seek to undo what I have done, to heal Tyrol as she has healed me time and again. When that is done, after seeing Charles crowned Roman King in Frankfurt, I wish nothing more than to die in my own bed in Innsbruck. Perhaps, after I have fulfilled my promises to her, I will be granted that. I must see to my will, and finish such pieces of my remembrance that can be completed in a few months.

Though I was weary of the Diet and all its stresses, taking leave of Augsburg was painful. I wished to hear Mass and visit the grave of my blessed ancestor, St. Ulrich. As soon as I entered the courtyard there, I was overwhelmed with emotion, remembering laying the foundation stone for the rebuilding of the choir in 1500, and many other meaningful times. I could barely keep my mind on the holy service, but rather found myself looking at each object and person in view, in turn, as I took my final leave. My premonitions are always with me now. My dear Augsburg, how many happy times have I spent within your walls? Now I will never see you again.

23

Innsbruck, I Must Leave You

The rolling landscape south of Augsburg leads to a thrilling sight. Catherine stares at a gray mass on the horizon, assuming it to be low-hanging clouds. When she was a child in Flanders, longing for something more exciting to look at than flat marshlands, she used to pretend cloud banks were mountains. Now she realizes that she's doing the reverse, and she's just had her first view of the Alps. The highest peaks have snow on them already.

At dinner that evening, Maximilian beckons to Catherine. He looks triumphant.

"I noticed you have finally decided to obey me, and travel by coach," he says.

"Yes, Majesty." She knows he's trying to goad her, but she is sick at heart as well as in pain, and cannot banter with him.

His smile fades. "You are not well. That's why you're not on horseback. I will have my physician examine you."

"Please Majesty, no doctors. This will heal on its own, in time," Catherine says.

Maximilian's face shows his disapproval, but he simply says, "Tyrol will heal you, dearest."

They cross the mountains at the Fern Pass, and descend to follow the Inn River.

The green foothills are painted with dots and swaths of color: gold and red. The clouds cling to the mountains like a gauzy scarf. The hillsides remind Catherine of a beautiful but shy girl, wrapped in an ermine mantle with a high collar, obscuring her from curious eyes, except for a few tantalizing glimpses. Catherine laughs at herself. I sound like the emperor, she thinks, comparing a landscape to a woman.

Torches are lit when dusk descends. It is nearly midnight when they cross the bridge over the Inn. Catherine had been dozing in the coach from time to time. The pain in her *achterwerk* is at least temporarily masked by the numbness there. Probably for the best, she thinks.

They ride into the courtyard of the Hof at Innsbruck, and she climbs stiffly out of the coach with the help of a servant. The emperor is passing a few paces from her.

"Can you walk, Catherine? Then come. The little queens will be waiting."

The little queens aren't actually queens yet. Four years ago, Maximilian brokered a double wedding between his house, and the royal house of Hungary. Anna, the daughter of the Hungarian king, was married by proxy to one of Maximilian's grandsons. Whether Ferdinand or Charles would claim the bride was to be determined later. The emperor himself stood in at the ceremony in Vienna, which little Anna looked none too happy about. Both members of the other couple were physically present, with no proxy necessary: Maximilian's granddaughter Mary was married to Louis of Hungary. All the participants were children, so Anna and Mary were sent to Innsbruck to finish growing up, and to be educated, until the time when the marriages could be consummated.

Mary had been brought up at Duchess Margaret's court in Mechelen. She was about ten years younger than Catherine, but despite the age difference, the two girls had always had an affectionate relationship. Mary looked up to Catherine as a sort of idol. Mary was always a very active girl, who loved to hunt, run around, and get her skirts full of dirt. She was also musical, and had learned the viol from Catherine and the clavichord from Hendrik Bredemers.

The emperor, Catherine, and a handful of courtiers enter the small audience hall of the Innsbruck Hof, where the little queens and their retinues are waiting. The young women curtsey before Maximilian; he gives them each a kiss, and allows them to take him by the arms and lead him to the high table. Supper is waiting, and soon they are all seated.

Before sitting down, Mary breaks protocol and runs into Catherine's arms. She is all energy and fire, with nothing frivolous about her, just a driving intensity. She inherited her grandfather's spirit and intelligence, but not his humor or charm. She isn't beautiful, having inherited Habsburg flaws like the protruding lower lip and forceful chin, but her face holds a person's interest. Catherine hopes that the friendly affection that Mary and her child-husband Louis had built up during the month-long marriage festivities, as children playing together, will be a solid foundation for affection in marriage when they eventually come together.

The little queens bombard the emperor with questions while they eat pea soup with sour cream and bacon.

"Tell us about the new fashions that the patrician ladies are wearing in Augsburg, Majesty!" Anna says. Mary seeks Catherine's eyes, and doesn't bother to hide her exasperation.

"Oh Nannerl, what must we say about fashions?" The emperor's smile is weary. "Though I will tell you a story. Augsburg is famous for the dances that the patrician families give, *Geschlechtertanz*, they call them." Maximilian breaks a white roll in small pieces; he eats only a few spoonfuls of soup. "Good spirits, fine dancing, music provided by the city pipers, who are actually good compared to others I have heard, though vastly inferior to the music we enjoy at our court." He tips his silver goblet in Catherine's direction. She bows her head to him, but cannot hide the pleasure his words give her. "What more could one want to pass a pleasant evening?"

"Pretty girls!" Kunz calls out.

"Exactly. We were certain there was no shortage of pretty burgher's daughters to admire in Augsburg, but where were they all hiding? We could not see them, because they were hidden behind heavy veils. No trace of a sweet smile, white neck or… other charms were to be seen. Well, we decided that imperial intervention was called for. So, I had the trumpets sound a fanfare, stood in the middle of the dance floor, and invited all the girls to draw near to me, where we had a quiet talk. I told them in all seriousness, that if they felt that their modesty would not be compromised, they must feel free to remove their veils while dancing. Nearly all of them did, and then I asked the prettiest one to do me the pleasure. My leg was not so bad that day, I was able to acquit myself quite well. And how pleasant to have a beautiful face to look at, instead of a curtain. And that, Nannerl, is all I can think of to say about fashions."

"Will you be hunting while you are here, Monseigneur?" Mary uses the freedom she has to address her grandfather in a slightly more casual way, and Catherine sees Anna stiffen a little; a little sign of a struggle for supremacy.

"If our health permits it, Marieke. Whether or not we hunt, we hope to see you ride out. You must be using a full-sized ladies' crossbow now that you are so tall," Maximilian says.

When she smiles, Mary is almost pretty. "Thank you, Monseigneur! We are all ready for some amusement, since we have had nothing but—"

Mary can't finish her sentence, due to a disturbance outside. Catherine hears loud voices, but can't discern any words. Kunz is on his feet so quickly that Catherine jumps just as she did the first time she met him. He jerks the double doors open, and closes them behind him. Almost immediately, the doors open again, and a short, round man in an apron shoulders his way into the room, carrying an armful of papers.

"Now just hang on—" Kunz is on his heels, red-faced and shouting. Hofmeister Firmian follows them, eyes fixed on the floor, as though divining his future in the pattern of the stones.

"I am here on his Majesty's business, and you won't stop me, doorkeeper!" the round man's Tyrolean accent is nearly impenetrable to Catherine, but she understands from context what is happening. The man stops in front of Emperor Maximilian, bowing deeply.

The emperor speaks first. "Firmian, what is the meaning of this? And you, we know you," Maximilian addresses the round man. "You are the landlord of the Golden Angel. What is your business with us? All matters of the Hofstaat should be handled by the Hofmeister."

"Mayrhofer, Majesty." the landlord bows again. His face is red, but not from fear, Catherine thinks. This man is pushed to his limit, and is demanding his say. "I wanted to settle it with Firmian, but I got the same answer from him I always get. I'm sorry, Majesty. Something has got to change."

With these words, the room becomes absolutely still. Not a breath, not a sound of cutlery.

The landlord holds up his armful of papers. "These are outstanding bills, Majesty, totaling 25,000 Rhenish guilders." He selects one at random. "This one's dated 1508, Majesty. 1508! I went to the treasury—the treasury has resigned. Your Majesty has emptied the coffers yet again."

"This is outrageous!" one of the courtiers shouts.

Mayrhofer's face changes from red to nearly purple. "What's outrageous is that His Majesty has left honest tradesmen in this town shouldering a burden they shouldn't have to, going back years. If a working man leaves a tavern without paying his bill, he's thrown into prison, and rightly so. When the emperor doesn't pay the bill for himself and two hundred courtiers, he gets off scot-free with another banquet waiting for him in the next town besides. We've reached our limit, Majesty."

Firmian sidles forward, finally raising his eyes, not to the emperor's face, but rather somewhere in the region of his breastbone. "Er, Majesty… the landlords of the town decline to offer hospitality until these debts have been settled. The horses and pack animals are still standing in their traces outside. The servants are practically fainting from hunger, and the animals are fractious. No one can buy food for himself, since they also have no money. I fear there's going to be a riot if no one does anything."

Catherine is glued to her seat, and doesn't dare move. Even swallowing the mouthful of food she's chewing seems to make an unbearably loud noise. Hostility has the texture of molasses, she thinks, and the room is sticky with it. She can't take her eyes off the emperor's face, which has gone paler than snow. She remembers something Ludwig said about Maximilian's capricious moods: 'He'll either fall weeping into your arms, or hurl something sharp at your head.' Everyone at the table seems tensed to duck, to avoid the latter option.

Maximilian stands. "Anna, you will offer Herr Mayrhofer some refreshments, and have the chamberlain sent to me. Kunz, Firmian, come with me."

Servants make room at the end of the lowest table for the landlord, who seems to feel that he's not going to let his emotions stand in the way of a good meal. He tucks into roasted venison, meat pies, rolls and rice pudding as though he hasn't eaten for weeks, a thought made impossible by his capacious belly.

Catherine hears shouting from a distant room; it sounds as though heavy objects are being flung and clattering to the ground. The dull scraping sound could be furniture being shifted. Kunz reappears a few minutes later, clothing stained and rumpled. He speaks to Anna, the de facto head of the household.

"The Hofstaat will be housed here tonight. The chamberlain is making arrangements to feed the horses and servants. The lords must seek lodging at various castles and hunting lodges in the area. His Majesty and I are leaving for Burg Martinsberg."

"In the morning, surely," Mary says.

"No, right now. He says he will not stay here after this insult, and I can't say I blame him." Kunz walks around the table. "Madam, your presence is requested," he says, gently drawing Catherine's chair away from the table. She looks back as she leaves the room, her eyes seeking

Mary, who hadn't risen from her place. The girl raises her right hand, then the door shuts behind Catherine and Kunz.

"I've never seen him like this. He'll fret himself into a fever," the jester mutters, looking down at his tunic in the dim light of the torches on the walls of the courtyard. "He threw a jug of wine at Firmian, though it's nothing to do with him. The jug hit Firmian, but the wine hit me."

"How far is this place we are going?" Catherine asks. A horse has been saddled for her, and she stares up at it in dread.

"Not far. A couple of hours, over mostly flat countryside." Kunz says.

Someone is running across the stones of the courtyard behind them. They turn to see Mary with Catherine's travel cloak. "I so much wanted to talk to you, Catherine, and play some of my new music for you! I hope I can come up to Burg Martinsberg tomorrow. His moods never last long." Catherine and Mary hug once more, then Kunz heaves Catherine into her saddle.

"Kunz!" She catches him as he's about to mount. "He's sure to want me to play—my lute is with the baggage somewhere."

Kunz nods. "I'll find it."

"One more thing," Catherine fumbles with her purse, and retrieves the pouch with the money Fugger gave her. "Give this to him."

Riding in near total darkness, with only small circles of light cast by torches, Catherine fights off sleep. In order to stay awake, she asks Kunz where they are going.

"We are going to a place very dear to his Majesty's heart. The site of his miraculous rescue, or something very like it." The light of the torch makes him look even more like a wild man of German legend. "Something happened up there on the mountain, known only to his Majesty. I was on the ground. I'm a keen hunter, but you won't catch me climbing a cliff. A chamois will always be a better climber than a man, and it never pays to give an animal the upper hand."

"Kunz, you're not making sense. Though why that should surprise me after all this time…"

"You're learning!" He grins at her. "Something happened, as I say. His Majesty was quite changed by it. For a time. You can read the official version in Theuerdank."

Catherine sighs. "I tried to read Theuerdank. Forgive me, but it's repetitive, and you just want to shake the hero for falling for the same ruses over and over again."

Kunz makes a noise like a small explosion. "Don't tell his Majesty that. It's his paean to his own heroic steadfastness, or so he thinks."

It is nearly dawn when the emperor, accompanied by Catherine, Kunz and a handful of guards, arrives at his hunting lodge called Burg Martinsberg. Catherine's impressions, half-formed by exhaustion, include a toy stone house guarded by an angry giant. Or maybe she dreamed it. She is aware of the steep path up to the lodge, walled in like a miniature fortress, the flash of torchlight on the facade—stones of different textures and sizes, as though the house had been built from the rejects of another, more important building project.

She slides out of her saddle, lands heavily, and sees Kunz in the flickering light. Like the magician he is, he has found her lute, and brought it along. The emperor has been freed from the confines of his litter, and is being helped up the shallow stairs and through the arched stone doorway. Kunz hands Catherine her instrument. "Sorry, Songbird, you're on duty now. Time to drive away some demons. There will be a room ready for you."

She nods, trying to keep hold of her instrument with her stiff fingers. "I don't suppose you could find a measure of wine and water for me?" The jester nods and disappears into the darkness.

Catherine follows the guards to the emperor's room. What a difference from the dazzling splendor of his lodgings at the Fugger palace: this one is almost without adornment. No carpet or tapestry to dull the sound of the bare stone, or lend the room some warmth. The ceiling is low and dark, made of rough wooden beams. There's a simple bed with plain curtains, suitable for the bed of a laborer, plus a chair, a writing table, a rough wooden chest, and a low couch. There's a fire in the hearth, but she is too far away for it to warm her. Two candles are lit, and Catherine sits in the chair, waiting for the emperor to be ready. She massages her fingers to warm them. It's a vain gesture, since the temperature in the room feels like a wine cellar. Kunz appears with a jug of wine and water, and she gratefully accepts a cupful from his hand.

When Maximilian has finally settled into bed, he speaks to her. "I won't ask you to play for me, Kathl. You must be exhausted. Will you just sit with me for a time? I feel restless, and would appreciate the company."

"Of course, Majesty." Catherine sets her lute on the table.

"Do you know where we are?" the emperor asks.

"Kunz just told me you experienced something here, and it changed you." Catherine says.

"Tomorrow you will see the Martinswand. When I was young, I climbed so high while pursuing a chamois that I could not get down again. Two days and two nights I spent on a narrow ledge of rock, unable to advance or retreat. I spent most of that time on my knees in prayer." The emperor sighs, and Catherine can hear him shifting around in bed behind the curtains. "On the morning of the third day, I looked up and saw a young man, dressed like a peasant. He spoke to me in the dialect of this region, which I know well. He said I was to follow him, and he showed me a way to descend the cliff in safety. When I reached the ground, I was thronged by those who had been waiting anxiously for me. I turned to find my rescuer, to thank him, to find out where he lived so that I might reward him, but he was gone. No one had seen anyone else come down from the mountain. They saw only me."

Catherine stares into the glow of the hearth while listening to the emperor's story. While she's fascinated, she cannot keep her eyes open any longer. She is on the edge of sleep; his voice calls her back.

"Stay with me, Catherine. I cannot be alone. Share this space with me, like we are two pilgrims on a journey."

Catherine blows out the candles, and curls herself on the small couch, with only her cloak for cover.

She wakes from a dream of battle: shattering sounds, percussive metal on metal, screams of felled horses and impaled men, and the overwhelming drone of a huge cannon firing. They shudder the walls of the besieged fortress not only with well-aimed shots, but the sheer noise of the attack.

She opens her eyes, and sees the dim daylight on the chamber walls, but the noise of battle continues: a droning explosion of sound at regular intervals. Not cannon fire. Snoring. Maximilian is snoring, and the stone walls of the chamber reflect the noise. She throws off the cloak she covered herself with on her improvised bed and rises, stiff and achy from the cramped couch. She wraps her cloak around her, and silently exits the emperor's bedchamber, rubbing her eyes. There's a pressure like a millstone on her bladder.

Unsure of where to go, she walks down the short hallway. There's a bedchamber there; the door is open, the bed undisturbed. She peers in cautiously, and sees her own wooden chest waiting for her under the window. Her viol is there too. After closing the door, she gropes under the bed for a chamber pot, but can't find one. Then she remembers that the emperor, ever vigilant against bad smells, had secret chambers installed in all of his residences, even in simple hunting lodges like this one. She finds the small door, raises the lid, and sits. Her release feels like grace.

She finds a ewer of water and a basin, and washes in the chill water, then quickly changes into a warm woolen gown and heavier cloak. She goes in search of breakfast, blowing on her frozen fingers as she walks.

She can smell roasted meat and baking bread, and finds the small dining room by following the odors of cooking. Kunz von der Rosen is finishing his breakfast, and greets her cheerfully.

"So you found your room, then?"

"Yes. Eventually."

"Cold sort of place, isn't it? It's one of his Majesty's favorite hunting lodges. We're in for some fun today. *Schaujagd*. Must get Himself on his feet. He doesn't want to miss a moment." Kunz tosses his napkin on his plate and departs.

Catherine makes a plate of food for herself: roasted venison, stewed apples with raisins, and bread. She doesn't want to eat the greasy-looking soup, but at least it warms her. She sips her wine and water, and puzzles to herself about *Schaujagd*. *Schauen* is to look at or watch. *Jagd* is a hunt. How can the emperor watch a hunt without being in the midst of it himself?

She glances around her at the dining room, which is too small to be called a hall. Three of the walls are decorated with frescoes of scenes much like she'll witness today, she imagines. The candelabra are fashioned from the trophies of autumns past. A verse is stenciled in calligraphy, decorated with elaborate scrolls. She reads it and smiles to herself. How like *him* it is:

I know not how long my life will be
Nor when I'll meet my end
I know not where my journey leads
the wonder is how happy I've been.

Outside she can hear the approach of a barking pack of dogs, and voices shouting. She quickly finishes her meal and steps outside. The first thing she sees is a pretty white chapel next to the house, but then something immediately takes her attention from it, the swarm of hunters and dogs, and general noise.

Last night's angry giant is a mountain. The house squats at the base of a stark wall of gray rock, so tall that the top disappears into mist. She arches her neck, staring upwards.

She feels a warm presence at her side, and a voice near her ear says, "You look like a woman in love, Catherine."

"I think I am, Majesty. Until this moment, I thought the Kemmelberg was a mountain." She hopes to make him smile by referring to a small bump of rock and trees that passes for a mountain in Flanders.

"You know the words, 'The eye is not satisfied with seeing'?" Maximilian asks. "Old King Solomon obviously never saw Tyrol, or he would never have written them."

A group of riders winds up the path, and stops in the courtyard. Anna and Mary dismount, along with several other courtiers from Innsbruck. Mary curtseys to her grandfather and kisses his cheek before running up to Catherine. She moves like an athlete, but not without grace.

They walk down the stone path to a place where they have an uninterrupted view of the rocky face of the mountain. It seems impassable, but hunters and dogs can be seen scaling it, along narrow paths and ridges. Chairs have been set up, and Anna, always looking for ways to take precedence, makes herself agreeable to the emperor. Mary sees this, and breathes a sigh of relief. "Thank God, we will just have to do without her nonsensical conversation. I want to hear about the Diet," she rolls her eyes, "and *not* the fashions!"

Catherine laughs. "I'll tell you all I know. But first you must tell me what I am seeing here. This is my first *Schaujagd*."

Mary grasps her arm and points to the wall of rock. "Look, there are two or three chamois. There are dozens more you can't see."

"Won't they just climb higher and higher, eluding the hunters altogether?"

"A contingent of hunters starts at the top and climbs down. The chamois will be trapped between two forces." Mary smiles proudly. "This is why the emperor says hunting is such good preparation for warfare."

"But how can the hunters move on such smooth rock?" Catherine asks.

"The soles of their boots have spikes on them. They use their spears for balance, and that is also how they kill the animals. Watch. It will happen soon," Mary says. "So when will Charles be crowned?" Her voice betrays the almost worshipful respect she has for her older brother.

Catherine shakes her head. "Apparently it's not settled yet. The emperor obtained the votes he needed, but the problem, as always, is money. The Spanish treasury refuses to send the capital in advance. If the emperor dies before Charles is crowned, everything he worked for in Augsburg will have been for nothing. The crown will again be within reach of the highest bidder."

Mary is silent for a moment, and they watch the spectacle on the wall in front of them. "Watch! The kill is coming," Mary says, pointing.

Catherine watches a hunter brace himself by positioning his legs on two different levels of his stony perch. His hunting spear is more than twice his height, and she wonders how he can exert enough force to pierce the animal's hide. She opens her mouth to ask, when she sees him grasp the end of the spear and drive it into the animal's breast, pulling it out again nearly as quickly. He then hugs the wall as the animal falls past him to the valley floor.

"He has to pull the spear out as quickly as he thrusts it, otherwise he risks being pulled down with the animal's weight. We've lost a few hunters that way." Mary turns to Catherine with a look of satisfaction. "What else happened in Augsburg, Catherine?"

"I received a letter from a colleague of mine, the Hofkomponist, about something very interesting that we just missed. The emperor wasn't interested in an argument between monks, as he called it, but Herr Senfl says Doctor Luther is making a great stir. He had dinner with him, at Dr. Peutinger's house. Luther has become a celebrity, and has been invited to dine at all the best houses," Catherine says.

"I read Luther's theses after they were published," Mary says. "Did you get to meet him?"

"No, we left before he arrived. But Ludwig—Herr Senfl—attended his interrogation by the papal legate, Cajetan, and he wrote to me about it. Luther was the complete master of the interrogation. Ludwig said Cajetan was forced to invent things on the spot, in order not to look a complete fool. Luther's knowledge of scripture is comprehensive."

Mary raises her sharp eyebrows at Catherine's use of Senfl's first name. "Ludwig? That's my husband's name," she smiles a little. "Well, it's really Louis, but we call him Ludwig."

It's my husband's name too, Catherine thinks, but decides not to burden her young friend with the knowledge.

"Did he get to converse with Luther at the dinner? What's he like?" Mary asks.

Catherine pulls Ludwig's letter from her cloak, and sees Mary's curiosity catch fire like dry kindling.

"He says, 'There's something rocky in his features. I picture his Creator hewing him out of Saxon rock with a hammer and chisel. Strong bones: square chin, cheekbones which protrude, but not unpleasantly. The mouth is surprisingly delicate, surprising in that it can be a sharp and powerful weapon when he chooses.

Besides his lively conversation and novel use of language, one thing I will always remember about Dr. Luther: his eyes. His eyes say, "I know the terrors of hell—nothing temporal or earthly has the power to frighten me. But I also know the nearly unknowable goodness of Heaven, so nothing on earth will ever give me true joy, either."

In short, it is the face of a zealot, but fortunately one who likes to sing, drink, and laugh. I like him immensely.'

"He also says that while his scholarship and knowledge is all-encompassing, he's a modest man, who points to Christ and scripture, rather than himself." Catherine folds up the letter again. "He's afraid Cajetan has already written to the pope, recommending that Luther be excommunicated and declared a heretic."

"I don't see how he can. Doctor Luther supports all of his theses with holy scripture."

"But he doubts the infallibility of the pope, and that is the entire problem." Catherine says.

"Was Luther arrested? Does he have to go to Rome now?" Mary asks.

"Senfl says Luther wrote to the cardinal, apologizing for speaking disrespectfully during the heat of the debate. He was allowed to leave Augsburg and return to Wittenberg. Luther asked Senfl to send him some of his music."

"Your Ludwig writes beautifully," Mary says, clearly propping the door open for more information.

"I'm more interested in *your* Ludwig. Do you hear from him?" She hopes to deflect the girl's attention.

Mary shrugs. "He's not much of a letter writer. I don't suppose many twelve-year-old boys are. We've seen each other a couple of times since the wedding. We have fun hunting."

They continue to watch the action on the Martinswand. Chamois come flying down the cliff by the dozen, then are loaded onto carts by servants, and wheeled away to be processed. She can hear Maximilian shouting directions, and giving a running commentary of the performance of his 'soldiers'.

Being so far from Ludwig and discussing him under a cloud of forced calm stirs a need in Catherine to talk to someone about her ordeal. He body is healing, but her mind is still raw from the experience. But she cannot unload her pain on this young girl. For no treasure in the world would she raise the specter of fear in Mary's mind about what she may face when she is old enough.

The clouds part gradually during the hunt, and the late autumn sun warms the air enough for the emperor to order an outdoor feast. Large cauldrons have been erected, and tables brought from the lodge and set up. Fresh fish is brought up the hill from the Inn and fried in pans. Game is roasted and baked in pies. Dozens of courtiers arrive from Innsbruck and Fragenstein, along with court musicians. Catherine makes a move to go to collect her lute and give them a song, but the emperor tells her to stay where she is. This evening, she is his guest.

The emperor is a changed man: energetic and happy, as though his appetite for life and food has revisited him with force. He eats game pie, dumplings, and stewed apples, while shouting at his physician that he told him so, Tyrol heals him faster than any of the doctor's nauseating concoctions.

24

Mixing Together the Subtle Cup of Desire

It's a dream. She knows it, but the knowledge brings no comfort. She tries to tell her dream-self it's just an image she has seen somewhere. It is not real. The knight is in no danger. The two hideous shapes pressing and crowding him in the narrow gorge cannot hurt him: not the mocking figure crowned with a snake, holding an hourglass. It would be leering if it had lips, but no skin or muscle sheaths the bones of the face.

Another apparition jostles the knight from behind, a malevolent figure like a ram with a curved spiking horn at the crown of its head. This one manages to smile with its imbecilic animal face. A clawed hand reaches up; it smiles because it thinks the knight will fall.

Horse and knight are unperturbed, but she, the viewer, wants to shout: Get away. Spur your horse and go.

Her dream-self can speak. She opens her mouth and tells him very plainly to be gone. But he can't hear her, and she can't hear herself. The creatures cry a terrifying antiphon to one another, using no language or words, just a bestial sound that calcifies her blood, making it brittle to the point of breaking. The sound is the roar of an animal, but with some human timbre, as though a demon bull were lowing from the gates of hell. The lingering cry arcs higher, then drops off to rasping, guttural depths. Sometimes short, thrusting croaks punctuate the prolonged cry.

Catherine opens her eyes, but there is no relief in being awake. The sick feeling of her dream has followed her into wakefulness, and worse, she still hears the hellish roaring. She sits up in bed, groping in the dark for the rough curtains. She nearly tears them down in her panic to get away. She forgets to use the steps to reach the floor, and falls. The darkness is profound, and she doesn't know the configuration of her room. She runs into the door, struggles with the old iron latch, and finally throws it open. Even if there had been light, she would still have been blind with tears.

In the corridor she sees a dim flicker, and runs toward it. Maximilian stands in the doorway in his dressing gown, candle in hand, peering out of the open door into the courtyard. As she approaches him, she sees the torches of the two guards outside, a yellow, warm, human light that makes her want to sink to the floor in gratitude.

Maximilian turns to her. "Isn't it splendid?" Then he sees her face. "Sweetheart, what has happened?"

Catherine rubs her eyes so hard they squeak. "What is that horrible sound? I thought it was the nightmare I was having…"

The emperor doesn't laugh. His eyes skim her from head to toe, and only then she realizes she's standing there in her sheer white chemise. He hands her the candle, and drapes her in his dressing gown. The motion stirs the air, and carries a trace of his scent up to her. Safely covered, he draws her near to him, and to the door. The bellowing ceases momentarily, then begins again.

"The stags are roaring—of course you would find it terrifying. I have heard it since birth, or very nearly, and to me it means one thing: the chance to vanquish a creature like that." He points to a painted stag with real antlers mounted on the wall. A twelve-pointer. "The deer are rutting, and the sound you hear is the males calling to one another, attempting to warn each other away from the females simply with the power of their voices. Of course that rarely works, and they do battle. Their antlers are their weapons; they clash with amazing force."

"There's something almost human in the sound," Catherine says.

"That is your fancy. Few things sound more bestial than that."

One of the guards in the courtyard shifts his position, and moves around a bit, presumably to stave off deadness in his legs. Catherine sinks behind Maximilian. The emperor closes the door and grasps her elbow, moving her back down the corridor and into his room. He stops again just as suddenly.

"Catherine, you have not been happy since we left Augsburg. You have been too quiet, and there is pain your eyes. Won't you tell me what is wrong?"

"You won't like it, Majesty," she can't manage more than a whisper.

"This melancholy of yours I also do not like. Tell me."

Catherine moves away from him, pacing the floor nervously. She can't keep it contained anymore, though she fears the emperor will fire away like his largest cannon. But this is no time for cowardice. She raises her head, and meets his eyes.

"I married Senfl in a clandestine marriage." She badly wants to look away, but makes herself hold Maximilian's face with her eyes. He hasn't moved a muscle. She draws breath to continue her story, but he interrupts.

"And he was brutal with you." His voice is low and unemotional, the rasp in it slightly deeper than usual. It must be the dampness.

She nods, slowly leaking tears, unable to speak. The emperor limps toward her, and embraces her. She doesn't shrink from him. His touch brings warmth and calm, and a memory that her body recalls more clearly than her mind.

One of his hands is on her hair, the other between her shoulder blades. He speaks softly to her. "It isn't always like that. It's not all *brauten*, you know. The man who restricts himself to that, well, it's like eating the same food for every meal, every day, for years."

She lowers her head to his shoulder, face pressed against his neck, tasting the flavor of his skin. She can smell the human comfort of his body; sweet with a tang of sweat, like pungent greenery wet with rain. For the first time since that horrible afternoon with Ludwig, her pulse brings the promise of something other than pain.

My beloved put his hand by the hole of the door, and my depths were moved for him.

His lips are gentle on hers, his tongue in her mouth a sweet intrusion. She gasps in pleasure and surprise; he pulls away.

She pulls him back. For a moment, her mind places her back by the riverside with Ludwig; she gives him a different answer. At the same time, she wishes nothing more than this seeking embrace.

"Let me show you." He climbs into bed, and holds out his hand. "Come, sweetheart."

She follows him, uncertain.

"You may leave your chemise on, if you like."

He has left the candles burning, but once she climbs into bed next to him, and closes the curtains, she can no longer see.

He tells her where he wants her to sit. "No, not there. Up here."

Catherine's heart pounds in her chest, her throat, and her groin. She sits on his chest, so that his head is between her knees. His hands grasp her hips and pull her toward him. She steadies herself on the headboard, while Maximilian pushes her chemise away from her thighs. His fingers peel back the folds of her flesh, and he feasts on her. Shock makes her body rigid, and she clamps her lips together.

"Relax, dearest. You will feel nothing but pleasure. My pleasure is to give this to you, and to hear you. Let me hear you."

She squeezes her eyes shut, sensing nothing but the building brightness in her body; it fuels a blaze mirroring sun upon sun. His tongue parts her from herself; it feels like a brief, entire death, a sacrifice by fire in ecstatic flames. Her back arches, and her neck and shoulders jerk backward, as though strings had been pulled by an invisible god. Her lips eject his name without thought.

The death has taken the vigor from her limbs. Her strength seeps from sinew and marrow, *anima mea liquefacta est.* Maximilian eases her down to him; she kisses him, shocked and aroused again at the taste of herself on his tongue.

Time is now measurable only by the number of times she feels his hand stroking her hair. The house is silent. She no longer hears the stags.

"Do you love him?" His voice surprises her.

Catherine tries to recollect who she is, and what he means. "I thought I did, Maxi."

"This is why young people should not be allowed to decide who to marry themselves, especially not young women. You love me, you love him…"

"Barbara has many months to wait before she becomes a mother again. And you accuse me of being changeable?" Catherine says. There's no heat in her voice. She's just stating facts as she understands them.

"It is unseemly in a woman, Kathl… yet, there is a solution for everything," Maximilian says.

"But we married before God…" It sounds weak in her own ears. And I don't know that I want it to be solved, she thinks. He just didn't know what he was doing.

"We will simply deny it ever took place," Maximilian says.

"Like a man would?" Catherine asks.

Maximilian ignores her. "You should have a husband who is suited to your heritage. I will arrange for Margaret to give you a large dowry."

"Who will want me as I am? There might even be a child."

"That is what the dowry is for." Maximilian's fingers have unwoven her braids, and slide between the loose locks of hair. "I have always respected the Italians, and their arrangement of matters like this. Take the duke of Milan, the uncle of my second wife. When he married, his wife insisted he release his favorite mistress. He married her off to a count, even after they had a child together. So civilized, the Italians." Maximilian kisses Catherine again. "Now go, and wash yourself with vinegar and water. You will sleep in your own bed."

"I want to stay with you," Catherine says. A hazy, somnolent urge for him nudges her; she runs her hand down the length of his body. Maximilian's hand clamps her wrist. The signet ring he always wears on his right index finger digs into the thin skin of her arm. The double-headed eagle, looking forward and back.

"Go." He gives her a gentle shove, and she obeys.

Catherine wakes with a jerk, nearly thrashing out of bed and onto the floor. Except she's not in bed, she's on the emperor's tiny couch again, covered with cloaks. She had been dreaming again, and before she is fully awake it strikes her that she has never dreamed so vividly, nor had such a clear remembrance of her dreams. It must be this place, she thinks. Something has roused the part of her mind open to the holy gift of dreams.

Last night, she left his room and washed herself as ordered, but she couldn't face sleeping alone in her damp bed. She waited until he was asleep, then crept silently back into his room.

The first thing she notices is the silence. Not only is there no sound of snoring like heavy artillery, there's no sound at all, not even of soft breathing. A dim light glints from the windows.

"Maxi—" Catherine stands beside his bed before she realizes she has moved. The curtains are parted; he is not there. There's no reason for the clamminess that suddenly settles on her skin, no reason for her innards to feel near total revolt. All his life, he's slept hard for short periods of time. Since his illness he sleeps fitfully and wakes often, and has taken to demanding music, or Kunz's company, at any time of night. She knows this, yet her arms fling the door open, and she runs to her room to dress. Her legs take her out of the house and into the courtyard. The world seems to have lost its color; there is only the gray stone of the house, the outbuildings, and the towering wall, seen through a pall of mist.

She heaves the dark heavy door of the chapel open; it closes with a hollow thud. She crosses herself and moves carefully through the dimness of the small nave. St. Martin, for whom the Burg is named, permanently rends his cloak in two in a fresco on the wall. Catherine approaches the altar, staring at a dark shape arranged in front of it. A carpet? She's sure it wasn't there when she prayed here yesterday. She's in front of the altar now, on her knees, negligent of how hard she falls on the stone floor.

The emperor is lying prone before the altar, arms outstretched in the shape of the cross. His body is positioned on the floor, while his head rests upon the sharp stone step upon which the altar stands. The contortion of his neck in this position seems calculated to give pain. She takes his hand; it feels searing despite the chill.

"Maxi," Catherine brushes his hair from his face; his brow is slick with sweat.

"Leave me." His irregular breath toils in and out of his chest.

"You have a terrible fever. I'm going to get Kunz to bring you inside."

"Leave me!" Catherine knows what she is hearing: not rage, or impotence, or a whim of illness. Desperation.

From the Emperor's Book of Days

HOW can I relate what happened to me? Doctors were called from Innsbruck, and they brought my fever down, but what I saw during the night is yet before my eyes, even when they are open. What I see when I close my eyes I cannot bear to contemplate. How can I write these things, when words stretch inadequately, when their meanings are only half right, like a sculpture badly cast? The burden I carry now makes my worries about the empire, and Charles, and bankrupting my government here in Tyrol, seem like the memory of a pleasant afternoon of games.

In my dream, I was once again high up on the Martinswand. I looked down and saw the abyss. I saw into the profound darkness and knew what was there. My soul's eye could see it. I saw the damned suspended in nothingness, eternally waiting for solace that they know will never come. They are eternally alone, yet eternally confronted with their sins. There was no physical torment; no flames or torturing demons. There were no screams, but what I heard was worse—I heard the silence of despair. It was infinitely cold, the damned were naked, exposed, unable to warm themselves. I have been lonely in my life, but this severance, this rupture from the One who is with you even when you are most alone... and there, my words break down and show their insufficiency.

I saw the souls of the damned, but I also saw my sins—all of them, with total clarity, as though they were being acted out before me. What is there for me now besides penance for what I have done? How can this debt be expunged? God saved me once here, and I took that costly gift and squandered it, then plundered for more and more.

I do not fear death. If I feared death, I would not have lived as I have. If there is anything about death that I fear, it is the protracted tedium of dying—the inertness, and the waiting. My fear mirrors what I felt up on the Martinswand on the occasion of my first salvation: God will not allow such a sinner into Paradise. I shall not be counted among the living on the Day of Judgment.

I have called for my confessor, Gregor Reisch. I will read Lamentations and hear the penitential Psalms. Above all, I will attempt to make amends, now, while I still live, and after death. My remembrance is a hollow, vainglorious thing. What am I, that I should be remembered, that I should continue to exist upon the earth after death in some way? I have brought ruin to my lands, like the daughters of Jerusalem, heaping dust upon their heads. I have brought death and barrenness upon my house: Mary, Philip, Margaret's children, and Bianca. Through my actions, thousands have met their deaths, for my vanity, my reckless craving for revenge upon my enemies. I have already been punished for my fleshly sins, but I have not repented. No, I honed my lust for women until the appetite was with me night and day, until I went to a second with the taste of one still in my mouth. The marks of my sin are still on my body, yet I went to them; another, and yet another. That is now at an end.

Two days ago, I rejoiced in my vanity. Dürer sent a finished portrait, based on the sketch he did in Augsburg. He works so quickly, yet with a skill that is almost a kind of sorcery. He followed my instructions to the letter, but he did more than that. Not only did he remove all traces of sickness and infirmity, he transfigured me in a way that I thought only the hand of God could. He gave me my wish, that someone in the future, who is open, who is looking, might know me. I looked at it, and wept in my vanity. More than that, I immediately wrote to Dürer, and sent to him, with my most trustworthy messenger, some very costly jewels in payment, since I have no money.

Tomorrow, I will have Kunz sharpen my dagger, and I will destroy this painting with my own hand.

I had intended for Dürer to create my final portrait, but I cannot bear to have anyone look upon this lie. I have always sought to employ the best artists to glorify me. Now I need only a simple craftsman, and he will honor me with his work, though he might feel honored by the commission. He will honor me by telling the truth. He will not portray an emperor, but a simple, penitent sinner, at the hour of his death.

25

The Beat of Deceitful Wings

It has become increasingly lonely in the imperial entourage. Maximilian has been disposing of followers like a newly converted eremite sheds the trappings of the world. They now number no more than thirty: a few key advisors like Dr. Mennel, indispensables like Kunz, and a few dozen servants. If he wants you near him, you stay where you are: his cook asked permission to visit his wife, since the entourage was traveling near his home. "You will wait, because I need you to help bury me." Never mind that the emperor hadn't eaten solid food since they left Martinsburg. Even Barbara is dismissed, shunted her off to her husband's family in Carinthia to have her baby, presumably with the promise of a generous living. Her group of ladies is dispersed.

Some strange restlessness still drives the emperor from place to place: Gmunden, Enns, Steyr, the Salzkammergut. Traveling must be intensely painful, with each jolt of the litter causing suffering to his inflamed innards. His trusted courier Berhardin von Herberstein rides next to the litter, and reports each evening that his majesty looks weak, yellow in the face, but refuses to show any outward sign of discomfort.

They arrive in Wels, the ancient market town on the Traun River, on December tenth. They trundle over the long wooden bridge, past barges loaded with lumber, barrels, and the cloth Wels is known for trading. Finally, they enter the walls of the city through the Traun gate. From there it's just a short ride to the imperial residence, which Catherine is relieved to see is a small, cozy building, which looks as though it has been recently restored and modernized. She has had her fill of cold, drafty hunting lodges, where one could just as well sit in the wine cellar to warm up. There's talk of moving on to Linz in a few days, once the emperor has rested.

Catherine climbs out of her cart and stretches her back. Kunz von der Rosen has already dismounted, looking fresh and rested as though from a short country ride. He leans close and whispers to her.

"I bear good tidings of great joy: his majesty has ordered the Hofkapelle to report to him here. He wants them to start rehearsing his funeral motet, I suppose. They'll be here in a few days. I thought you'd be happy to hear it."

She just smiles and nods her thanks to him. She knows her voice will betray her, if her face hasn't already done so.

From the Emperor's Book of Days

WHEN we arrived, I could not rest because of the pain. The pressure in my bowels increased until the doctors were forced to purge me. The purgatives were too strong, and the next day I moved my bowels one hundred and eighty times, according to Collimitius' records. They thought it might kill me, but I have my father's constitution, and his drive to live. I survived, though I emerged looking like a rendered down remainder of myself. Once this initial crisis was vanquished, I resumed work. I still begin each day by being carried to Mass in a chair, then I return to bed to be hovered over by secretaries for hours. Collimitius interrupts regularly with medicaments and strong beef broth with a little bread soaked in it, and admonitions to rest, which I ignore. When I am forced to rest, Dr. Mennel is my constant companion. He reads aloud from the ancestry book he wrote for me.

I refuse to see Catherine. I tell myself I am ashamed of the stench, of my weakness, and the nearness of Death. But I am simply delaying the inevitable. I must tell her.

After a few days, I felt well enough to hobble to the window, where I sat watching falcons being flown in the garden below. Of course, in order to see them, the window needed to be open. I sat in the wintery air over Collimitius' strenuous objections, bellowing when anyone came near me. My room boasts one of the few external ornaments the Burg has to offer, an oriel window, over one hundred years old, preserved in the recent restoration.

The fresh air must have revived my appetite. I became ravenous, and wanted a Tyrolean specialty: *Krauttascherln:* dumplings with cabbage. My cook can justify his presence at last. I ate them like a starving man, but the cancer did not allow my body to digest them. They streamed away again from both ends.

I fear there will be no more good days. I await the arrival of the Hofkapelle to give Senfl my orders regarding my funeral motet. I wish to hear it before it is too late.

CATHERINE has been trying to see the emperor since they arrived in Wels, but has been refused. Finally, Collimitius admits her and retires to a small room next door.

Maximilian greets her, and she hopes he does not see her flinch when she looks at him. While sickness and pain would have made another man splenetic, they seem to soften him, like metal resting in fire. The impatience, the hurry, the restless race from one place, project, or woman to another are gone. He appears calm and resigned.

"I have been designing almshouses with Treitz. Look," he pushes some documents across the bed in her direction. She sees floor plans for dormitories, refectories, gardens, and a small chapel. "One of my houses will be built in all the major cities of my empire: Vienna, Antwerp, Augsburg, Innsbruck. The residents will be registered, deserving poor, and they will receive clothing, and a small allowance. Here I have ordered what they will eat: bread, vegetables, and a special health-giving drink I invented years ago, a concoction of juniper, boiled water, and lingonberries, with a little honey to make it tasty. And here is the design of a bronze statue of myself that will be erected in each almshouse. They will attend Mass every day, and pray for my soul, especially on the anniversary of my death.

"The almshouses are part of the path of penitence I must walk before God will allow me into Heaven. My sins are like grains of sand in the wilderness, and I must beg forgiveness of those I have wronged. Even by omission."

Catherine sits and grows very cold. The dense atmosphere of the room closes in on her, with its layers of smells: herbal preparations partially banishing the stench of uncontrolled bowels and sour flesh. It had not bothered her before, now she fights against the upward force in her throat. She watches as Maximilian slides the sleeve of his gown up to expose his forearm. His bones seem to strain at the thin layer of flesh encasing them. She stares at the constellation of small scars on his skin.

"Do you know what this is?" he asks.

She shakes her head, but she knows.

"The French sickness," Maximilian says. He leans his head back on the bolster, as though too tired to hold it up. She feels he's too ashamed to look at her. "I caught it in a brothel in Italy. I was on my way back to Germany after fighting the French with Ludovico Sforza. I stopped at a monastery in Füssen, to take hospitality there. That is where the attack struck. My mouth felt as though it had been slashed with a knife. The monks knew what they were seeing: *morbus gallicus*. All I wanted was relief, of which there was none. Afterwards, I gave the monastery a valuable gift of land, benefices, and some relics, to keep them quiet. I also issued a broadsheet with a hastily cut print, showing me kneeling before the Blessed Virgin, receiving a crown, while on the other side, pox sufferers languish with no comfort. The message being, the emperor is as unblemished as the Virgin herself. We can't have the Holy Roman Emperor suffering from a whore's disease, now can we?"

Catherine springs up with a cry which brings Collimitius running from the next room. Maximilian waves the physician away.

"Do I have it now, too? Because of what you did?" Her breath is shallow, her vision has narrowed to a point in front of her.

"Of course not. I would never have done that to you, Catherine. You can only get it from *brauten*," Maximilian says.

"Why are you telling me this?" Her voice is unrecognizable: thin, broken, cut with anguish. She does not pity him or herself. The thing burning in her throat is rage.

"I am telling you this to do penance. I can only prostrate myself before God and beg to be forgiven and admitted into His company of saints. Will you forgive me, Catherine? Will you pray for my soul?"

She could not speak, even if she knew what to say. She is choked by something that feels like a physical blockage in her throat. She wants to say there is one he has wronged far more than her, whom he needs to beg for forgiveness.

Catherine goes next door to Collimitius. She walks in without knocking and shuts the door behind her.

The physician is grossly fat, and the pale skin of his face is a canvas for a network of tiny, hair-like red lines. He has not slept for two days due to the care the emperor requires, and lack of sleep makes him harried and gruff.

Her shame makes it difficult for her to speak with him, but she must know, for Ludwig's sake. She doesn't care what happens to her, but her redemption must begin and end with protecting him. Her fear for him works on her like a poisoned arrow: a sharp pain in her heart, spreading waves of sickness inside her. If there's even a chance, she must go. He must not touch her again. But if it were true, only from *brauten*...

She calms herself and speaks to the physician. She hides behind Latin while discussing the sickness. Speaking a foreign language puts everything at a remove, and she is able to distract the agony of her mind with grammar, at least temporarily.

"Is it true what the emperor said, you can only catch *morbus gallicus* from *brauten*?" A small ember of hope glows in the ashes.

If Collimitius pities her, he does not show it. He heaves himself from his chair, and moves to a side wall where three large wooden chests stand, lids open. They are full of books and pamphlets. He stoops, breath coming in gusts as he roots through them. He returns to Catherine and places a stack of pamphlets in front of her. His thick finger points to the one on top.

"A report from an Italian physician who reported on the spread of *morbus gallicus* after the initial outbreak. He reports cases where the only contact consisted of kissing with the tongue." His watery gray eyes fix on hers.

We kissed before, she thinks. When we first got to Augsburg. A deep kiss. I did not become ill.

The small ember kindles.

"It is known to spread through other types of contact than just *brauten*." Collimitius pushes the tract aside and points to two others. "Reports from two men from the emperor's immediate circle: von Hutten and Grünpeck. Firsthand accounts of the ravages of the disease. There is no cure, aside from divine healing, of which I know not a single case. Some believe the Almighty is punishing sinners with this curse; if that is the case, why would he cure them? Mercury and the wood cure are entirely ineffective." He shoves his bulk away from the table. "Read them if you like."

Her finger traces the title on the cover page of one of the tracts. "How soon will I know?"

"Soon." The physician is already out the door.

She reads Grünpeck's account of when he was stricken with the disease. She sighs as she reads that he caught it at an imperial banquet where, as he said, 'Venus and Bacchus were both represented.' He lists his symptoms in detail; she does not dwell on them. His friends and relations leave him to his misery, and he suffers alone, comfortless. He wonders why he was afflicted with the disease at that banquet, and not during previous sexual encounters. Catherine holds her breath and straightens her spine. He places the blame with an unfavorable alignment of the planets, and, naturally, an imbalance in his humors.

Catherine closes the pamphlet and stares at the cover. Maximilian had been complaining ceaselessly about having to conduct the Diet under such adverse astrological conditions. The eclipse he saw in June augured only doom, in his opinion, and the opinion of his astrologers.

D EATH is a public act. What good does it do to die well, with courage in the face of fear and pain, if no one is there to see it? The entire household is packed into Maximilian's room, but he is no longer the emperor. The day before, while he was still able to speak, he relinquished his title, and gave the imperial seal to Abbot Schrein.

Everyone in the household is invited to come to his side, and call him by his name, like a common man. Stable boys, washerwomen, and scullery maids stand shoulder to shoulder with the grandest names in Austria. There are too many people, it is unbearably hot, and the room still smells like a cesspit.

Catherine can't see him unless she stoops and peers through the tangle of arms and elbows in front of her. She's been standing for five hours straight, sometimes sagging against the wall when her legs weaken. Soon she won't be able fight sleep any longer.

Earlier that evening, Maximilian suffered a stroke, which took away his ability to speak along with the use of his right hand. After that he began communicating by writing with his left. His mind is mostly lucid, though he occasionally writes things that make no sense. Mennel reads the things he writes out loud for the whole company to hear.

Maximilian dies at three o'clock in the morning on January twelfth. He passes quietly, like a child falling asleep. His last words, read by Dr. Mennel, are, 'With God's grace, I am fully prepared for this journey.'

A sheet is spanned across the room, to hide the body from the onlookers. Maximilian's confessor, Gregor Reisch, and his body servant Wuestin are charged with carrying out his final instructions regarding the treatment of his body.

He had recounted them to Catherine at one of their stops along his final journey, relishing every detail. Smiling, he quoted Horace,

No dirges at my insubstantial funeral,
no elegies, and no unseemly grieving:
suppress all the clamor, not for me
the superfluous honor of a tomb.

But she knew he was exaggerating for effect. Both his dirge and his tomb were of prime importance to him.

"Reisch will read scripture passages I have selected to go along with each step in the process. First, my body will be stripped and washed. Reisch will read, 'I am stripped of my glory, the crown has been taken from my head.' Then, he will flog me until the flesh of my back is opened, and read, 'And that servant, which knew his lord's will, and prepared not himself, neither did according to his will, shall be beaten with many stripes.' My head will be shaved. 'Mine iniquities have taken hold upon me, so that I am not able to look up; they are more than the hairs of mine head: therefore my heart faileth me.' My teeth will be removed, while he reads, 'He hath also broken my teeth with gravel stones, he hath covered me with ashes.' Finally, they will sprinkle me with ashes and lime, to slow the onset of decay, since it will be many weeks before I am interred in Wiener Neustadt. I refuse embalming. My shroud will be of the simplest linen and damask. My coffin you have seen already. I will approach the Almighty as a penitent. I will be laid to rest in the chapel of St. George, where I was baptized. My body will be buried in front of the altar, so that the priest will stand over me while saying Mass."

As soon as Reisch and Wuestin are finished, they take down the sheets that had shielded the body. The silence in the packed room is profound.

They all look at him, but he is all but unrecognizable. The removal of his teeth has caused the lower part of his face to collapse, distorting the architecture of the face that had been so familiar. Another shocking lack is the curling, shoulder-length hair. It has been replaced by the cap of a penitent. His nose protrudes from the sunken face like a mummery mask.

After an interval of respectful silence, one of the servants raises his head and speaks to Mennel. "It's customary for the staff to be allowed to take a memento…" Mennel nods.

They swell forward; not just the servants, but Maximilian's secretaries and advisors. They try to maintain a discreet silence by not speaking, but to Catherine, that makes the rustling, scraping, tearing and wrestling for items even more deplorable, nearly bestial. Bed curtains, bolsters, cushions from the bay window, candlesticks, ewer and basin, bottles of medicaments, chairs, the crucifix on the wall, even the tables next to the bed. In just a few minutes, the room is completely stripped of every furnishing, and Maximilian lies alone in poverty. Catherine sees that the paintings, the Virgin and Child by Gerard David, and Maximilian's favorite portrait of Mary, had already been removed, probably as a measure against the plunder.

Afterwards, she stands near a wall, thinking she's alone, except for Mennel and Reisch, but she sees sudden movement in the shadows. She turns and sees Kunz. The jester is staring at the body, not weeping, or making any sign of grief. She looks into his eyes and sees a void. His entire life, nearly every waking moment for the past forty years, had been devoted to Maximilian. How do you say farewell to that?

"Kunz," She says, stepping over to him, not knowing what to say, but feeling the urge to speak anyway. "You must mourn him. Don't let your grief eat you up."

"Don't worry about me, Miss. Anything that eats me up will find me indigestible. Besides, I have nothing to grieve. I'll be with him soon enough. He still needs me." Before Catherine can put her arms around him, as she wants to, he turns away and clomps out of the room.

Dr. Mennel approaches her with a sealed letter and the small box of pink and white marble she had seen in the emperor's *Schatzruhe* in Mechelen. "The emperor instructed me to give you these items. You'll find everything explained in the letter." As she takes the marble box, she notices it is sealed shut.

She moves toward the door, but something compels her to turn her head and glance at Maximilian again. She knows she will see him again, during the next few days of public viewing, and again when he is buried in Wiener Neustadt. Maybe the letter will tell her she is to dress as her alter ego once more, and sing at his funeral, which she is glad to do.

Before leaving, she stands aside as two young men enter the room. One carries an easel. The other, short and compactly built, with wispy hair the color of wheat, bows to Dr. Mennel.

"Andre Astel of Wels, painter."

She avoids Ludwig by staying in the locked ladies' wing, though she is the only lady present. She sings the emperor's funeral motet for him, standing next to Ludwig, then flees the room as soon as it is over. Finally, after the emperor's passing, Ludwig corners her. He marches her to the room that serves as the emperor's library. They are alone. It's a cheerless, blustery day, and what little light there was is waning already. There is no warmth in the library, and the chill is heightened by the dew of cold sweat on Catherine's skin. She stands with the closed door at her back, clutching the letter and the small marble casket, while Ludwig nervously crisscrosses the room.

Finally, he stops pacing and speaks to her. "Why have you been avoiding me?"

Catherine means to say as little as possible. The few words she has etched in her memory, the only ones she plans to utter, will make the rest pointless. He will never want to see her again, and that's what she wants. He must not touch her, not even a kiss. Grünpeck's gruesome description of how the pox ravaged him repeats itself in her mind like a stubborn melody you cannot shake. Abscesses, swelling of the sexual organs, skin erupting in pustules, excruciating pain. Ludwig must not touch her.

"So you won't even speak to me," Ludwig takes a few steps toward her, but she puts out her hand to halt him. "I can't believe this is still because of what I did to you in Augsburg. It isn't, is it?"

The shake of her head is almost imperceptible, even to her. But he sees.

"My God, Catherine. What happened to you? Why won't you tell me? I'm your husband—I want to help you."

She forms the words she's been rehearsing. "No marriage took place between us. You *brauted* me against my will, but I won't fight it in court. I'm leaving, and you'll never see me again." I only wish I knew how I was leaving, she thinks.

Ludwig stares at her. "No, this is not you. It's him, isn't it?" He moves closer, and she puts her hand on the latch. The message is clear—I will flee if you come any nearer. Ludwig goes on, nodding slowly. "He's got something over you, something terrifying, even though he's dead. You'd think he couldn't hurt anyone anymore. But we both know that's not true." He's been slowly advancing until he's just out of arm's reach of her. He speaks softly. "Please, whatever it is, we'll ride it out."

She cannot bear to let the hope in his eyes live. Hoping for the hopeless is more bitter than death. "There's no riding this out, Ludwig. This is life or death—yours and mine, not his. I'm not doing it for him, but for you. Please believe me." A muscle in her jaw twitches relentlessly.

"A broken heart, and severance from you, like having half of yourself hacked away... if that's what you're doing for me, don't bother. Let's face whatever it is together."

"There are worse things than a broken heart." Despair is all there is in her, and the wall she built is breached. She struggles with the door and runs.

Ludwig's last word to her, an anguished shout she can barely understand, sounds like 'coward'. Let him think that, by all means, rather than know the truth.

Safely alone in the ladies' wing, she lays on her bed and allows herself to contemplate what she has lost. After the period of mourning was over, they would have had their marriage blessed, and would have shared a bed openly as man and wife. She pictures Ludwig's bulk talking up most of the space. She pictures waking in the night, alight for him again, spending time doing what God gave men and women to do together. She imagines their house in Augsburg, and their little choir growing every year.

That future is irretrievable, and dwelling on those pictures will only drive her to despair. What can she do? How can she face the duchess, whom she loved like a mother? If she survives the sickness, she sees only one path. She will shave her head, and live as a man, like she said to Ludwig, but not in the way she imagined at that moment. She will earn her bread as the lowest of the low: an itinerant musician. She's glad the ladies' wing is empty and closed off. The noise of her grief would have caused alarm.

Catherine eventually calms herself enough to sit up, wash her face, and drink some wine and water. She breaks the seal on the emperor's note.

"Dearest Catherine, do you remember what you sang for me in Mechelen, the day you first saw this small casket in my *Schatzruhe*? I am now beyond the sorrows of this world, and what is inside this box is beyond the reach of pain. But I ask that you would take it to Flanders, and inter it with Mary in Bruges. Help me reach my final rest. We are still pilgrims on a journey, Kathl. But the tables have turned; now you hold my heart in your hands.

"You need never return to Germany. Margaret will make the arrangements. You will be cared for, and loved. This I promise you. Do this for me—for my remembrance."

Though he created the whole situation, he has also given her the way out she sought. For this, she is grateful. Dr. Mennel arranges a special guarded convoy to conduct her, and many articles of Maximilian's inheritance for Margaret, to Mechelen. An express messenger has already been dispatched, who, as part of a relay, will ride day and night, changing horses every twelve miles. The last rider will reach Mechelen in less than a week, to inform Duchess Margaret that her father has passed.

Catherine doesn't wait for the funeral. The convoy is ready in two days, and they leave on the morning of the third day.

*

Disgrace I do not wish from her,
I hope also that it will not be bestowed upon me.
Whatever is possible for me, I am ready;
In love and woe never shall I forget her.
All my life
I shall be thankful that she
Tender-hearted, Of noble nature,
Should have shown herself so friendly once,
and been no different until now,
As befits her.
Honorable and worthy she is reckoned,
Is called righteous, A crown of womanly beauty,
Her hope is solely to be pious, joyous,
As to a noble heart fitting is,
Although cruel cunning
Stands in her way,
Eager to oppose

Such joy,
Which by jealousy
Is condemned,
As occurs to me and my company.
Where uncouth nature rules at court,
Very rarely is found good governance.
The nobility thereby is despised;
As I see it, I must pay for this too
May that one day
Turn upside down,
Although today
I am forced out,
And no longer belong in this house.
It is all idle rubbish:
To serve her, I must be patient.

*

No love remains true,
it's as clear as the day,
that I've learned myself.
My dear's cunning and good word
beguiled and charmed me,
though I'd never done her any wrong.
Now I know too well that I shouldn't
risk such danger again
to believe her, who always has
received faithful counsel from me.
Everything has its purpose: my time is done.

THE EAGLE AND THE SONGBIRD

No one on earth can make me forget her.
She remains a full half of my heart.

Ludwig Senfl, Schweizer

25

Sorrow and Tears were His Food

June, 1520
My dear Herr Dürer,
I offer you greetings and the promise of my faithful good service. Please forgive me for writing to you in this manner, though we have not seen one another since our dinner at Augsburg with Dr. Luther. I was just with Dr. Peutinger, and he tells me you are planning a trip to the Low Countries, and may visit Mechelen on your travels. May I ask you, while you are there, to make inquiries into the whereabouts of my wife, Catherine de Croÿ? We were married in a clandestine ceremony at the Diet in Augsburg, but I have not seen her since she left Wels after the death of the late emperor. She left there on an errand for him, which he charged her with in his will, and went to Mechelen. I have not heard from her since then, and have all but given up hope. I have written repeatedly to her, to Duchess Margaret, even to King Charles, in my despair. I would travel there myself, but lack the means to do so. If you were to undertake this on my behalf, I pray I may one day do you a service which would help you as much. I wish you safe travels, and all possible blessings.
    Ludwig Senfl
    Imperial Hofkomponist

THE EAGLE AND THE SONGBIRD

*

NUREMBERG, *August 1521*

Ludwig Senfl knocks on the door of Albrecht Dürer's large corner house opposite the Tiergärtnertor, slightly out of breath from the long walk up the hill. While he's waiting to be let in, he studies the front of the house. It is large and impressive, and Ludwig is reminded again of his own appearance. His clothes were respectable enough when they were new, but now they are tattered and not very clean, and they hang loosely on him, as he has lost a significant amount of weight in a short time. He knows his face is marked by grief and the signs of too much drinking. By the time he's standing in Dürer's front hall, he wonders how they let him in at all.

He sees his host coming across the hall toward him. Senfl wonders how the wispy man he met in Augsburg could now be even thinner. He's pale, and dressed far too warmly for the hot August weather. The two men exchange bows, and Senfl speaks first.

"Herr Dürer, it's good of you to invite me here."

"It's my pleasure, Senfl. Please, let us speak on friendly terms. *Wir duzen uns.* Will you join me in my dining room for something to eat?"

They walk up the stairs, which Dürer takes slowly while clutching the railing. The dining room is long and paneled in dark wood with a beautifully carved sideboard. A *Lüsterweibchen*, a candelabra formed from an antler trophy with a female half-figure resting on it, hangs from the ceiling. Ludwig studies it, and guesses that Dürer designed it himself.

Dürer invites his guest to sit down at the table, which has been laid with platters of sausage, bread, and pitchers of beer. Dürer pours the beer himself, and the two men toast one another.

Ludwig's hands are shaking so badly that he spills beer on himself. He opens his lips to apologize, but Dürer shakes his head, signaling there's no need. He hands him a cloth.

"Would you like something stronger?" Dürer asks.

Ludwig grimaces. "It's that obvious? Yes, I suppose it is. No, thank you. I think I feel one of my periodic skirmishes with sobriety coming on."

Dürer leans forward. "What has happened to you, Senfl?"

"What *hasn't* happened to me? In 1519, I had everything: I was thirty-four, and at the top of my profession. Between the pension I was promised and several benefices, I had an excellent living to look forward to, and every hope of serving the next emperor. And I had a beautiful wife, a singer. You must remember her from Augsburg. You sketched her."

Dürer nods.

"We were going to create a musical dynasty to serve the House of Austria until doomsday," Ludwig smiles a little. "Now I have nothing. No pension, despite repeated appeals to the imperial treasury, and Duchess Margaret. The new emperor won't receive me or respond to my letters."

"But you will eventually succeed, I'm sure," Dürer says. "It's in the will, correct?"

"It was in an early version, which Dr. Peutinger drew up, but not the final one. When I consulted him as to what I should do, and he saw that my pension had been revoked, even he was outraged. You know how he reverenced the late emperor," Senfl says.

"How are you surviving?"

Ludwig lays his knife carefully on the side edge of his plate. "Comically enough, I live in a similar style to our late beloved patron: on borrowed money I have little hope of ever being able to repay. While that never seemed to bother him, it weighs on me. Dr. Peutinger and Hofhaimer have been my saviors, literally."

"Can you not seek employment elsewhere?"

"I was charged with disbanding the Hofkapelle last year. But the new emperor has stipulated that none of us can take a post elsewhere for four years, in case he wants us. Which is not likely. A German sound does not please him." Ludwig pauses, and fights a sudden urge to stand up and run. He knows he will not hear any good news—why put himself through the misery? On the other hand, not knowing has been a form of hell. He takes a breath. "Did you stop at Mechelen during your tour of the Low Countries?"

"I did. The duchess received me with great hospitality. She showed me her collection of paintings herself. I took many of my pictures along and—" Dürer sits up suddenly. "Wait a moment," Ludwig blinks and the artist is out the door like a slender gyre.

Dürer comes back moments later with a stack of sketches. He stands at the end of the table and lays them out, sorting through them with his thin fingers. Ludwig stands beside him. "The duchess wasn't interested in many of my pictures, unfortunately. I took her a very fine portrait I had made of the late emperor, similar to the one I sent him in Tyrol before he died. For some reason she disliked it. But one she was very taken with. In fact, it seemed to stagger her. Here's a sketch I made of it."

He holds out a sheet to Senfl, who takes it to the large bank of crown glass windows, to see it in the light. It shows a family group: St. Anne, the Virgin, and the infant Jesus, a blond cherub with a strangely bulging head. St. Anne, an older woman in a wimple, stands over the Virgin, a beautiful young woman with sculpted cheekbones and a high forehead. Her smile makes you imagine she had just thought of the most amazing thing, and was looking for the right person to tell.

Kätterlin.

Senfl stands in the light, not feeling much of anything, except it seems as though all the blood in his body has been removed in one hot rush. He tries to speak to Dürer, but his breath and tongue won't work together to form words, only sounds. He turns back to the window, and the artist turns equally quickly back to his sketches.

Senfl speaks once he's sure his voice is under control. "Did you see her in Mechelen?"

"No."

"What did the duchess say when she saw your painting?"

"She reacted much as you did. She went pale, and I could see tears in her eyes. But she was very quickly mistress of her emotions again. She asked me where I had seen the young lady. I told her I sketched her in Augsburg at the same time as the emperor."

Senfl restrains himself from taking the artist by his bony ankles, and holding him upside down to shake the information out of him. "And she said nothing else?"

"No, just that looking at my painting was like turning a corner and meeting her again unexpectedly. I'm sorry, Senfl. There were many questions I would like to have asked, but…" Dürer shrugs.

Senfl nods, lower lip clamped between his teeth. Subordinates at court speak when spoken to, and do not ask questions.

"But my curiosity was roused. Dr. Peutinger told me a little about your difficulties, though not that you were married to the young lady. It would have ended there, were it not for an opportune meeting I had that evening."

The two men move back to their places at the table. By some beautiful sorcery, a flask of brandy has appeared at Senfl's place. He looks at it, and then at Dürer, who snaps it up and pours a good measure into Senfl's glass. He takes a gulp, and the curtain comes down, mercifully dividing him from the world. Everything feels a bit blunted, like hearing yourself sing in a small room softened by cushions, carpets, and draperies.

"You know the name Petrus Alamire?" Dürer asks.

"Certainly. The imperial library is full of his manuscripts."

"We met by chance after the duchess was finished with me. My guide was Tommaso Bombelli, and we were invited to visit Alamire's workshop. Then we had a friendly glass together. He's from Nuremberg, and we have several connections in common."

The brandy is taking effect, and just barely prevents Senfl from shouting at Dürer to ask him what in the name of Christ's wounds Petrus Alamire has to do with Kätterlin. He just nods and sits, sipping sedately.

"Did you know that Alamire is… a man of information, for whom walls and closed doors do not exist?"

Senfl stops sipping. "A spy?"

Dürer nods. "After our friendly glass, we had another, whereby we got down to business. He showed himself to be trustworthy, so I told him about my encounter with the duchess, and the painting, and what I knew about Miss de Croÿ."

The composer can no longer lift his eyes, or wishes to conceal what the artist might see in them. Senfl fixes them on the floor as he speaks. "Where is she now, Dürer?"

"She is in Spain, at the new emperor's court."

"As a musician?"

"I don't know." Dürer lowers his head, and his shoulders fall slack. "I only know she's there with her husband. He is one of the emperor's advisors."

Ludwig's hand is no longer under his control. It usually only shakes like this when he's *not* drinking. He sets his cup down. "I am her husband, Dürer," A sharp cracking sound in his temple makes him stop clenching his jaw.

"According to Alamire, Maximilian wrote to the pope to have your marriage annulled on the basis that you had become a heretic," Dürer says.

Ludwig can only sit and stare, mute.

"It was known that you were in contact with Luther," Dürer says. "He had been declared a heretic, along with his adherents, all those who helped him, or were his friends."

"Who is it? Who is her husband?" The raspy noise coming from Ludwig's mouth seems to have nothing to do with him.

"The emperor's son. Dietrich. Before the marriage, he was legitimized, and given the name von Österreich, and the Habsburg coat of arms. They already have a son. I'll spare you having to hear his name."

"Now he can lie in his grave happy in the knowledge that his little fantasy of his love for Mary continuing on is playing out. He gave Catherine the arms of Burgundy, and fabricated some relationship to Philip the Good of Burgundy," Ludwig says.

"According to Alamire, it is true," Dürer says. "Duchess Margaret heard from Catherine's father, Philip the Good's natural son."

"Whether it's true or not is almost beside the point. His son would have her, so in some way, he would too." Ludwig's vivid imagination conjures the emperor's voice in Catherine's ear. *'When he takes you, I will be there. Any children you bear will be mine too. I get my wish, to be reborn of your body.'*

"Ludwig," Dürer is standing beside him, hand on his arm. Ludwig's nails dig at his scalp. He has been tearing his hair by the roots without even noticing. His teeth feel worn down with grinding them. "Come," the artist leads him back to the table, and helps him to sit down again.

"So I blunt my mind with drink, and occupy it with writing songs," Ludwig says, not caring that the artist has seen the depth of his loss. He speaks through his tears. "I haven't written a single piece of sacred music since the emperor's funeral motet. It is simply no longer in me. Maximilian labeled me a heretic, but he made me something worse." Godless, he thinks. Probably damned.

"Ludwig, don't lose your faith, whatever you do. Your bereavement, as terrible as it is, is nothing to life without God. Read Dr. Luther's writings. I have found comfort in them during many times of trouble in my own life—after the death of my mother, and working for three years for the late emperor, to my own financial loss, with no payment and no hope of any. How can a man who bases his entire theology on the Bible be a heretic? He is the voice of God's truth."

Ludwig remains silent for a few moments, pushing pieces of sausage around on his plate with the tip of his knife. "Did you happen to hear a rumor or suggestion that Catherine might have been ill when she returned to Flanders?"

"No, nothing like that. Alamire would have told me, I'm sure. Nothing seems to escape his notice."

Ludwig picks up the sketch again, and stares at it while he speaks, as though Dürer is not really his audience. "There once was a king who betrayed a servant who was nothing but loyal to him, served him faithfully, gave him everything. The king desired the man's wife, so he sent him to the frontline in battle, and he was killed. The king took the man's wife as his own. The king was a favorite in the eyes of God, but God was displeased. He sent a prophet to the king, and the prophet told him a parable.

"'There once was a poor man who had nothing but one perfect ewe lamb, which he carried in his bosom, fed and raised as his own child. In the same country there was a wealthy man with fields, servants, flocks almost without number. He was visited by an important guest, but he didn't wish to sacrifice any of his own sheep, so he took the poor man's ewe, slaughtered it, and fed his guest with it.

"When the king heard the prophet tell this story, he was enraged. 'Who is this man? Tell me, and I will punish him many times over.' When the prophet told him, he wept bitterly.

"The emperor was the perfect penitent when he died. Confessed and was absolved of all his sins. I have no doubt he will be numbered among the righteous on the Day of Judgment. No doubt the king was penitent also, and God forgave him. I know it's just a parable, but I always wondered what happened to the poor man. He probably died destitute, bereft of his one valuable possession. The lamb would have provided young to sell or slaughter, and milk to drink. But above all, he loved it. We pay for the sins of others, Dürer."

Ludwig hears the chimes of St. Sebaldus, and stands.

"Formschneider will be closing up soon, I'd better be on my way." The curtain has thickened, and he's no longer certain what his business with the printer is. He wobbles down the stairs, out the door, and into the street.

When he turns he doesn't see Dürer, but rather Frau Agnes. He recognizes the features of St. Anne from the sketch. Even though he knows she has never been in the same room as Catherine, let alone posed with her hand on Catherine's shoulder, they are now linked in his mind. He wants to embrace Agnes, and he wants her to comfort him. She does, but not the way he was expecting.

"My husband didn't want to tell you, Herr Senfl, but… she tried to get back to you. She pawned some things, cut off her hair and escaped from Mechelen. She got as far as Cologne, working as an itinerant musician. Somehow they found her and hauled her back, and Margaret forced her to marry the emperor's son."

The artist appears next to his wife. Ludwig stares at him, unable to speak.

"I'm sorry, Senfl. I thought knowing would hurt even more," Dürer says.

Agnes sniffs. "A woman knows better, Albrecht."

She hands Senfl a small pouch. His trembling fingers struggle with the cords, but finally he opens it. It holds more money than he has seen in years, at least two guilders.

"We know all about butting heads with a so-called patron who won't pay. Albrecht had to fight for his pension as well," she says.

"Frau Dürer, it's too much."

She shakes her head. "We have so much, Herr Senfl, and we want to help."

He's still staring at the pouch when the artist hands him a folded sheet of paper. This he does not need to open. His mouth has gone dry, but he manages to thank them both.

"Auf wiedersehen," he says, and makes his way slowly down the hill.

THE EAGLE AND THE SONGBIRD

*

Munich, *Autumn 1538*

Ludwig Senfl hears a soft noise at the door of his study. "Come in, my dear," he says, recognizing his wife's gentle knock.

Maria Senfl appears at the door. Or rather, her brown head, glossy like a chestnut, appears first, with a sly smile of anticipation on her face. The rest of her follows soon after. They have been married five years, and Ludwig still can't resist grabbing the curve of her hips as soon as she is within reach. She screeches and swerves away, teasing him, and then he sees the package she is holding behind her.

Before he can say anything, something else at the half-open door takes his attention from Maria and her bundle. He holds out his arms, saying, "Come here, *Äffchen*. What's my little monkey up to?"

His little daughter, his first and only child, toddles over. She seems to be doing her best to fall on her rosy face, so he ensures that she falls into his hands. Ludwig hoists her up onto his lap. She sits there, content for one moment, then squirms and reaches for his pen. He gives it to her, along with a piece of blotting paper so that she can scribble as much as she likes without marking up his score.

Ludwig Senfl is forty-eight years old, husband to a young wife, father to a young daughter, a homeowner, and finally content.

Soon after he came to Munich, he'd been invited to dine with the Halbhyrns, the wealthy burgher family of one of his pupils. He met his pupil's sister Maria, a young widow.

It was a small gathering, with no more than ten guests present, and after dinner his pupil had urged his sister to play and sing for the company. Her reluctance to make music in front of so many (not to mention the Duke of Bavaria's own court composer, who had once served the late emperor) revealed itself in her glowing face and lowered eyes. Ludwig found her modesty attractive, or so he told himself, and before he knew what he was doing, he stood up, took a seat at the clavichord, and invited Maria to sing while he played. He was never quite sure what the fatal blow had been; her rich alto voice as she sang *O Rosa Bella* or the effect of her deep brown eyes when she looked at him, like the heat of a good fire on his skin. Whatever it was, it made him join her in singing the quodlibet, where their two different songs melded into one:

In fiery heat, so burns my heart, my dearest love.
I suffer so much: help, and stand by me.
I once saw perfect beauty, success, happiness and salvation in my heart:
I was forgotten – O, the power of yearning!
Open up, open up, my beloved love!

They were married three months later.

She'd had no children with her first husband, and it took four years for her to become pregnant with their little daughter. After her long labor, she held the child in her arms, exultation outshining exhaustion in her face. When Ludwig came in, she hid her face a little. "I'm sorry dearest, it's only a girl..." Had he been able to speak, Ludwig would have told her not to talk nonsense. He sat behind her to hide his emotion, while stroking her unbound hair.

She wanted to name the baby after her mother, and Ludwig couldn't think of a way to refuse this request. His own mother had been named Adelberthe, after all. His joy in his daughter could not have been greater. As she grew and became more of a little person, the nicknames came: *Äffchen*, little monkey, Käthe or Kitty. But never Kätterlin.

Ludwig kisses her fuzzy blond head and looks up at his wife. "What do you have there, Maria my sweet?"

She places the package carefully on his desk, after setting aside the note paper he'd been working on, so she wouldn't crease it. "It's finally come, Ludwig. A messenger brought it from Nuremberg just now."

Maria plucks little Catherine out of his lap, who whimpers a bit at the abrupt removal from papa, and they leave him to open the package alone. He knows what it is and had been anticipating this moment for months.

He removes the book from its wrapper and studies the title: *Johannes Otto's Second Book of New Musical Works*, printed in Nuremberg by Hieronymus Formschneider.

Five of his motets are included in the volume, and they are in exalted company: his master Isaac is represented, and his idol and compositional model Josquin is the author of the greatest number of motets in the volume, with ten of his works gracing its pages. Ludwig works his way through the book, carefully separating the pages with his paper knife. He notes with interest the three works by a young man named Gombert, who serves Emperor Charles V in the very position that Senfl had long striven to occupy.

He continues separating pages until he reaches the piece he is looking for. *Quis dabit oculis*. Motet for four voices by Ludwig Senfl.

Who will give our eyes a fountain of tears to weep...
Alas for our lord Maximilian...

Ludwig stands up and walks across his study, a bright corner room on the second floor of his house, with rows of casement windows. The west-facing windows overlook the garden of his friend, the author Simon Minervius. Ludwig hunts for a small key in his purse and unlocks a plain oak cabinet, which holds a few valuable objects, but also the only two items besides music he'd kept from his years serving Emperor Maximilian. He had sealed them in an envelope, and then ignored them for nearly twenty years.

Ludwig slowly opens the envelope and removes the items. They look paltry enough in the bright daylight: a jagged fragment of charred paper with a few musical notes, and a sketch of a woman's face. But despite their trifling appearance, seeing them again nearly staggers him.

He does not like to think of those dead years, 1519 to 1523, a blur of tears and drink. The only bright spot had been the publication of *Liber Selectarum*.

In the spring of 1518, Emperor Maximilian saw an eclipse and became obsessed with death. A comet had been visible when he was born, which portended his great reign and the mighty works he would accomplish, while the eclipse augured doom, downfall, and decay. Maximilian saw alpha and omega in these two heavenly manifestations, and his astronomers confirmed this in their ponderous prophecies.

Always vigorous, energetic, and in moderately good heath, except for the chronic colds which plagued him and his old leg injury, the emperor seemed to sicken into old age almost overnight. The whole court murmured about his broken-down appearance, lapses of memory and judgment, and even the possible onset of senility. His scrupulous attention to the bureaucratic running of his empire waned, and he began to cancel appointments, to the point of sending away delegates who had traveled for weeks to meet with him.

But the work on his remembrance continued, even intensified. He wrote to his daughter, Duchess Margaret, at her court in Mechelen, requesting that certain funeral motets from her library be copied and sent to him, "so that We might present them to our court composer, that he might study them, and learn what kind of music We desire to have connected with Our name for eternity."

This was marked 'Urgent'.

Senfl received a bundle of about ten motets in due course, rehearsed them with the Hofkapelle, and performed them privately for Maximilian in a sort of serial lamentation.

Gradually, all but one of the funeral motets had been performed in the emperor's presence; a work by an unknown Italian. Ludwig told Maximilian what he was to hear, and mentioned as an afterthought that the composer, named Festa, had recently been called to the French court.

The emperor straightened in his seat. While listening, he leaned forward toward the singers, coveting the notes, as though he were trying to pull them out of the performers, as though the music didn't come fast enough to match his greed.

Who will give our eyes a fountain of tears to weep before the Lord?
Brittany, why do you weep? Music, why do you keep silent?
France, why are you in mourning and spent with grief?
Alas for our lady Anne!
The joy of our hearts was turned into mourning;
The crown has fallen from our head.
Therefore, boys howl, priests weep,
the singing men lament, the nobles weep and say:
May Anne rest in peace.

"This, Senfl," Maximilian said after hearing the last note shimmer and fade into nothingness.

The emperor stood up slowly, every movement marked by pain, and limped toward Ludwig. Lacking the large wooden stand used in church to hold up the music, large enough for all the singers to crowd around and read while singing, the massive volume was held aloft by three servants. The singers gave way as Maximilian came to stand in front of the volume, thumping it with his flat hand. The servants weren't expecting the music to fight back, and staggered a little under the blows.

"Write us something like this. The poetry and music are exactly what we desire. The depth of feeling in this section," he paged backward in the manuscript and jabbed his finger at the part he meant, "is exquisite. We love how the name of the monarch is interwoven with the words 'the joy of our heart'. This is fitting for us since we are the joy of the empire. More fitting than for the unworthy ruler for whom this jewel was written. 'The crown has fallen from our head'. This too is utterly appropriate, for our successor, though he is our flesh and blood, is not German. We love the ambiguous ending—it sounds bereft, searching, unsure how to go on, as the nations will be after our death. It is perfect. Go now, and write something like it for us."

Ludwig surfaces from memory, aware of the sound of his small daughter wailing somewhere in the house, far away from his study. Maria is probably forcing her to eat mashed peas or something equally revolting; Ludwig can't fault her for her reluctance.

Ludwig hears the bells of the Frauenkirche chime two forty-five; it's time to leave to meet with his employer. He gathers up the new edition of music, stuffs it in the wrapper without bothering to tie it up with string again, and leaves his study.

Maria and little Käthe are in the kitchen by the fire. His daughter's face is smeared with unsuccessful attempts to maneuver mashed peas into her unwilling mouth, but she's no longer crying. She points at her father and shares several important items of baby news with him. Ludwig blows them each a kiss. "It's time to meet the duke. I'll be back before supper."

Ludwig conceals the envelope under his clothes, between linen and skin. As he walks along, thinking of *her*, he places his hand over the envelope through the good cloth of his cloak, pressing her face against his breast again. Her cheek had rested on his bare flesh just once, on their night by the river. The questions seethe in his mind as they always do, though all the answers have long been known to him. He tastes bile through his clenched teeth.

He knows exactly where to look for his patron on a beautiful day like this. He passes through the ducal residence without hindrance; he knows where he is going, and the servants know him. Hofkomponist is an honorable title, and they greet him respectfully as he passes. He walks out into the vast garden, and sees activity and a handful of figures in the distance.

Duke Wilhelm is practicing. He stands next to a large pond, where two servants with long poles stand thigh-deep in water. They beat the rushes with their poles, causing ducks to take flight. The duke takes careful aim with his crossbow and releases an arrow, then quickly takes ready-loaded replacements in turn from servants on either side of him. He is a fairly good shot, but still misses more than he hits.

The duke notices Ludwig's approach and calls for a break. Ludwig greets his employer with a respectful bow. He calls him 'My Lord', and is careful to observe protocol, but aside from these nominal courtesies, the two men approach each other on level ground.

"Herr Senfl, you are a welcome sight! Nature is my mistress today, and a straight shot is beyond me. At this rate, I will never equal my uncle's record of felling one hundred ducks in one hundred and four shots." Duke Wilhelm gives Ludwig a friendly smile and invites him to sit on a nearby bench. Wilhelm sits next to him in a wide-legged stance, with his unloaded crossbow across his knees.

"But you still look as though you enjoyed it," Ludwig says.

"I do. With all its frustrations, there's nothing I'd rather be doing on a day like this. You still won't be persuaded to join me?"

Ludwig shakes his head. "Oh no! Your uncle convinced me to go on a hunt one day. I slipped on a wet rock, dropped my matchlock, and it fired. Luckily, the aim of the masterless weapon was as poor as my judgment: it hit me in the foot. That injury plagued me for a full year; I couldn't walk properly until the Diet of 1518. In Augsburg."

The duke laughs softly, shaking his head. "My apologies, Ludwig, I'm not laughing at you, but rather at my uncle's powers of persuasion. He had wiles like the devil. Of course I don't need to tell you that—you know more about it than I do. I only saw him about once a year, if that. I loved him when I was a boy, you know—when he was younger he was always ready to wrestle or practice sword fighting. My own father, a duke, was too grand for that kind of thing, but emperor or no, Uncle Max was fun."

"Strange that he should be the topic of our conversation today," Ludwig says, handing his employer the heavy volume of music. "This just arrived from Nuremberg."

Wilhelm sets aside his crossbow and takes the book, laying it carefully across his knees.

Ludwig watches him as he pages through the book. The duke isn't handsome; his eyes have an asymmetrical cast, and his long face makes him seem melancholy even when he isn't. Even so, there's something pleasing in his face, especially since he had obviated the fearsome Habsburg chin by growing a beard.

At length Wilhelm finds the motet Ludwig had marked with a small piece of paper. "The funeral motet you composed for him?" he asks. He stares down at the notes, then shakes his head and hands the book to his court composer. "As I've said often enough, music is in my heart, but nowhere else. Not my head, my tongue, or in my fingers. Notes look like hieroglyphics to me."

It's not a long piece. Ludwig begins in the middle and sings through the rest of the work, alternating between the alto and tenor parts at whim, hearing the other voices in his head as concretely as though the singers surround him. He never understood singers who only learn their own part. That seemed to him as absurd as only reading every fourth line of a poem. He wonders what the duke is hearing.

Wilhelm exhales at length when Ludwig finishes singing. "Stunning, Ludwig. It's a masterwork."

Ludwig is silent for a moment. He looks out over the pond where the ducks had begun to regroup on the water, convinced of their safety once more.

"It *is* a masterwork. I can say that in utter humility, because it is not my music, they are not my words, and it was not composed for Maximilian at all."

The duke stares at him for a long moment, then rises, beckoning to his servant to collect his crossbow. He takes his court composer by the arm and leads him into the palace. "Come, Ludwig. You will tell me the rest in my library, over a glass of wine."

Ludwig always counts himself fortunate when he enters the duke's personal library. It is a handsome room, full of books, good pictures, a comfortable fireplace, everything one would like, besides light. His own music library is not as large, but it is a corner room, and manages to feel light and airy even in mid-winter.

The duke offers him a comfortable chair, and they sit together, sipping wine.

"You say you did not write that masterpiece, Ludwig?"

"That is correct. I labored over his motet, day and night, for nearly a week. He wished to hear it, of course. I chose a text from the gospel of John, the angel at the tomb.

They have taken my Lord,
And I know not where they have put him.
The angel said unto her:
Woman, why do you weep?
He has risen, as he said,
And he goes before you into Galilee
Where you will see him. Alleluia.
And as she wept, she stooped

And saw two angels who said to her:
He goes before you into Galilee
Where you will see him. Alleluia.

"By that time I could do nothing right in his eyes. Maximilian lay there in silence, then sighed and said, 'We had wished for more than this, Senfl, but time has run out. My time, and yours.' In front of everyone—the singers, Dr. Mennel, and the few courtiers who remained at the end. I was beside myself with rage, but contained it, of course. Murdering an emperor, even one half-dead already, would not have gone well with me." Ludwig glances at his patron, as though just remembering who he was. "I apologize, my lord. That was disrespectful, and I humbly beg your pardon."

Wilhelm makes an impatient motion with his hand, as if to say, never mind that, get back to the story.

"He was right, time was short. He died a few days later. My motet was performed at his funeral, and universally praised by the singers and all who heard it. One singer in particular, whose voice I had in mind when I wrote the superius part. And when I chose the text."

"So what happened to that motet?"

Ludwig balances his goblet on the arm of his chair, and reaches into his cloak, extracting the fragment of charred paper, and hands it to Wilhelm. The duke glances at it. His next words explode from his mouth.

"You did not burn such a beautiful work?!"

"That is exactly what I did." Ludwig can no longer sit still, so he stands and paces in front of the duke. "That hunting accident I mentioned earlier—they amputated my toe. Cut it right out of my foot, and debrided the wound, while I was conscious and sober. Burning my work hurt much worse."

Wilhelm makes a questioning motion with his hands.

"Maximilian took everything from me, my lord duke. He promised me a living of one hundred fifty Rhenish guilders per year after his death. I never saw a *Kreuzer* of it, despite making a pest of myself at the imperial treasury of his successor. He took my prospects for earning and doing my job in the future. And he took away the most precious thing of all."

"Ludwig, do not think I don't believe you—I do. I know you to be honest beyond all doubt. But at the same time I cannot believe such… paltriness on his part. What could have made him act in such a way?"

Ludwig reaches into his envelope again, and silently hands the duke the sketch. Wilhelm stares at Catherine's face. "I should have known. What better way to make a man the enemy of his best self, and of other men, than fighting over a woman."

"She was my wife, my lord. He took her from me. So, I was petty in return. I struck out at him with what means were at my disposal. Granted, they were few in number, and not very impressive."

Wilhelm stares at the sketch for a few moments longer, before handing it back to Ludwig. "She is lovely. Is she the singer you wrote the superius part for?"

Ludwig nods.

"What happened to her? How did Maximilian take her from you? Surely, he never married her himself, on his deathbed?"

Ludwig shakes his head, not looking at his employer. "Worse, if you can believe it. I will tell you the whole story, but let's finish the bit about the motet first."

"So, whose motet did Maximilian end up with? The one that survives, in that volume?" The duke points to the book which Ludwig has propped next to his chair.

Ludwig grins like a man recalling a delicious prank he pulled as a child.

"That was written for Anne of Brittany."

The duke breathes in sharply. "His stolen bride."

"Maximilian never forgave Charles, King of France. He never neglected an opportunity to decry French treachery or bring up all he had suffered at their hands, in purely general terms. He would never speak of those mortifying events, naturally."

"And now, Anne and Maximilian are linked for all eternity, sharing not a marriage bed, but a funeral motet." The duke tries to hide his smile by sipping his wine.

Ludwig shrugs. "In a way, he chose it himself. He heard it, and told me to go and write something like it for him. I tried, and failed apparently, and eventually gave him what he wanted."

"And the other matter?" Wilhelm says.

As unemotionally as he can, Ludwig tells Wilhelm how Maximilian tore Catherine away from him.

The duke is no longer sipping his wine. During the story, he places his goblet on the table beside him, and now sits with his elbows propped on his knees, studying his hands.

"And you still love her." Wilhelm says after a few moments of silence. It is not a question.

Ludwig can't look at him. "Does music lose its power after the last note is sung?"

Wilhelm sits up straight again with a sigh. "I must say, you did well, Ludwig, with what means were at your disposal. He treated you infamously. By stealing your bride, did he mean to somehow avenge the humiliation he suffered at the hands of the French?"

"No doubt that was part of his plan. But he also wanted her for his memorial, and he succeeded. She married his son and brought forth another little Maximilian von Österreich. He got the last word. He will always get the last word."

"Ludwig," Wilhelm reaches for the music volume again. He rests it in his lap and taps the leather cover with his fingers. "Unless I am mistaken, there's more than one way to do that."

THE EAGLE AND THE SONGBIRD

*

Now I thank God that I
am so well provided for here.
For He never abandons one who prays to Him,
which everyone should note and think of often.
Princely grace has come my way,
for I devoted myself
to serving my lord
most obediently and shall not cease
in future, if I
see that people can
still make use of me to God's honor
with choral music, which I have now long
practiced, and do every day.
It also pleases me much above other things
that are now pursued in this world,
for he who understands it values it highly,
although it does not please everyone.
That does not concern me;
so long as I have
my lord's grace and favor,
I take no heed
and make do;
I shall be grateful to God all my days.

Ludwig Senfl, Schweizer

EPILOGUE

Shall I weep? Shall my art fail to work on you alone?

OCTOBER, 2013
Blanton Museum of Art
University of Texas at Austin

"Audio guide?" A smiling young woman hands me a ticket. Juggling the handset and headphones, ticket, and notebook, I walk through the atrium—wide, bright, white and blue tiled, and up the wide stone staircase. At the top, a man checks the ticket, and sees my notebook.

"No pens in the galleries," he says, fishing in the pocket of his suit jacket. He hands me a stumpy yellow pencil that I associate with church pews. I thank him and turn into the gallery.

Prints have never excited me, but I'm eager to get a preliminary look at this artwork before my lecture.

The lecture had been my boss's idea. I came back from vacation to find a brochure for an exhibit called *Imperial Augsburg* on my desk with a Post-It note stuck to it: 'We pimped you out. Hope you don't mind.' I didn't mind either being volunteered for the lecture or the curious phrasing of my boss's note. I was ready to go to great lengths to promote early music, which was my personal passion, and had often joked to my husband that I was willing to be a whore for my art. Or other people's art. I make none of my own.

Early music could be a hard-sell, so any opportunity to raise awareness was welcome. Early music has no composers with the level of name recognition of Bach or Beethoven. There are no hundred-piece orchestras to bowl people over. And sometimes it can sound flat-out weird, if you're not used to it. The names sound funny (sackbut, anyone?) But once those sounds have found a resting place in your heart, they stay there. I believe Bach and Beethoven have enough cheerleaders, so my radio show focuses on the not-Bachs of music history, composers of the Middle Ages, Renaissance, and early Baroque who could certainly use the support. Though they rest in partial obscurity now, they were once celebrated, hired at great expense, sometimes fought over. By people like the Habsburgs, I think, turning my attention to the art before me in the gallery.

I settle the headphones on my head and press the green arrow button on the handset, and get my notebook ready. I'm surprised to see more than prints; there are also a couple of books: a first edition of *Weiß Kunig*, Emperor Maximilian's fictionalized autobiography, first published in 1775. This book gave rise to his most often quoted words: '*He who does not create remembrance during life will have none in death, and will be forgotten with the tolling of the bell.*' Scholars are divided on whether Maximilian dictated the text to his secretary, Marx Treitz, or whether Treitz was actually a ghostwriter.

I see a rare copy of the first printing of *Theuerdank*, the romanticized telling of Maximilian's journey to Burgundy to claim the hand of his first wife Mary, the only one of his books to be published during his life. I lean over the small volume, tucked into its glass case, and try to puzzle out the script. The typeface was developed especially for this book by one of Maximilian's artists. The audio guide tells me that *Theuerdank* never entirely disappeared from public consciousness. It was published many times in subsequent centuries, and was popular in the eighteenth century. One of Goethe's plays bears witness to this phenomenon; in *Götz von*

Berlichingen in 1771 he wrote of 'girls reading *Theuerdank*, wishing they had such a man themselves.'

Then it really gets interesting. I turn up the volume a little. The emperor's love of music was well-documented by contemporary chroniclers. He wanted music in his environment constantly, even when he was alone.

There's a print by Burgkmair, showing Emperor Maximilian surrounded by his musicians.

I peer at it, getting closer than is comfortable to admire the precision and the detail of this page, which originated from an intricate carving on a slab of wood five hundred years ago. I scribble the title in my notes: '*How the young White King learned to know music and stringed instruments*'.

The instruments are rendered exactly; an organologist's dream: a tromba marina, a lute and a sackbut leaning against drums in the right foreground, a young man playing a clavichord, which sits on a table. Behind the clavichord some wind instruments rest on the table: crumhorn, recorders, shawm. I glance back to the clavichord player's face; to my eye it looks delicate, soft, almost feminine. But this of course is wishful thinking. A high-level organization like the Imperial *Hofkapelle* would have been made up of men only, like much of public life in the early Renaissance. Women might have made music in the private sphere, or at small gatherings, but never in public.

To the clavichord player's right sits a man whose function is not clear; we can only see his head and shoulders. There's a viol on the table next to him, maybe in the next moment or two he will reach for it, and begin to tune. In the center foreground, a harpist plays, looking out toward the viewer. He faces an organ; the organist's face is turned away, but it's probably Hofhaimer. The bellows-pumper gazes down; all I can see of him is his very festive hat. In the back, in front of a window showing a mountain view, three singers crowd around a small music book (singing looks like a very intimate activity, when all share the same book!). A man playing a mute cornetto stands next to them.

Maximilian, the young White King, stands in the midst of them all. His head is at a slight angle, he's clearly listening intently. His right hand makes a gesture; is he marking time, or signaling to one of the singers (probably the tenor) that he's overpowering the rest? His left hand holds what might be a cantor's staff, used for pointing to huge music volumes resting on tall music stands. I've seen contemporary pictures of Renaissance choirs in which the choirboys seemed barely able to see the music, since it was so much higher than they were.

Maximilian is listening, but he's not playing anything. I know from long years spent trying to learn an instrument, the only way to learn is to practice. I'm already getting the picture of this monarch's need to be shown being the best at everything. Why not portray himself playing, even if it wasn't true? Who would know, five hundred years down the line? Maybe in this, the art form he loved most of all, he graciously stepped back, and let his musicians shine. Maybe, with all of his love for it, the mechanics of music were as mysterious as heaven itself.

The crown jewels of his *Hofkapelle* were Heinrich Isaac, Paul Hofhaimer, and Ludwig Senfl. I hear samples of their music: a grand six-voice polyphonic piece by Isaac, probably the emperor's coronation motet, a short organ work by Hofhaimer, and a song by Senfl. The one I want to hear again is the song, and I press rewind again and again. I quickly jot down some lines of the English translation:

> *In love and woe never shall I forget her,*
> *although cruel cunning*
> *stands in her way,*
> *eager to oppose such joy,*
> *which by jealousy is condemned.*
> *Where uncouth nature rules at court,*
> *very rarely is found good governance.*

The nobility thereby is despised.
I too must suffer in this case.
I am forced out, I do not belong.

This kind of highly personal text is surprising for a Renaissance composer. A composer with a broken heart might not be unusual, but calling your boss uncouth in a song certainly is. The audio guide tells me about Maximilian's second-hand funeral motet, long attributed to Senfl. I puzzle over why a music-loving monarch with a world-class court composer ended up with a worked-over piece intended for Anne of Brittany, of all people. His stolen bride.

Next, I pause in front of an etching of Kunz von der Rosen. He is remembered by history as Maximilian's jester, but he was more than that—a trusted companion who had saved the emperor's life, and the only one, it seems, who could tell the unvarnished truth, both about the emperor, and *to* him. The audio guide states that he died the same year as Maximilian did, and is buried in the chapel of St. Anne in Augsburg.

I turn to face another woodcut, this one by Albrecht Dürer, from a sketch he made in Augsburg in 1518, at the emperor's last imperial Diet. Dürer made Maximilian look mighty and imposing, with his shoulders filling the frame of the image. (I had seen Maximilian's suit of armor in the previous gallery. If that armor had been made to fit him, he had been slender, and not very tall, and this portrait might be viewed as idealized.) At first glance, the face seems remote and closed; I'm looking at the stereotypical monarch. Was that nose a product of nature, I wonder? Only his lips seem real and human: they look sensitive, despite the firm set of the mouth. I stare a bit longer. There seems to be a plasticity to the mouth. The more I stare, the greater the feeling I have that the lines framing it will contract, and he will smile. The grooves around his eyes are not just from squinting into the sun while on horseback, I'm sure of it. Dürer the magician.

According to the audio guide, Dürer created various works of art from the final sketch he made of the emperor at the Diet in Augsburg: several woodcuts, and three oil paintings, two of which hang in museums in Vienna and Nuremberg. It is unclear what happened to the third. It is missing and presumed lost.

The emperor is the last stop on my journey today, and finally I turn away from him. I make another circuit of the gallery, and linger in the doorway, unwilling to go. I turn my head again and see the emperor, already laughing at myself for being absurd. Eyes across a nearly empty room. The monarch is there to be gazed at, not interacted with. But why does it seem like something tugs at me; that I hear a whisper where no one is? The sense of *presence* mystifies me. Not physical presence, something far more compelling. *Dasein*. Being here. To express a world in a word, only German will do.

I leave the gallery, sad but also buoyed, like something is just ahead of me, and if I pace my steps just so, I might catch up to it around a corner.

A few weeks later, I give my lecture to an overflowing crowd in the portrait gallery. I am done, but it's not done with me. Usually, I'm quite tired of a subject after giving a lecture, ready to move on. This won't let me. I buy books and exhibit catalogs, and stacks of CDs. There are few English language histories about Emperor Maximilian I, so I take lessons to brush up my rusty German. I force my eyes to read a five hundred-year-old version of an already complicated language, and its bewildering typeface, so I can read facsimiles of *Weiß Kunig* and *Theuerdank*. It's like learning to read all over again, but I persist. I wonder if Treitz was this invested.

Finally, I write.

Finis

ACKNOWLEDGMENTS

In 2013, the Blanton Museum of Art at the University of Texas at Austin hosted an exhibit of prints and drawings called *Imperial Augsburg*. I was invited to give a gallery talk about music at the court of Emperor Maximilian I. This book began there and then.

In 2015 I participated in an online novel writing course with the Faber Academy (now Professional Writing Academy); I am indebted to tutors Tom Bromley and Paul Kingsnorth and my fellow students for their critiques.

This book could not have been written without historians and art historians whose research focused on Maximilian's life and 15-16th century German history in general, specifically the works of Hermann Wiesflecker, Steven Ozment, Larry Silver, and Jeffrey Chipps Smith.

The artistry of ensembles like Capilla Flamenca, and singers Tore Tom Denys, and Charles Daniels brings the music of this period to life so exquisitely. Their recordings provided the inspiration for the music described in this book.

I am also grateful for A.S. Kline's open access poetry archive, poetryintranslation.com, for helping me become acquainted with the writings of Ovid, Horace, and Virgil.

I'd like to extend my personal thanks to:

- My German tutors, Olga & David Wise

- David Wise for translating the poem in Chapter 16
- Marlys Boettner for keeping things organized at home while I was living in Germany
- Dr. Jeffrey Chipps Smith & Kathleen Berg for insightful interviews
- Karen McLinden for being my very first reader
- Karen Pope for proofreading assistance
- my friend Ann Kelble for line edits and advice

I lovingly dedicate this book to my late husband, Jim Schneider, with gratitude for his love, support, and boundless patience. He passed away suddenly while I was completing the final edits. I couldn't have done it without him.

ABOUT THE AUTHOR

Sara Schneider's love affair with early music began in a classroom at the University of Amsterdam, when she first heard music from the 12th century Notre Dame School. After earning her master's degree in historical musicology, she moved to Austin, Texas, where she works as a host and producer on KMFA, Classical 89.5. She also produces and hosts the nationally syndicated show *Early Music Now*.

Her research for *The Eagle and the Songbird* took her to Augsburg, Innsbruck, Nuremberg, and Vienna (not unlike the emperor's itinerant courtiers). She even hiked the steep switchbacks of the *Martinswand*--the site of Maximilian's legendary rescue, near Zirl, Austria.